Confession

"Care?" said Constance. *"Care?* I've cared so much that I've drenched my pillow with tears night after night. I've cared so violently that I made a fool of myself trying to forget you because I was sure you could never care for one like me. I've cared ever since that first morning on the hillside with the little blue flowers . . ."

His arms were about her now, her face buried in the dear roughness of his coat. But he lifted her face and laid his lips on hers.

"My darling, my precious beloved! Tell me that you love me," he said.

"I love you! Oh, I do love you!"

Bantam Books by Grace Livingston Hill
Ask your bookseller for the books you have missed

Grace Livingston Hill
Matched Pearls

BANTAM BOOKS
TORONTO · NEW YORK · LONDON

MATCHED PEARLS

*A Bantam Book / published by arrangement with
J. B. Lippincott Company*

PRINTING HISTORY

Lippincott edition published 1933

Bantam edition / November 1971

2nd printing .... February 1972	6th printing .... May 1973
3rd printing .... February 1972	7th printing .... January 1974
4th printing .... May 1972	8th printing .... June 1975
5th printing .... May 1973	9th printing .... May 1979

ISBN 0-553-12227-4

Published simultaneously in the United States and Canada

PRINTED IN THE UNITED STATES OF AMERICA

CHAPTER I

CONSTANCE COURTLAND came smiling into the living room humming a gay little tune. She had just been lingering at the front door with Rudyard Van Arden, a neighbor's son, with whom she had been to ride, and her brother. Frank looked up with a whimsical sneer.

"Well, has that egg gone home at last?" he drawled. "It beats me what you find to say to him. You've been gassing out there for a full half hour. Why, I c'n remember when you wouldn't speak ta that guy. You said he was the limit. And now just because you've both been ta college, and he's got a sweater with a big red letter on the front, and a little apricot colored eyebrow on his upper lip, you stand there and chew the rag fer half an hour. And Mother, here, ben having seven pink fits for fear the Reverend Gustawvus Grant'll return before she has a chance ta give ya the high sign."

The mother rose hurriedly, embarrassedly, her face flushing guiltily, and began to protest.

"Really, Frank, you have no right to talk to your sister that way about her friends! When she's only home for this week-end you ought to make it as pleasant for her as you can. You don't see much of your sister and you oughtn't to tease her like that. She won't carry a very pleasant memory of her home back to college if you annoy her so whenever one of the old neighbors comes in to see her a little while. You know perfectly well that Rudyard Van Arden is a fine respectable young man."

Constance stopped humming and looked keenly from her brother to her mother.

"Never mind Ruddy Van," she said, coolly sweeping

1

her mother's words aside without ceremony, "What's this about Dr. Grant? You don't mean to tell me, Mother, that you've invited him to dinner one of the few nights I have at home, when you know how I detest him?"

"No, of course not, dear!" said the mother hastily and placatingly, "Nothing like that at all. He just dropped in to see you this afternoon. He was very anxious to talk with you—" The mother stopped abruptly.

"To talk with me!" said Constance narrowing her eyes and looking from mother to brother again, "What could he possibly want to talk with me about? If it's to sing in the Easter anthems, or a solo, no I won't and that's flat! I can't and won't sing with that Ferran girl flatting the way she does. There's no use asking me. If that's what he wants I'll slide out the back way and go over to Mabel's for a little while. You just tell him I've got bronchitis or any other efficient throat trouble. I simply won't discuss it with him. He always acts as if he wants to chuck me under the chin, or pat me on the head as if I was still five. My, how I used to hate it!"

"No, dear, it's nothing like that. He didn't even suggest your singing."

"Well, then, what is it? Let's get it over with."

"Why, dear, you see they're having a special communion service to-morrow, Easter you know. It's such a lovely idea, and all your Sunday School class are uniting with the church. He wanted you to join with them and make it a full class. It seems a rather lovely idea I think myself, so suitable you know."

"Me? Join the church? Oh, Mother! How victorian!"

"Oh, but now, Constance, don't try to be modern. No, wait! I really have got to tell you about it, because he may be here any minute now, and Connie dear, your grandmother has quite set her heart upon it."

"Grandmother!" laughed Constance, "What has she got to do with it? My soul! It sounds as if my family were still in the dark ages."

"Well, but Connie, you'll find your grandmother is very much upset about it. You see she's been scolding me ever since you first went off to college that I let you go without uniting with the church. She thought it would be such a safe-guard. And now that you've almost finished she is determined that you shall be a member of the church before you graduate. She says she did and I did and it isn't respectable not to. And really, my dear, I think you'll just have to put your own wishes aside this time and humor her."

"How ridiculous, Mother. Join the church to suit Grandmother! Just you leave her to me. I'll make her understand that girls don't do things like that to-day. Things are different from when she was young. And by the way, Mother, do you think she's going to give me that string of pearls for a graduating present? You promised to feel around and see. I'd so much like to have it for the big dance next week. It's going to be a swell affair."

"Well, that's the trouble, Constance dear. I've been trying to find out what she had planned, and it seems she's quite got her heart set on that string of pearls being a present to you when you join the church. Her father gave it to her when she joined, and she has often said to me: 'The day that Constance joins the church I shall give her my string of pearls.' I really believe she means it, too, for she has been talking about your cousin Norma, and once she asked me if Norma was a member of the church."

"Mercy, Mother, you don't think she's thinking of giving a string of matched pearls to a little country school teacher with a muddy complexion and no place in the world to wear them?"

"You can't tell, my dear, what she may not do if you frustrate her in this desire of her heart. She's just determined, Connie! She told me your grandfather had always said that he wanted to see you a member of the old church and be sure you were safe in the fold before he died, and she had sort of given him her word that she would see to it that you came out all right. Connie, you really mustn't laugh so loud. If she were to hear you—!"

Constance stifled her mirth.

"But honestly, Mother, it's so victorian, so sort of traditional and all, you know. I'd be ashamed to have it get back to college that I had had to knuckle in and join the church to please my grandmother. Why, everybody would despise me after the enlightening education I've had. It's a sort of relic of the dark ages."

"Aw, you don't havta believe anything," put in the brother amusedly, "Just havta stand up there a few minutes and then it's all over. Doesn't mean a thing and who'll ever think of it again? Gee if Grandmother'd buy me that Rolls Royce I want I'd join church any day! I don't see whatcha making sucha fuss about."

"Franklin! That's irreverent!" reproved his mother coldly, "Of course Constance would do anything she did sincerely. Constance has always been conscientious. But Connie, dear, I don't see why you object to something that has been a tradition in the family for years. Of course you're a thoughtless girl now, but you'll come to a time when you'll be glad you did it, something to depend on in times of trouble and all that. You know, really, it's a good thing to get a matter like this all settled when one is young. And of course, you know, that college-girl point-of-view isn't going always to stay with you. You just think you've got new light on things now, but when you get older and settle down you'll see the church was a good safe place to be."

"Oh applesauce!" said Constance merrily, "Mother, what good has it ever done you to be a member of a church I'd like to know? Oh, of course you've pussy-footed through all their missionary tea-fights and things like that, and everybody puts you on committees and things. You may like that sort of thing but I don't. I never could stand going to church, and as for Dr. Grant I can't endure his long monotonous preaching! No, really Mother, I can't! Let me talk to Grandmother. I'm sure I can make her see this thing straight."

"No, Constance, really you mustn't talk to your grandmother! Indeed my child, you don't understand. She's quite in a critical state. I'm not sure but she contemplates writing Norma this evening and committing herself about those pearls. She feels that Religion is being insulted by your not uniting with the old family church. And you know, my dear, in spite of all the modern talk, one really does need a little religion in life."

"That is nothing but sentimental slush!" said Constance indignantly.

"Well, I'll grant you your grandmother is a trifle sentimental about those pearls," admitted the mother, "she feels that they are a sort of symbol of Innocence and Religion. She said all those things this afternoon. In fact I'd been having a rather dreadful time with her ever since Dr. Grant called, until I told her that he was returning to arrange things with you and I was quite sure you would be willing to see things as she wanted you to."

"Oh, Mother!"

"There's the reverend gentleman now," said Frank amusedly, gathering up his long legs from the couch where he had been stretched during the colloquy, "I'm going ta beat it. He hasn't got a line on me yet, not until Grand talks about that Rolls Royce, anyway."

"Oh, Mother, I really can't stay and see him. Let me get up the back stairs quick," said Constance.

But her mother placed her substantial body firmly in her path.

"No, Constance, I must insist! This really is a serious matter. You are not going to let those ancestral pearls go out of the immediate family I am sure. Listen, Connie, he's merely coming to arrange a time for you to meet the session. It's only a formality you know, just a question or two, and it's over. There won't be time for anything else. He said the session had a meeting this evening. Some of the girls will be there then."

"Indeed I can't go this evening," blustered Constance breathlessly, "I'm going to that dance at the country club, and I promised Ruddy I'd ride with him in his new car beforehand."

"Well, we'll fix it somehow. To-morrow morning you could go a little early, before the service. It's only a formality anyway."

"Oh, Mother!" wailed Constance softly as she slipped through the door, "I was going to play golf with Ruddy all to-morrow morning! Must I, Mother? Can't I get by without it?"

"I'm afraid you must, dear," said her mother firmly, even while she arranged a welcoming smile on her lips for the old minister who was being ushered in.

With a whispered moan Constance had slipped up the back way to her room where she remained out of call during the minister's stay.

As Constance answered the call to dinner ten minutes after the minister's departure she saw her mother and her grandmother at the foot of the front stairs talking.

"It's all right, Mother dear. Constance is going to join," said Constance's mother to the firm-mouthed little old lady in black silk with priceless lace at her throat and wrists.

The little old lady had keen black eyes and she fixed them on her daughter warily.

"You're sure she's doing it of her own free will, Mary?" she asked. "I wouldn't want any pressure to be brought to bear upon her in a thing like this."

"Oh, yes, Mother dear, I'm quite sure Constance sees the fitness of it all, Easter Sunday, too, so appropriate!"

Relief came into the bright eyes, the tenseness of the thin lips relaxed.

"Then she'll meet the session to-night?" she asked eagerly.

"Well, not to-night," said the mother warily, "Dr. Grant has arranged a special session meeting early in the morning before the service."

"Oh," said Grandmother suspiciously, "Why was that?"

"Well, he said they often did," evaded Constance's mother. "I think it's most appropriate at that hour just before the service."

The old lady studied her daughter a moment speculatively, then apparently satisfied she said:

"Well, then I shall give her the pearls in the morning. I'd like her to wear them to the service. I'd like to see them on her the first time in the church. Easter Day. Her first communion. It will be lovely, Mary. It will be just as I have hoped and planned. Her grandfather would have liked it so."

"Yes!" said Constance's mother crisply, "So appropriate! And so dear of you, Mother, to give her the pearls. I'm sure she'll be deeply grateful."

Constance smothered a mocking smile and came ruefully down the stairs, wondering what some of her professors at college and various fellow students would think if they could know that she was succumbing to tradition and family pressure just for a string of pearls. Well, the pearls were worth it! Matched pearls, and flawless. The only really worthwhile heirloom in the family. Grandfather's taste in adornment had been severe simplicity and pearls!

The sun shone forth gorgeously on Easter morning. Constance groaned softly as she saw it, looked forth from her window and noted the far stretch of the golf links in the distance. Such a day as this would have been to play golf! And to think all the morning had to be wasted!

Yet of course she was to wear the string of pearls!

She went about her dressing with more than the usual care. Was she not to be the cynosure of all eyes to-day? Even the eyes in a country church, that had been her greatgrandfather's church in the past, were worth dressing for.

She picked her garments all of white, heavy white silk with a long fitted coat, white furred to match, white shoes, even white stockings, though the sun-tan would have been more stylish, but she must not have the look of a sportsman this morning. Grandmother was even capable of coming right up to the front and taking those pearls off her neck during service if she suspected all was not utmost innocence.

She dressed her golden hair demurely, in smooth braids coiled low over her ears, with a little tip-tilted hat of white showing a few soft waves on her forehead. With her gold hair, the white hat and the sweet untinted cheeks and lips au naturel for the occasion, she looked like some young saint set apart from all the world.

Her grandmother felt it when she came down the stairs and met her with a sacred smile and a look of satisfaction in the keen eager old eyes. She clasped the pearls around Constance's neck and kissed her tenderly.

"Dear child!" she whispered, "How your grandfather used to talk about this day, and pray about it!" And then half frightened at her words she retreated back into her silent reticence and hurried out the door to where the car waited to take them to church.

And Constance, following, felt a sudden smart of tears in her eyes in spite of her cynicism. She remembered words of one most modern professor in talking once about sacraments, how he had advised them not to throw away old sacraments, even if they meant nothing anymore, but to keep them for the sweet sentiment they had had in former years. Constance thought she understood suddenly what he had meant. She caught a brief vision of what all this meant to her grandmother and was really glad she had done it. Even without the pearls she was glad she had done it just to please little sweet hard bright old grandmother.

So with virtue shining from her lovely ultramarine eyes she entered the lily decked aisles and took her place in the house of the Lord.

The windows in the old, old church were lovely Tiffany windows. They cast opalescent lights across the sanctuary and touched lightly like a halo the gold of Constance's hair, they lighted up her unpainted face till she attained an almost holy look in her white garments, her gold hair, her blue, blue eyes, and the pearls about her neck with twinkles of the beauties of all the world in their polished depths.

The music was angelic, and the words the monotonous old minister read and said were sonorous and musical. They meant nothing much to Constance. She was seeing herself with the pearls at the next week-end party. She was conscious of the crowded house, and of being the best dressed of the whole class of which she was a member.

When the time came she went sweetly, demurely up to the front of the church and stood with just such a demure and prayerful attitude as did her grandmother years and years before, and people whispered "Isn't Constance lovely? I never knew she was so serious, did you?"

Constance stood before the altar and kept her eyes upon the white haired Dr. Grant whom she detested, watching his lips half fascinated, wondering if the wave in his white hair was natural, bowing her head when the prayer began, and studying the toes of two well polished shoes and the neat creases of the cheap dark blue serge trousers that stood next her white suede slippers, and wondering idly who was their owner. Was the serge a bit shiny, almost shabby? That was the impression she got from her brief glance as she closed her eyes for the prayer.

The ceremony was over and they were seated for the sacrament. Constance noticed as she sat down that the man beside her was tall and had a courteous bearing. She had not noticed his name as it was called. Doubtless some newcomer since she had been away.

The solemn ceremony proceeded amid soft music from the fine organ, tender old melodies that reminded her of her childhood days, exquisite fragrance from the lilies in the chancel, blended prisms of color flung across the perfumed air from the Tiffany windows, scraps of white bread on silver plates, tiny tinkling crystal glasses like ruby jewels passing, blood red wine against the whiteness of the lilies in the chancel, soft cool polish of matched pearls against the softness of her neck. It all was a lovely dream to Constance, just a picture in which the colors and setting harmonized. It meant nothing in her life, a brief incident, and pearls. What did it matter so she had the pearls for her very own? She had a passing moment of wonder as she touched the tiny glass of wine to her lips. Memory flashed back to a Sunday long ago when she had wept bitterly into her grandmother's lap that she could not have this privilege, and now here it was hers and she was reluctant. Was all life like that she wondered? Nothing attained until desire had passed!

At last the final solemn march and passing of the mystic symbols was complete, the painful stillness, soft-music-laden, was over, the final hymn and benediction finished, the minister admonished the members to greet one another with a cordial right-hand-of-fellowship be-

fore they left, and the organ burst forth into a tri-
umphal Easter paean of victory.

Constance lifted up her head with a relieved breath
and glanced about her. She was free now for the rest of
the day. Her penance was over and the prize was upon
her.

Then a voice beside and above her spoke, a pleasant
confidential voice that yet was clear above the trumpet-
ing of the organ, with something throbbing, deep and
stirring in its lilt.

"I guess that means that we're to greet one another,
doesn't it?" the voice asked. "We're members of one
household now, members of the Body of Christ."

Then Constance was aware of a hand, shapely, well
cared for as a woman's, yet firm, big, strong, the hand
of a real man. And it was obviously being held out to
her in greeting, a kind of holy greeting, it seemed. She
was suddenly aware that all the people around her were
shaking hands and offering congratulations, just like a
wedding reception! Heavens! Did one have to endure
another ordeal also? And who was this presumptuous
person who seemed determined to shake hands with
her? A stranger!

She lifted haughty eyes and met the very handsomest
brown eyes she had ever looked into, young, friendly,
pleasant eyes; and then without her own volition she
found her hand folded in a strong quick clasp.

The stranger was taking almost reverent note of the
sweet line of forehead under gold hair and little tilted
hat brim, lovely curve of cheek and lip and chin, the
soft white neck above the lustrous pearls, and doing
them homage with his glance.

"My name is Seagrave. May I know yours?" he
asked with utmost courtesy.

Then Constance remembered her patrician birth, the
pearls she wore so regally, the shabbiness of the blue
serge trousers she had glimpsed through prayer time,
and lifted her patrician chin stiffening visibly, and answering in a voice like a clear lovely icicle:

"I am Miss Courtland."

"Thank you, Miss Courtland, I am glad to know

you," he said with quaint old time formality, "I hope we'll meet again."

Constance gave him a little frozen smile and swept him an upward appraising glance.

"I'm afraid not," she said haughtily, "I'm going back to college Tuesday."

Their glances met for just an instant, a puzzled questioning gaze, and then her girl friends surged between them; when she looked again, wondering if she must introduce him, he was gone.

"Who's your boy-friend, Con?" whispered Rose Acker, one of her most intimate friends, "Isn't he perfectly stunning looking!"

But Constance only smiled and went forward to her grandmother who was waiting with proud eyes and sternly pleasant lips.

As they drove along in the car toward home Constance looked for the stranger among the people on the pavement, but he was not anywhere among them. She wondered if she would ever see him again. He was impertinent of course, or perhaps only ignorant, she decided, but nevertheless interesting. A new type.

"Well," said her brother Frank, coming down the steps to fling open the car door for them when they reached home, "Is the grand agony over?"

"Do you see my lovely pearls?" asked Constance quickly with a warning look at her brother as she noted the wicked twinkle in his eyes.

"Some pearls!" said the reckless youth, "cheap at the price I'll say! What do I get, Grand, if I go and do the same sometime?"

But the little old lady with the keen dark eyes shut her thin lips in a firm line, and spurned her grandson's offered arm, tripping up the steps like an indignant robin, holding her black taffeta shoulders irately as she marched into the house without answering.

CHAPTER II

CONSTANCE came downstairs early the next morning.
She had promised to play a set of tennis with Ruddy
Van Arden. She wanted to get in touch with the brightness of the morning and stretch her wings a little just to
feel how good it was to be at home again and have it
spring.

Her father and mother were not down yet, breakfast
wasn't ready, and Frank of course would not even be
awake. By and by perhaps she would go up and lay a
nice cool dripping wash rag across his eyes and forehead, and call good morning as she slipped away
again, before he roused and threw it at her.

But first she would bring in the morning paper and
just get a glimpse of the yard. She had caught a glim-
mer of daffodils down near the walk, and was the
forsythia bush really out in bloom?

She opened the front door and picked up the paper,
glanced idly over the headlines, then looked toward the
daffodils. Yes they were out. She would go down and
look at them. So tucking the paper under the arm of
her pretty sports knitted costume of blue and white
she started across the lawn.

She was half way down to the walk before she saw
Seagrave coming up the street with something in his
hands, carrying it wrapped in white like a cake. She
paused irresolute, the color coming to her cheek, then
hastened on. Why should it be anything to her that he
was passing her father's house? He was a stranger. She
need not recognize him. It was not likely he would
know her again, she told herself and hurried down to
where the daffodils made brave array along the path to
the street.

Her face was down among the daffodils, pretending
to be inhaling their delicate fragrance, her golden head
among the golden flowers. The morning paper slid into
the grass.

She heard his footsteps pass on the pavement and turn in at her father's gate. Could it be possible that he would presume upon a mere church acquaintance? Would he dare? Her indignation grew. Now, she must say something to put him in his place. Yes, his steps were coming across the young springy grass, walking confidently and unafraid. What should she do? Freeze him? One would have thought that she had made it plain yesterday.

But now he paused above her and his voice had again that soft indescribable gentleness that strangely took away the idea of presumption in spite of her. Was it a touch of the south in his accent? She wasn't sure. But there was a courtliness, a refinement about his voice that calmed her indignation and forced her attention.

"Good morning," he said like a gay boy, "I hardly hoped for such good luck as this. I've brought you something. I hope you don't mind. You see you're the only girl in town I know even a little, and this was too pretty to keep to myself."

In amazement Constance straightened up and looked.

He was opening the white bundle that he carried like a cake, and now she saw it was his big clean handkerchief with the corners folded over, and it was full to the brim of the loveliest blue and white hepaticas, lying on a bed of delicate maidenhair fern. They were fresh with the dew upon them and they seemed as she looked to be the loveliest things that Constance had ever seen.

"Oh, the lovely things!" she exclaimed in wonder, "Wild flowers! What are they? Where did you find them?"

"Aren't they lovely?" he answered with eagerness, "Why, they are just hepaticas. I found them in the woods just over on that hill beyond the golf links. I've been out taking a little tramp and I came upon them. Isn't our Lord wonderful to trouble to make such beautiful little things, and each one so perfect!"

Constance looked up at the young man and stared in wonder. She had no words to answer such a remark as this.

"I couldn't help picking them," he went on earnestly. "It seemed to me I must show them to some one else. I'm glad I found you. It seemed somehow as if they sort of belonged to you. They reminded me of you when I saw them."

Constance did not know what to make of such homage as this. If he had said: "They're not so bad, are they, old girl?" as some of her college acquaintances might have spoken freshly she would have thought nothing of it, but this old time courtesy and homage she did not understand. She wondered how he came to be that way and what she ought to do about it. She felt almost uncomfortable under such open yet reverent admiration.

"But you didn't mean these for me," she said, as if he were offering her priceless jewels that of course she could not be permitted to accept.

"If you'll take them," he said humbly, "I wouldn't have any way of looking out for them myself now, I'm on my way to the office to get acquainted with my new job before things start off to-morrow. I'd hate to see the brave little things droop."

Constance was filled with sudden pity for the flowers as if they had been lovely little children uncared for. His tone had invested them with personality.

"Oh, I'd love to have them," she said quite simply now. He had been so humble she must put him at his ease. He had not meant to be presumptuous. He was just counting on that mystic bond of religion, that church stuff, probably. Queer a young man in these days could be so childlike. But he was probably brought up in the country. He would get over it.

"I don't believe I ever saw them before," she went on to cover her own embarrassment.

"I wish you could see them growing," he said, watching her with unveiled admiration, "They're like a little sea of blue, blowing and nodding in the grass, with these maidenhair ferns in a little huddle behind them like a miniature forest on the bank."

"I'd like to see them," she said frankly. "They must be a wonderful sight."

"You couldn't spare the time to go?" he asked wistfully, "I'd enjoy showing you just where they are."

Constance glanced at her watch and shook her head. "I have an appointment at the country club at nine."

"Oh, not now," he smiled, "I couldn't go to-day at all, I thought perhaps, to-morrow morning—early, could you?"

"It would certainly have to be early," laughed Constance and wondered why she dallied with this handsome ingenuous boy. She had lost all sense of his being presumptuous now.

"I'm quite respectable you know," he said wistfully, and flashed her a smile. "I could get Mr. Howarth to introduce us rightly. I'm with Howarth, Wells and Company you see—"

Constance flashed him a smile herself now. The Howarths were all right people. He must be respectable she felt sure. Yet he was queer, and different from her other men friends. She wondered why she was interested.

"Could you go as early as half past five, or would six perhaps be better?" He fixed his brown eyes on her face now and gave her another of those radiant smiles, and suddenly she knew she was going to see those flowers to-morrow morning.

"I'm not sure," she said thoughtfully. "If you are going anyway and happen to be passing by here about that time I might come along. I can't really promise. Something might make it impossible."

"Thank you," he said with another of those grave smiles, "I'll just be hoping. It's very pleasant to have found a Christian friend right at the start in a strange place. I'm praising God for that. Now, I'll bid you good morning. I must hurry to the office."

Constance stood with the bundle of flowers in her hands and watched him walk away in wonder. What a strange unusual young man he was. She had never seen anyone like him before. Heavens! How very good looking he was. It seemed too good to be true, such looks on a man! And yet he wasn't one bit effeminate.

At the gate he turned and lifted his hat in a princely

fashion. Constance stood still, smilingly nodded a friendly good-by, and then wondered at herself.

It was not until he was out of sight that she realized that she was still holding his snowy handkerchief in her hands with its mound of ferns and flowers. Then suddenly her cheeks grew hot. Why had she been so very friendly as to let him give her flowers, and promise to take a walk with him to-morrow morning when she had resolved before he came in to put him in a stranger's place? Well, there was one thing, she didn't have to go and take that walk. She wouldn't of course. She had left herself a loophole. She had not promised.

Then with her cheeks still hot she hurried into the house. She must get those flowers out of that handkerchief and the handkerchief out of sight before the family saw it.

She tipped the flowers into a large plate and stuffed the handkerchief quickly into her sleeve out of sight just as her brother Frank amazingly appeared in the dining room door.

"Who's your comely giant, Connie," he asked with a twinkle, "You certainly like 'em tall, don't you?"

Constance looked up with a smile that was meant to be natural, but her cheeks were still hot and needed no rouge and she knew that the watchful eyes of her brother would not let that little item pass.

"Oh, he's just a man I met in church yesterday," said Constance indifferently, "fill that glass bowl with water for me, Frankie, that's a dear."

"Hmmm!" murmured Frank wisely as he returned from the butler's pantry with the big crystal fruit bowl filled with water, "You only met him yesterday and yet he gets up at all hours to pick dewdabs out of the woods for you! You certainly fetch 'em quick, don't you, sister?"

The color flew into Constance's cheeks again to her great annoyance.

"Oh, for sweet mercy's sake, won't you stop being ridiculous? He happened to be passing and I admired them, and of course he had to give them to me."

"Oh, was that the way it was?" mocked the imp of a brother. "I thought you were stooping down with your

back to the street smelling daffodils when he went by
and he had to come away around through the gate in
the hedge and walk across the grass. But I must have
been mistaken. Probably you called out to know what
on earth he had done up in that handkerchief and he
had to come in and show you. However, I should say
in any case he was getting on fast."

"Oh, shut up will you?" said Constance quite vexed,
and devoting herself to placing the airy stems in the
fern-fringed bowl. The entrance of the family created a
diversion, and Constance's mother exclaimed over the
beauty of the center piece.

"Wherever did you find them, dear?" she asked.

"Just an offering from one of her throng of admirers," answered Frank quickly with an eloquent look.
"They begin quite early in the morning you perceive.
I'm just wondering what it's going to be like around
here this summer if they come as thick as this in the
spring."

"Frank!" said his mother in a reproving tone, "You
promised me last night you wouldn't tease your sister
any more."

Frank opened his eyes wide in wonder.

"Why, Muth, dear, I wasn't teasing, I was just admiring her tactics. She certainly has acquired good
technique while she was at college."

But Constance with a murmur about washing her
hands hurried upstairs, and when she returned with
coolly powdered cheeks and a placid exterior her brother had somehow been subdued, till only a pair of
dancing eyes reminded her that he had not forgotten.

They sat down to breakfast, bowed their heads for
the formal mumbling of a grace by the head of the
house, the same old mumbled blessing he had used
since Constance was a baby and his wife had told him
it was not seemly to bring up children at a table without some sort of grace being said.

During the grapefruit and oatmeal, the passing of
cream and sugar and hot rolls, the serving of eggs and
bacon, there was pleasant converse. Grandmother was
not present. She took her breakfast in bed. They could
speak about her freely.

"She was so pleased, Constance," said Mary Court-land, "She's been all strained up over this ever since she heard you were coming home at Easter and the girls in your class were all joining the church."

"Well, I suppose it was an easy way to please her," laughed the girl. "Of course I wasted the whole morning, but then it was worth it. Mother, it's going to be simply great having those pearls right now before college closes."

"You forget, Connie," put in Frank, "the comely giant. You wouldn't have met him, remember, if you hadn't gone to church. Pearls and a giant all in one morning. I'll say the time wasn't wasted even if poor Ruddy Van did have to cool his heels at the country club with Mildred Allison."

But nobody was listening to Frank. His father was reading the morning paper, his sister acted as if he didn't exist, and his mother went right on talking, deeming it the best way to get rid of the pest, to just ignore him.

"You'll have to be very careful about those pearls, you know, dear," her mother warned Constance, "They are valuable of course. Your grandmother will probably tell you before you leave just how valuable they are. You'd better arrange to keep them in the college safe. And be sure you don't tell people promiscuously that they are real. For really they are very valuable."

"Yes, and Connie," chimed Frank again in his nicest tone, "you better be careful about that good-looking giant too, he might turn out to be valuable you know. You never can tell when you have the real thing in a man right under your thumb you know."

Something in Constance's mind clicked at that, but she went right on ignoring her brother, even though she did register a wonder whether he might not happen to be right concerning this particular young man.

Then Ruddy Van Arden slid up to the door in his new gray roadster and Constance drew a breath of relief and hurried off after her racket and presently was gone into a great bright day of her own world. A world that had nothing to do with queer strangers who made odd remarks, and gave lovely gifts of sweet wild flowers done up in fine linen handkerchiefs that smelled of lavender and had a hand-embroidered initial G in the corner.

All day long Constance enjoyed herself, playing tennis with Ruddy Van Arden in the morning, taking lunch at the country club with a gay party of young people, golf in the afternoon with Sam Acker from Harvard, and then another eighteen holes with Ruddy to make up for Sunday morning, a hurried dinner at home with her stately little grandmother in black taffeta watching her across the table in her new rose evening frock and the pearls, a rush to the theater train for the city with a Mr. Montgomery whom she had met at luncheon and with whom she attended a play, and then late supper at a roof garden and home long after midnight. Constance really had very little time to think of hepaticas and handsome presumptuous strangers. The little hepaticas in their crystal bowl on the dining room table were all curled shut into sweet buds against the lacey green of the maidenhair when she stopped in the dining room for a drink of water before going up to her room. Little sleepy buds. Probably they would be dead in the morning. Flowers of a day. Like the handsome stranger-acquaintance of a morning.

As she tumbled into bed Constance remembered the half appointment for the morning. Half past five! Well, she never would make it now even if she wanted to, and of course she hadn't meant to any of the time.

And then she fell asleep.

But strangely enough a young early robin, or was it a starling, or some other bird with a heavenly voice, flew down on a twig beside her open window and trilled out a bit of celestial song just at quarter past five. The clear sound dipped deep into her sleep and brought Constance back to earth and day again. She tried to turn over and go to sleep again, tried to tell herself that of course it was absurd to think of getting up at that hour and tramping off to the woods with an utter stranger who said and did queer things. But all the time that fussy little bird by the window sill, trilling out a love song of blue hepaticas growing on a hillside, against a tiny forest of maidenhair blowing in the breeze, dew pearled and lovely with the rising sun upon them.

The morning breeze blew the curtain in at the window, blew sweet breath of flower-laden zephyrs into her face, reviving her, and suddenly she wanted to see that flowery hillside very much, and to see if that young stranger was really as interesting as he had seemed the day before. She opened one eye, stole a glance at her clock, and then she was wide awake, stealing about her room. She found the little nymph green knitted dress that fitted an early trip to the woods, the soft brown suede tramping shoes, gave a hasty rumpling to the big gold waves of her hair, and was ready.

She thought she heard footsteps coming down the pavement in the stillness of the morning, as she stole into the hall and down the stairs, softly not to wake that dreadful brother of hers, and when she opened the front door ever so silently there was the stranger lingering down by the group of hemlocks beyond the daffodils. He gave her his brilliant smile and a quiet lifting of his hat for welcome and seemed to know they would go quietly and not disturb the sleeping town as they walked through it.

Out beyond sight of her father's house Constance drew a breath of relief. Her brother hadn't wakened. It wouldn't matter whether any one else saw her or not, although it suddenly occurred to her that it was rather odd to be walking off with a stranger at this early hour in the morning.

"This is simply great of you," said Seagrave looking down upon her, his eyes full of light. "I've been wondering all night if you would come."

"Why, so have I," gurgled Constance with a breath of a laugh "or no, not wondering," she corrected herself, "I was very sure I wouldn't of course," she laughed. "You see I really haven't time. I'm leaving in about three hours."

"I know," he said gravely, "I'm sorry."

"I just couldn't resist the desire to see where those darling flowers live when they are at home," she said quickly to hide the commotion she felt in her mind at the serious way he took her going. This really was all wrong she told herself, but it was fun, and of course it would soon be over.

All too soon they arrived at Hepatica Hill and dropped down to worship the beauty. It seemed to Constance that she had never been in such a beautiful spot before, and she drank her fill of the day, and the hour, the sky, and the wonderful flowers.

Then they grew silent sitting on the hillside with the blue flowers at their feet and the fringe of fern beside them. Looking off over the valley, the town in the distance, taking deep breaths of fine air, thrilling with the song of a bird in the top of a tall tree, they were filled with the awe of the morning.

Suddenly he turned to her with that grave sweet smile she had seen first on his face at the church.

"How long have you been saved?" he asked, as simply as if he had asked how long before her college would be over.

Constance looked up in a great wonder and stared at him.

"Saved?" she echoed, and again "Saved? I—don't know just what you mean? Saved from what?"

He gave her a startled look, and then a great gentleness came upon his face. As if she had been a little child he explained, simply:

"Yesterday we united with the church," he said slowly.

"Yes?" she said with a sharp startled catch in her voice and giving him a keen look. Had he seen through her plavacting? Did he know how loth she had been to parade before the world in that way.

"You united on profession of your faith, not by letter from another church as I did. I was wondering— perhaps I have no right to ask on such a short acquaintance—but I was interested to know if you had been a Christian a long time or had just come to know the Lord?"

He waited in a sweet silence for her answer, and Constance looked up and then down in confusion.

"I—oh, I—why—!" and then she stopped with a half embarrassed laugh, "I'm not very familiar with those phrases you have used," she said, and tried to give a glibness to her speech, "they don't talk much of such things in the college I attend. But I suppose you must mean something like what they used to call in old-fashioned camp meetings being converted? Well, I'm afraid then I'll be quite a disappointment. I haven't really ever given much thought to these things. You see it was rather sprung upon me, this thing of uniting with the church—" she glanced up with a lift of her dark lashes that gave such a piquancy to her lovely face, and the look she saw in his eyes made her hurry on anxiously, speaking rapidly, trying to get the old time snap into her words and somehow not making it.

She hurried on determined to make a clean sweep of it and end this nonsense. After all the truth was best. She hated to pose as something she was not. That was why she had not wanted to join the church. It seemed to her hypocritical.

"You see my grandmother was determined I should join. The rest of the girls in the Sunday School class to which I used to belong were joining and she simply had her heart set on my joining too."

The young man was so still that she felt uncomfortable. She was afraid to look up and see the look in his eyes. She somehow felt a disapproval and she did not like it. Her young men friends were not apt to express disapproval of her. She resented it. She tried to put on her world drawl.

"I didn't see joining the church. It seemed rather archaic to me. I tried to get by without it, but it simply didn't go down. I had to either give in and join or hurt my little old sweet grandmother—" She finished her explanation flippantly and looked up with what was meant to be a daring glance at her companion, and she found such a look of sorrow in his eyes that her tone failed miserably. After an instant she dropped her eyes again and sat there, with all the still breezes, and the vaulted sky, and the blue bed of flowers at her feet dropping away from her and leaving her a lone little arrogant atom in a world that had just been full of song and sunshine, and now seemed to have withdrawn from her its joy.

After a little, that seemed a long while, the young man beside her uttered a single syllable, just a long drawn breath of a word, that almost sobbed as it became audible, like the sound of a soul who was pulling from his own heart a barbed weapon that had gone deep, and trying to be brave, but the pain of it made his breath quiver.

"Oh!"

CHAPTER III

FOR a long moment she sat there suddenly covered with shame. She had hurt him. She had pulled down the beautiful vision of herself that he had conjured up and dragged it in the dust.

Why had she been so foolish? Why had she not just kidded him along, asked a few questions, anything to keep him talking for the few minutes they would stay here, and let him think her all that he seemed to want to think? What difference did it make what he thought about her anyway? This was only one morning out of her life. She would likely never see him again or if she did their ways would not touch again. This was only an incident. Why did she have to be so awfully honest and spoil all their nice time? It was ridiculous. What was it all about anyway?

And then she looked up to try with bright words to regain her place in his estimation. What was he? A country innocent apparently. She must make him snap out of this, show him how foolish and archaic and childish his present attitude was. And so she forced her eyes to look into his and see all the pain, and all the disillusion, and all the actual dismay that her words had brought him, and she was covered with a shame she had never known before.

She perceived that this attitude of his mind was a basic part of him, something she would never be able to reason out of him nor change, and she had shocked him. He had set her up as a sort of saint, had idealized her, and she had made him understand that she was just a flesh and blood girl, a modern person of the world. Well, he had to learn sooner or later that dreams and visions did not go to make up a world in these days. Best laugh it off. He was flesh and blood himself. Couldn't she laugh him out of this?

"You take it as solemnly as if you were my father confessor," she said in a flippant tone.

"No," he answered quickly, "It's not what you've done to me—though I didn't know that anyone, not anyone with a face like yours, could stand up and take solemn vows upon them that they didn't mean—but it's what you've done to my Lord! You've mocked Him! You've taken vows upon you that you did not mean to perform. You have desecrated the cup of the blood covenant."

There was such deep pain in his words that Constance was almost stunned for a moment. She drew herself up and looked at him half bewildered.

"I don't see why that's such a dreadful thing to do!" she said crossly, "If it pleased my grandmother I think it was a good thing to do."

"Would it have pleased your grandmother if she had known that you were only playacting?"

The brown eyes looked searchingly at her and she shivered. She felt as if there was suddenly a God though she had not so believed for a long time, and that He was standing right there beside her looking into her soul and seeing all her empty vanities, tossing aside her foolish worthless virtues on which she had so greatly relied.

"She will never know," said Constance with a toss of her head.

"Perhaps not," said the young man sadly, "But God knows. It is He after all that is hurt. It is He that matters. Not I! Not your grandmother!"

Constance was still a long time. Her throat was hot, her eyes were smarting, the great vaulted sky and the valley were blurred into one with the blue flowers at her feet. She wished very much that she had not come. She wondered what time it was but she would not look at her watch. She wanted this to be over but she could not go until she had somehow made this young man think better of her. Even if she missed her train she must do it. She could not stand the thought of his disapproval. She was utterly unused to disapproval.

She cast a quick furtive glance in his direction. He sat with his face half shaded with his hand, his head bowed, his eyes closed, almost as if he were praying.

"I'm sure I don't know what you mean at all!" she burst forth in a vexed tone, "What do you mean by 'saved' anyway? Why should I have to be saved? Saved from what? And how? I never in all my life heard anybody talk the way you do. How do you get that way?"

He raised his head and looked at her gravely and she had a fleeting thought of how very sweet was the look in his eyes, almost it seemed a holy look.

"Saved from death," he said quietly, "eternal death. That means eternal separation from God you know, not extinction. We are all sinners and under condemnation of death for our sin."

"I don't see that I'm such a terrible sinner!" said Constance indignantly with an upflinging of her patrician chin. "I don't see that I should be condemned to any kind of death."

Seagrave looked at her again with that grave sweet smile.

"And yet you are a sinner condemned to death," he said impressively. "Please don't mistake me though. No one could take one glance at you and not know that you are different from the modern girls. I cannot imagine your allowing in your life the things that I know most modern young people delight in these days. Such things would be repulsive to your tastes. But what I mean is this. Ever since Adam's sin we all were born with dead spiritual natures, you, I, everybody. And a dead thing cannot be improved or made over. The only way that we could get into the presence of God is by being born again, by acquiring a new nature."

"Just how could one go about doing that?" asked Constance regarding him with a cold sarcastic air.

"Simply believe what God says about His Son, that Jesus Christ took our place, suffering on the cross the penalty for our sins, and rose from the dead as proof that God's justice was satisfied as to the sin question. God Himself comes to dwell in every one who believes that, and makes of him a new creature."

"I told Dr. Grant I didn't believe things," mused Constance a little bitterly, "He said that was all right. He said the church was the place to bring your doubts."

Seagrave considered this a moment gravely, then answered earnestly:

"The only place where we can bring doubts and have them cleared away is to the Lord Jesus. When one really comes to Him with a will to believe, He makes it all clear. One look into His face, face to face and heart to heart, is enough to satisfy doubts. But you have to come with the will to accept what He has said and trust yourself to His promises. Believing, you know, is something we will to do. Believing is not a conviction of the mind as a result of reasoning. It is swinging off and trusting to something you haven't yet proved. The proving comes afterward."

"How could one ever be willing to trust in something one wasn't sure about?"

He smiled.

"Did you ever take a ride in an airplane?"

"Oh yes, two or three times. In fact I've been considering whether I won't go back to college that way."

"But have you tested the machinery? Did you go over the engine? Do you know the mechanic who made it? Can you be perfectly sure there is not a flaw somewhere that may cause a terrible accident?"

"Why no, of course not. But others have gone up and come down in safety. The planes are tested. The accidents are very few."

"Ah, just so. You believe the plane is all right. You do not know yourself but nevertheless you are willing to trust yourself to the plane. Well, take this matter of trusting God the same way. Others have tried Him. Old saints throughout the ages have given witness that He has sustained them through trials, has always kept His promises even unto death. Sinners have accepted Him and been utterly changed by Him. Why could you not swing off and trust Him in the same way? Haven't you known some one that you are sure has been happy in trusting God?"

"Oh, yes, Grandmother, I suppose. At least she banks a lot on such things, although she doesn't talk as you do. I don't believe she even knows that line you're giving me. She thinks if you join the church the trick is done. But she's old, of course. She's about come to the end. Maybe when I get there I might feel that way too."

"I wish you knew me well enough to believe what I say." He smiled his winning smile, "I'd like to tell you what the Lord Jesus has done for me, has been to me, since I've taken Him for my Saviour. I'm young. And I can testify that I've never had such joy in my life as since I knew the Lord."

Constance with a deep restlessness in her soul studied the face of the young man before her.

"You're different from anybody I ever met," she said speculatively, "I wonder why?"

"If I'm different it's only because He's saved me."

"Do you mean you've always been this way?" asked Constance studying him thoughtfully. "How come?"

"No," he said, "Only about two years."

"But," she said, frowning, puzzled, "Don't you miss a lot out of life taking a line like this?"

"Not a thing," he said earnestly, "I'm finding out every day how much I missed before I was saved."

"But I don't understand," said Constance after a moment's puzzled silence, "You speak as if you were perfectly sure you were saved. How can you possibly know that?"

"Because He has said it and I believe Him," said Seagrave jubilantly, "Look, here are the words:" and he drew out a little soft leather book from his inner pocket and fluttered over the leaves:

"Here it is: 'He that believeth *hath* everlasting life, and *shall not* come into condemnation, but *is* passed from death unto life.'"

Constance took the book and read the passage over slowly, and at last handed it back to him.

"A great many people don't believe the Bible is anything but a book," she said with a superior tone.

"Yes, and a great many people don't know what it means to be saved. Listen to this one:" he fluttered the tiny leaves again and read: " 'If our gospel is hid, it is hid to them that are lost!' Spiritual things are spiritually discerned. The people who do not believe the Bible do not know it. They may have studied books about it. They may have studied the language and poetry in the Bible, they may have even learned by heart some of its most beautiful passages, but they have never taken it from the angle of acceptance as a perfect plan of salvation for themselves. They have never known how it all fits together without a single break or inconsistency, how gloriously it opens up when one studies it with the help of the Holy Spirit."

"You're talking in an unknown tongue to me," said Constance staring at him again half wistfully. "You look happy. You sound sincere, but I don't see how you make the grade among other people if you live on such a different plane. Aren't you terribly lonely? You don't find other people who talk this way do you?"

"You'd be surprised how many there are," he flashed at her another of his dazzling smiles that lit up his whole face. "Why, back in the city where I've been this last year there were so many of them, group after group! I used to meet them at the different Bible Conferences, and we always had such glorious times together. There's no fellowship like the fellowship of those who love the Lord Jesus."

He said that name "the Lord Jesus" in such a tender beautiful way that it seemed to put her afar and make her a stranger.

"Oh, old people I suppose," she said half contemptuously. "I can't imagine young people—excuse me, I'm convinced you're one of a kind. I'll admit you're interesting, but I can't imagine a bunch of young people getting together and being interested in such things."

He flashed a look at her, with a slight lifting of the eyebrows, but his voice was steady, his lips were pleasant as he said:

"No, they were young people. Many of them young people who were studying in one of the big Bible Schools getting ready to do Christian work."

"Oh! Missionaries!" said Constance patronizingly, "but aren't they usually awfully dumb, and kind of frumpy?"

"No, I didn't find them so," said the young man, "I'd like to take you to some of those gatherings. It would surprise you."

"Are you getting ready to be a missionary?" she asked him suddenly.

"No," he said, "I felt I could perhaps witness better at present in business. And you? Are you planning some big life work?"

"Me? Oh, I don't know what I shall do. Dad's offered me a trip to Europe next summer. All the world's before me. I'm only planning to have a good time. You think I'm a selfish little heathen I suppose but I've been under school and college life and discipline for a long time and I want to get out from under and just do my own way."

"I used to think that," said Seagrave thoughtfully, "but God showed me there was a better way."

"A better way?" she said.

"Yes, just put one's self in God's hands and let Him have His way. I've had more peace and joy since I learned to do that than ever I had in all my life before. But see, that plume of white smoke down yonder in the valley! Wouldn't that be the morning train, and aren't we getting rather late for our various appointments?"

Constance looked quickly at her wrist watch.

"Oh, my goodness!" she cried and sprang to get up. "Think of my packing, not half done! However has the time flown?"

He helped her easily to her feet.

"I'm sorry," he said, "I should have been watching the time more carefully. But it's been good to have this talk with you. I'm a stranger in town yet you know. It was most gracious of you to come out with me."

"Why, it's been beautiful!" said Constance heartily. "I didn't dream it would be so lovely up here. And I've enjoyed the talk. It certainly was a unique subject. I'm sorry I couldn't have been more in harmony with the theme and the hour. I'm rather a heathen you know, in spite of your gracious judgment of my unmodern face. But the flowers have been a wonderful sight."

She stooped and touched them with her finger tips, and then brushed her palm lightly over the fronds of the ferns.

"Good-by, little flowers," she said softly, "When I come back you'll be gone I suppose, but perhaps another year I'll see you again—" Then she turned and hurried down the hill.

The young man watched the sweetness of her face as she touched the flowers, and something very wistful came into his own eyes. He helped her carefully down the hillside till they were come to the road again, and then both fell into a quick stride knowing that the time was short. They were silent till they came into the edge of town again, each busy with his own thoughts. Somehow they felt as if they had known one another a long time, each dreading to have this pleasant intimacy come to an end.

Constance as she neared her home reflected that everybody was up now, breakfast would be almost over. She must run the gauntlet of her acquaintances who happened to be on the street, and she must meet the tantalizing questions of her brother, and perhaps also of her father and mother. They would be a little hurt that she was late to breakfast on this her last morning. How crazy she had been to go off on this queer wild goose chase with this unique stranger.

And yet as she looked up at him with a swift furtive glance there was something compelling in his gaze, something so strong and sweet and dependable about him that in spite of herself she had to be glad she knew him. It was nice to know there was one such man in the world. She wondered if he would stay so? If he could possibly survive the times and keep his faith.

They had come to her father's gate now and she paused, unable to say the bright flippant words that she felt would be appropriate to end such a very irregular acquaintance as this had been.

Seagrave put out his hand.

"I'll thank you again for this beautiful morning," he said with a gravely sweet look.

Constance had a strange impulse to cry.

"In spite of the fact that I'm only a little unsaved pagan," she asked archly with a long sweep of her dark lashes and an upward look that she had found most effective with other admirers.

But he did not laugh away her words. He only looked long and earnestly at her.

"I shall be praying that my Lord Jesus will meet you, somewhere, somehow!" he said gently.

It was just at that moment when her soul was most touched that Ruddy Van swept up to the sidewalk in his new roadster and called loudly to Constance.

"Hello, Con, got your baggage ready? I've come to take you to the train."

Constance looked up annoyed, and Seagrave with a courteous good-by marched away down the street, leaving her with a strange unfinished feeling, as if something rather wonderful and interesting were gone out of her life.

CHAPTER IV

IN the end Constance did not go until the noon train, and Ruddy Van Arden went back to his office crestfallen, for there was no way in which he could get off at noon to take the lady to the station without running actual risk of dismissal. He could not expect leave of absence twice in one day.

So it was Frank who drove his sister to the train after all, and gave her an unpleasant fifteen minutes until the train came, asking if she had remembered to pack the blue flowers from the dining room bowl, and if she didn't want him to send them on to her afterwards.

Ordinarily Constance did not mind teasing. She wondered why she minded it so much this time. Perhaps it was that she was annoyed with herself for having gone off to the woods that morning at the beck and call of an utter stranger, and thrown the whole morning out of its neat and orderly calculation. Or, perhaps it was because she found herself thinking wistfully of the pleasant brown eyes, and the earnest converse. She had never met a man like this one before.

"He's all right, Kid," said Frank suddenly, watching his sister with approving eyes. "No kidding, he is. Bill Howarth told me last night he's A number one. A real man. He has no end of honors from his college, both scholarly and athletic, and they say he's a whizz at business. Only thing is, his dad lost all their money just before he died. So of course that'll put him outta the running with you."

"What on earth do you mean, Frank, you crazy boy?" she asked sharply, "When did I ever act like a snob?"

"Oh, not a snob exactly," said Frank staring off down the tracks at the approaching train, "but of course anybody that is willing to change religions for a string of matched pearls wouldn't naturally be supposed to rush a fella that couldn't support matched pearls. You're outta his class, you know, Kid. You gotta live up to Grand's pearls—or down to 'em, I don't know which you'd call it. Supposed ta be up, isn't it?"

"Frank, you certainly are the most absurd and ridiculous boy," said his sister, trying to laugh it off. "As if the man was anything but a pleasant chance acquaintance!"

"Oh yeah?" remarked the implacable brother.

But Constance's cheeks were burning from an altogether new cause of disturbance which had suddenly entered her mind. Here she had been priding herself that she was honest anyway; she had confessed to the stranger that she had united with the church to please her grandmother. But she hadn't said a word about the real reason of her yielding, the pearls for which she would have gone even further if need be than just standing up before a congregation and taking meaningless vows upon her lips.

It was as if Frank's words had torn away a pleasant garment from her and laid bare her real self, the sordid self that was willing to sacrifice intellectual standards that she had with pride set up for herself, just for a costly trinket. It was as if her conscience had suddenly stepped upon a thorn with her first step into that parlor car and it limped all the way after the porter to her chair, pricked hard while Frank and the porter were settling her bags, and putting her coat in the rack overhead, hurt even as her brother kissed her and hurried from the moving train with a nonchalant wave of his hand, and a shouted promise to send the blue flowers.

Constance settled down into her chair, got out the magazine that she had saved to read on the way, took off her gloves, watched the familiar home sights fly by faster and faster till miles of green fields began to make her feel that vacation was really over and she would soon be back in the routine of college life again. Then she sat back and opened her magazine, but the thorn in her conscience continued to prick and she knew she must give it her undivided attention once and for all and get rid of it someway. So she closed her magazine and put it definitely down at her feet out of the way, letting her mind go back to that morning and the hillside with its carpeting of blue quivering flowers in the soft breeze. She went over again her confession. Had it really been a confession? Hadn't it been more in the manner of a defiant statement? Hadn't she really been trying to shock the young man out of his solemnity?

She closed her eyes and faced this thought, seeing herself in a new light. It had been a rather despicable thing to do when she remembered his true eyes, and the reverent way in which he had looked at her. Even yet the thought of the reverence he had given her made a warm glow about her heart. Most young men nowadays had anything but a reverent attitude towards girls. Maybe it was largely the girls' fault, but—well. To her surprise she rather liked to have this man regard her that way. And she had set deliberately about trying to shatter this illusion of his! What a fool she had been. A rare thing like that!

But yet she had not touched the crux of the matter, the real point of the thorn in her soul, which was that she had not really told him at all why she had joined the church. She had let him think that she did it to please a dear old lady whom she couldn't bear to hurt, and in a way, at least in a material way, that was a praiseworthy thing to have done. But she didn't really do it for her grandmother at all. Now she faced herself honestly and owned it. She had done it for the pearls. She wanted the pearls and she didn't want her cousin Norma to have them!

Suddenly she was quite ashamed of herself. She wondered why it hadn't seemed before to be rather raw in her to do that? But it hadn't. It had only seemed a good joke. She had even appreciated the sarcasms of Frank as he jeered at her.

But now, to-day, after her morning on the hillside, it all seemed different to her. Now why was that? Had that young man's queer ideas made a difference in herself? Had she received a new vision, a kind of a glimpse of what spiritual things might really be if one paid enough attention to them? She was inclined to laugh at the idea, and yet, she had to face the fact that she was actually ashamed of herself for having stood up before a congregation, beside a young man like that to whom the ceremony meant so much, and done it just for a string of pearls!

She tried to think what his face would have looked like if she had told him about the pearls. She recalled what he had said about false vows and her cheeks burned. She remembered the sadness of his voice, a kind of disappointment in it at what she had told him. If he had known about the pearls she knew it would have been even keener. And his words! They would surely have been more scathing. She knew enough of the shibboleth of religious phrases to think herself of things he might have said. "You have betrayed the Lord for a string of pearls." What was it Judas sold Christ for? Oh, yes, thirty pieces of silver! And she had done the same thing for matched pearls. Perhaps she was as bad as Judas. At least Seagrave would have thought so. What right had a man to be as good as that? Self righteous that was what it was, to set up a standard and go around making other people feel uncomfortable because they didn't believe in the same things! There was no sense to it. Why would she persist in thinking about that man any longer? She had nothing to do with him, would very likely never see him again. He would probably be sent off to some other city by the time she got back. People did that in business, got sent to a Western office or something. Well, she hoped she never would see him again. Prig! Going around and nosing into strangers' business. Scraping acquaintance with a girl in church when she was uniting with a perfectly respectable church and then daring to give her flowers, and leave his handkerchief—! Goodness! She had never returned that handkerchief! Where was it? Had she stuffed it into her suitcase at the last minute thinking it was something of her own, or had she left it lying on her bureau or floor for her brother to discover and send on with appropriate inscriptions of poetry or something? He was perfectly capable of course of doing that.

Well, she wouldn't return the handkerchief anyway. He would just think she wanted him to correspond if she did. She would forget it, and he could too, or else think he had put it in his pocket and lost it. Anyway it didn't matter what he thought. She must snap out of this. She was getting perfectly maudlin on the subject.

She sat up with a jerk and opened her magazine, absorbing herself as well as she could in a thrilling murder and detective story, but ever in between the paragraphs would come some sentence that Seagrave had spoken that morning. Some arresting phrase that kept her wondering. Born again. That was the thing he had talked about so much. She tried to think it out. What had he said was the way to get born again? Was it just that you had to believe something? That was absurd, of course. You couldn't believe a thing that you couldn't believe.

Of course he had used the illustration of riding in an airplane, but then that wasn't quite a parallel case. One rode in planes as a natural thing. Now if some special plane had been condemned, if it had even had a doubt cast upon its workmanship or mechanism she wouldn't go in it of course. And that was what had happened to her spiritually. She had been to college and found out that these things he talked about were myths, fables, legends, traditions. How could one believe any more in a fable after one had been enlightened? How could he? He had been to college too, and seemed more than commonly intelligent.

And yet he did believe with all his soul. There was no denying that. He was utterly sincere in everything he said.

During the whole of that five hour journey Constance debated with herself thus. She didn't even finish the detective story. It didn't somehow seem worthwhile. She finally laid down the magazine and closed her eyes. Too many times had a pair of brown eyes come across the page and interrupted the trend of the story. She was more interested in the stranger of the hillside than in the story.

Then she found herself recalling every trifling word or action of her contact with the handsome stranger, from the moment when he addressed her in the church to his farewell smile and the set of his fine shoulders as he walked away, when Ruddy Van so annoyingly appeared on the scene.

She remembered each expression of his face, each intonation of his voice, she thrilled at the memory of his hand clasp, and the almost reverent way in which he lifted her from the hillside and helped her to her feet. She remembered every word he spoke. Somehow the words he had read from his little Testament had gone deep into her heart. She could not throw them off though she tried hard to do so. It was not going to be pleasant having such words clinging in her mind when she got back to college. But of course college and a normal life would drive them out again, just as college had first driven away the early teaching of her grandmother and her Sunday School teachers.

Before her journey was over Constance had made the incident of the stranger into a lasting memory of her life. She thought that she was going to be able to shake it off as soon as she arrived at her destination, but she found herself succumbing more and more to the memory of the man. She even allowed herself to think wistfully what it would be to have such a man for an intimate friend, perhaps the most intimate friend of her

life. Of course it would be utterly unthinkable to live up
to such standards as he held, but there were ways in
which such a friend and companion would be wonderful. It would put living on an entirely different plane.
Of course she never would be willing to pay the price.
She was too fond of her world and its ways; too eager
for matched pearls and the like. Yet she found herself
thinking wistfully of a future in which there might
appear such a person who would yet be satisfied with
herself as she was.

She was roused from her absorption by the stir of the
passengers getting ready to get out, and the porter
appeared to brush her shoes, take her baggage and
receive her generous tip.

Half reluctantly she opened her eyes and came back
to her regular life again, knowing that Seagrave must
henceforth have no part in her thoughts and plans. He
was merely a pleasant romantic little incident, like the
flowers he had given her, that were likely withered by
this time, and would soon be forgotten.

Getting back to college again was always an interesting occurrence. There was the happy stir of fellow
students' greetings, the unpacking and getting in order
again, the running back and forth to other rooms to
chat and hear the news, to tell all that had befallen one
during the few days' absence. In the excitement Constance snapped back to normal and was as gay and
flippant as the rest. The hillside and the stranger, and
the lovely blue flowers, even the steady, earnest brown
eyes, were forgotten. Constance was her former self
again.

It was not until Doris Hampden, her roommate, after
a burst of confidence about a new admirer she had met
at a dance, said:

"Well, Connie, what's the news? Any great thrills?
Meet any new men?" that Seagrave's face came back to
her and his eyes seemed to be smiling at her again.

The color, to her utmost confusion, flamed into her
cheeks without warning. She was not a girl given to
showing emotion and it annoyed her.

"Oh, yes," she owned in a drawl of indifference, "one

perfectly stunning one, but wait, Dorrie, I haven't shown you my pearls yet."

"Your pearls? The real pearls! You princess! How come?" Constance twisted a little grimace.

"Oh, my grandmother gave them to me," she said lightly.

"But I thought they were to be a graduating present if you got them. You weren't at all sure when you went home you know."

"Well, there they are," said Constance proudly exhibiting them, "but I had to pay the price."

"What do you mean, pay the price?" asked her friend curiously, "was there a string attached to them?"

"Yes," said Constance shrugging her shoulders, "a theological string. Grandmother got these pearls herself the day she joined the church and she had set her heart on giving them to me when I joined the church. I found she was going to be quite stubborn about it. There was even danger she might give them to my country cousin who happens to be quite religiously inclined, so I gave in. I joined the church last Sunday. What do you think of that after all my noble renunciation of the faith of my fathers?"

"You don't mean it, Connie, you really joined church? Say isn't that rich? But I don't blame you of course for pearls like that. They're wonderful! I'd have done it myself of course. What harm could it do? It doesn't mean a thing of course."

"Of course not," said Constance, and felt suddenly a pair of steady brown eyes upon her soul, a keen disappointed look in them.

"But to think of you standing up before the congregation joining church! Con Courtland. It's a scream! What'll the girls say when they hear it?"

"It's none of their business of course," said Constance gravely. Somehow she wasn't enjoying the sensation as much as she had anticipated when she had thought of going back to college and telling the girls what she had done. She had thought it a good joke at first. But now somehow she shrank from it. Was she always going to have that man with his brown eyes following her around censoring her acts? She must certainly snap out of this and do it quickly.

So she joined in the laugh as two other girls came into the room and Doris proceeded to tell the tale and show the pearls. She even added grotesque touches, describing her nunlike appearance in white, and the throng of her former Sunday School mates, who were not her intimates any longer. As the thorn in her conscience stabbed her, and the prick went deeper, she grew more flippantly eloquent, until she had the girls in screams of laughter and the news was noised abroad that Constance Courtland had joined the church. They all flocked in to hear the tale and view the pearls, and added each her witty sarcasm, until suddenly Constance felt as if she were going to cry. She seemed to have cast aside all tender ties to home and family and fine true things. She knew she had said things she did not mean. She knew that if Seagrave could have heard her he would have turned away with hurt disappointed eyes, and would never have wanted to see her again. And he had said he would pray for her! Perhaps he was even now praying for her! The thought stabbed her like a knife.

Suddenly she snatched the pearls from Rose Mellen's hands and put them away, snapping the little case that held them sharply.

"Come, girls," she said breezily, "let's go down and take a walk."

So they all trooped down to the campus, and went gayly arm in arm down the broad cement walk. But Constance's heart was very sore. She was deeply ashamed of herself. She said bitterly to herself that she wouldn't wear her pearls. They were spoiled for her, utterly spoiled by the false light in which she had allowed them to place her.

She went to bed early that night professing to have a headache, and turning her face to the wall began to think again about Seagrave and all that he had said, and most of all about the steady true voice, and the deep look in his eyes, and the way he had seemed to expect the best and finest things of her. She felt somehow degraded by her own acts.

Never in her life before had Constance felt that sense of utter humiliation. It would sweep over her at times with a strange sick feeling in the pit of her stomach, and the hot blood of shame would burn in her cheeks against the cool pillow. It seemed to be an actual physical disability. It fairly choked her with a sense of her own worthlessness as she lay there with her face burning in the darkness.

She tried to summon her former self-respect, to call to mind that she belonged to two very old respected families. It ill-became a Courtland or a Van Vleck to discount herself. She had always been respected. Her family had always been respected. She had not done anything to merit this inferiority complex. She had merely lived up to the code of the day. And she had humored a dear foolish little old grandmother, pleased her beyond anything, and got the lovely pearls in return. Why should she have this feeling that she had somehow erred in a moral way?

Why, she had always been almost ridiculously moral in comparison to her comrades, and they were considered perfectly all right girls anywhere. Yet they did a lot of things that she wouldn't do. Surely she wasn't to blame, was she, that she couldn't believe in some fusty old traditions in which her grandmother was brought up? And just for that should she hurt the dear old lady? If, as she firmly believed—or had believed until she got all upset by that fanatical stranger—there wasn't anything in this religious stuff but traditions and dogmas, what harm had there been in going through the gestures just to satisfy Grandmother? It wasn't her fault either that the pearls were a part of the business. It was just her luck.

So she reasoned with herself hour after hour, and tossed cautiously upon her bed lest Doris across the room should hear her. And Doris finally did rouse sleepily and say, "What's the matter, Con? Have you got the toothache again? I thought you had it out!"

"I did!" snapped Constance taking a deep breath, "I guess I ate something that didn't agree with me!"

"Better get up and take a dose of soda," advised

Doris turning over her pillow and returning to her dreams.

But Constance continued to toss, and just when she would think she had exorcised this demon of wakefulness and would be dropping off to restfulness Seagrave's face would appear before her, his eyes looking trustfully at her as they had done on the hillside that morning. No, decidedly, Constance was not at rest.

CHAPTER V

SHE took herself severely to task next morning, when, having at last dropped into a troubled sleep she woke to find herself very late for the day, and was dressing with haste and annoyance.

"This is ridiculous!" she told herself. "It's just a case of nerves! I didn't have enough exercise when I was at home. I ought to have played tennis all Sunday morning instead of sitting in that melancholy church service and getting all upset. I always said religion was mainly a case of emotions, and now I know it! Well, this has got to stop! How absurd to let a fanatical stranger get hold of me in this way. What do I care what he thinks of me?"

And then suddenly she knew in her heart that it wasn't just what the stranger thought, it was this queer feeling he had given her that there was a God, and that God was looking at her and thinking about her and was not pleased with her attitude.

"And that too is absurd!" she said aloud. "There likely isn't any God, nothing but a Power somewhere, and if there is, He wouldn't bother about me. Of course Grandmother believes He does, and that likely has affected my imagination. I declare, it's a crime to teach little children such unreasonable dogmas!"

Later in the morning there came a dainty package addressed in Frank's scrawling handwriting, which when opened proved to be a tin box containing the last surviving blue hepaticas done up in wet moss.

Constance was alone in her room when she opened

them and a sudden constriction caught her throat, a
flashing memory of the giver as he had stood with his
hands full of them looking down at her that morning, a
breath of the hillside where they had sat and watched
the wind blowing the little frail blue cups, and the
maidenhair fern bending low in the breeze over them
like loving nurses over the baby flowers. Something
almost like a sob caught in her throat and she put her
face down for an instant on the brave little drooping
blossoms and cried a few tears, a great wistfulness
coming over her.

An instant later she dashed the tears angrily from her
face and going to the open window she threw the
flowers out of the window down behind the shrubs that
grew about the dormitory. A great panic came over her
lest Doris should come and find her weeping over dead
flowers. Doris could make a lot out of a thing like that.

She hurried to splash water in her face, dab it expert-
ly with a soft towel and then apply powder deftly till
all traces of her recent emotion were obliterated.

As she turned away from the mirror she experienced
a wild wish that she could as easily erase the memory
of those flowers from her heart.

But she went over to her desk with a firm resolve to
get to work and drive this nonsense out of her mind.
When Doris came in a few minutes later with her hands
full of letters she was working away at her thesis.

"Listen Connie," cried Doris sitting down beside the
desk, "pay attention! I've got a letter!"

"A letter?" said Constance looking up coolly, "Is
that unusual? You seem to have many letters. And
really I'm awfully busy, Dorrie!"

"But this is a special letter!" said Doris sparkling.
"It's from Casper Coulter!"

"Again?" said Constance coldly with disapproval in
her voice, "I thought you said you were done with
him."

"Oh, I am as far as that goes," laughed Doris gayly.
"I gave him back his pin before Easter, but it doesn't
seem to faze him in the least. After all, why shouldn't
I have a good time with him? He understands that I'm
not committed to him. Besides, Connie, he certainly

shows a girl a good time. But anyhow that's not the point. He's coming down for the dance at the weekend. I had to ask him down when I was explaining to him. He just pestered the life out of me. Besides, he has a new car that is simply sublime. I couldn't resist."

"He'll get drunk!" said Constance with a lifting of her chin and a slight curl of her lip.

"No, he won't!" said Doris, "He promised me! He hasn't been drinking at all since Easter!"

"He says so, I suppose," commented Constance loftily.

"Yes, he says so, but Sam Warner says so too. And anyhow, that's not the point. He's bringing a perfectly stunning man down with him and he wants to know if you'll let him take you to the dance. Now, Connie, don't begin that I-am-better-than-thou frown! Wait till you hear. He's not Casper's chum. He's ages older than Casp. He graduated four years ago. He's a perfectly stunning man! A real thrill! He's dark and interesting and tall. I saw him once while I was in New York last week, and Casper pointed him out to me. He's written a couple of successful plays, and he's all kinds of clever, musical and artistic, and awfully popular. Casper is just crazy about him, and he says he knows you'll like him. He's your line, clever and intellectual and all that."

"I'm sure I ought to be greatly honored that Casper Coulter considers me clever and intellectual," said Constance haughtily, "but really, I must decline to entertain his friends. I just can't stand Casper's kind of men."

"Now, Connie, don't be horrid. Just because you've joined church don't go and get disagreeable. You've practically got to do this for me, because you see I told Casper it would be all right and for him to bring him if he could. And you won't go back on me now after I've given my word, and he's already been asked."

Constance flashed a look of annoyance at her roommate.

"You had no right in the world to do that, Doris. You know Casper Coulter is not my kind, and I don't want to have anything to do with him or his friends. I don't like to go with strangers either. I hate this way of forcing a man to go with a girl he hasn't even met. I've always made it a rule to go only when the man himself asks me. I don't approve of somebody else picking out partners. And you needn't give that nasty fling about joining the church. You know it has nothing to do with that. I just don't like Casper's crowd or his way of doing things."

"Now, listen, Connie," said Doris settling down earnestly to plead her cause. "You're all mistaken about this man. Casper has been telling him a lot about you, how beautiful and clever you are, and he's wild to meet you. It seems he saw you last year in the distance and has been asking Casper to bring him down ever since. He calls you the girl with the gorgeous gold hair. And Connie, you needn't go again if you don't like him, but you won't let me down this time, will you? I've told the girls he's coming down to take you and they're all crazy to meet him. Rose Mellen went to the opening night of his first play and she says it was a wonder, just full of thrills and pathos. And you know, Connie, if you turn him down flat that way the girls will all say it's because you've got religious."

"I don't know why it should matter to me what the girls think," said Constance coldly, though she knew in her heart that it did. "If Rose Mellen is so crazy about him why don't you let him take Rose? Her hair is a much brighter gold than mine."

"Because Rose Mellen is going with Pat Fraley, of course. And anyway it's you the man wants to meet, not Rose. She's not his type at all. You don't know how interesting he is, Connie. It's not every day a girl can meet a man who is crazy about her before he even knows her."

In the end Constance gave in and promised, as Doris had been confident she would. But Doris would have been amazed if she had known what made her do it. Just the sudden sight of a little withered blue flower lying on the rug at her foot, a little faded flower that had slipped away from the rest and remained behind to linger with a memory of a wind-swept hillside, and the dawn of a dewy sunlit morning.

Constance saw it with a dart of remembrance, put

out her slippered foot quickly, casually, and covered the little crumbling flower grinding it into the floor. But the vision of the tall stranger with the light of the morning in his eyes and the blue flowers in his hand had done its work. All her worries of the night before seemed suddenly to rush back upon her. Well, why not one stranger as well as another? And perhaps this new one would be able to drive out the vision of the other and bring peace back to her soul again.

So, reluctantly, she consented, telling Doris firmly that she would do it this one time, but that she must never again make any promises for her.

Doris hugged her ecstatically, and went joyously on her way to her next class. Constance tried to bring her mind back to her thesis, but it would whirl on in circles, until she got up in despair and carefully brushed every vestige of the little dead flower from the rug. Then she sat down and went vigorously to work at her thesis once more, telling herself that she would simply refuse to think at all of that incident of Easter. She would plunge into work and play, any play that offered itself during the few weeks that remained, and get rid of this ridiculous obsession.

So with the lingo of the classroom and the patter of the campus Constance lashed her startled conscience into quiescence once more, and went forth into each day welcoming any diversion whether of work or play that would make her forget utterly her doldrums as she called them.

But college life began to sweep in a strong tide and left no room for repining. There was much to be done in the next few weeks for commencement was almost upon them. There were rehearsals and themes and invitations and clothes to discuss and plan. Each day was more than full. Slippers and gloves, white dresses and rainbow colored dresses, caps and gowns and all the other paraphernalia of commencement. There were class meetings galore, presents for teachers and graduating classmates, fraternity meetings and business, much discussion about pledging new members. It was all most absorbing and fascinating.

Constance was swept along with the rest with little

time for dreaming or harking back to Seagrave and what had happened at Easter.

One day she asked Doris:

"Well, how about this thriller that I'm to take to the dance Saturday night? You've raved a lot about him but you haven't even told me his name."

"Oh, surely I have!" said Doris laughing, "It's Thurlow Phelps Wayne." Doris pronounced the syllables impressively.

"Why the Phelps?" asked Constance dryly. "Wasn't Thurlow enough to uphold the Wayne prestige?"

"Oh, you, you make me tired!" said Doris in a vexed tone. "Here I've gone and got you a man with a real background and you make fun of him before you've even seen him."

"Well, isn't that better than doing it after I've seen him?" mocked Constance. It still went against the grain to take up with any of Casper Coulter's friends. She felt that Casper Coulter was a bad influence in Doris' life and she could see that more and more Doris was becoming deeply interested in him.

"Well, just wait until you see him, that's all!" said Doris petulantly, "And you may as well know that the Phelps is distinguished. He belongs to the old Phelps family of New England, an old old family, and quite notable. I believe they were all literary, and the Thurlows were distinguished too. I forget for what. But they are awfully smart and quite popular."

So for the next two days Doris began giving anecdotes and incidents concerning the Thurlows, the Phelpses and the Waynes whenever Constance was in the room.

"What's the idea?" asked Constance at last. "Are you afraid I'm going to back out, or are you aiming to make a permanent connection, a sort of quartette to bring about some of your own dates? Because I warn you that however nice this Thurlow person proves to be I'm done when this dance is over. He may be an angel in disguise, but anybody who makes it easy for you and that Coulter boy to get together again, would be my enemy. Because truly, Doris, Casper Coulter isn't good enough for you, and that's the truth. I do hate to see

you running around with him, and I'd take twice as
much interest in this dance and this unknown knight
you're bringing on for me if you'd just promise me
that after Saturday night you're done with Casper."

"For heaven's sake, Con, what's gotten into you? I do
believe there must be more in that church gesture of
yours than you're willing to own. I never saw you so
particular before. What's the matter with Casper? Just
because he took a little too much liquor once and went
with a girl you didn't like. All men do things they grow
out of. Besides, when a young man gets married he
generally settles down. If he doesn't one can always get
a divorce nowadays."

"*Doris!*" Constance swung around toward her,
"You're not going to marry him are you? And to marry
any one *that* way, talking about getting a divorce!
You've never talked that way before! I'm sure your
people are not that kind of people!"

"Oh, you and your kinds of people! What's wrong
with divorce I'd like to know? Everybody's doing it
nowadays," said Doris angrily, "But I didn't say I was
going to marry him, did I? But all the same you're
changed. I don't know what it is but you're twice as
finicky as you were before you went home this last
time. If it's religion I hope I don't catch it. For goodness sake cut it out! After Saturday night you'll understand that I'm really doing you a favor introducing you
to such a talented man as Thurlow Wayne."

"Thurlow *Phelps* Wayne, dearie, don't forget the
Phelps. It's hyphenated isn't it? Shall I have to call him
Mr. Phelps-Wayne did you say?" Constance's tone was
amused but there was a note of anxiety behind it. She
really was worried about Doris, for she was becoming
more and more absorbed in the young man whom
Constance felt was utterly unworthy of her. She was
still more worried when for answer Doris slammed out
of the room angrily. It was not like Doris to lose her
temper.

Nevertheless as the day of the dance approached
Constance's mind turned toward the stranger with more
than her usual distaste toward meeting a stranger against
whom she was already prejudiced. What would he be

like? How would he look? Was it conceivable that she could possibly enjoy the society of a man who was a friend of Casper Coulter?

Constance had by this time pretty well exorcised the memory of Seagrave, his blue flowers and strange conversation. She only thought of them occasionally, as one looks back to a book read or a picture seen which left a strong impression. Only, now and then, when she leaned forward to look out of her window, and glanced down at the shrubs growing luxuriantly there, she had a quick consciousness of the little dead flowers she had thrown down there, as if it were a grave below her, hiding something that had once been dear.

But Friday night she had a sharp vivid dream of Seagrave, dreamed she was telling him about the pearls, dreamed that his look had been even graver, sadder than she had feared, dreamed that her burden was even heavier than before, and woke up with a sharp memory of the sorrow in his face.

His look lingered with her through the day, though outwardly she was for the most part her gay crisp self, utterly sure of her own position in life, utterly strong and breezy and hard and bright. But in her heart a war was being waged.

Somehow the renewed picture of Seagrave had strengthened her dislike toward meeting Thurlow Wayne and going to that dance with him. The dance itself meant nothing to her. She had danced all her life. She was not especially interested in going even without him, but as the day waned and the time for meeting her escort arrived she developed such a strong dislike toward going that she half contemplated going to bed and pretending to be sick. Only somehow she could not quite bring herself to play such a trick on Doris of whom she was really very fond, and who was obviously so full of delightful anticipation that she could hardly contain herself.

So she arrayed herself in garments calculated to be the most impressive. Severe black satin, and her string of pearls. She hesitated a long time about the pearls. Somehow she shrank from the pearls because of the memories they brought up, which still were accompa-

nied by a keen feeling of humiliation. Then suddenly
she realized that if she were ever to get over that nonsense now was the time to do it, so she quickly clasped
them about her neck and turned away from the mirror.
She had not worn them since Easter Day, and somehow
she did not want to remember that now. This kind of
thing, this dance, was what she had wanted the pearls
for in the first place. Of course she would wear them.
They would help her to be impressive. And it just
might happen that Doris would need something impressive to hold her from doing something foolish.

So she went hastily out of the room and down the
hall, trying not to see Seagrave's face every time she
closed her eyes, trying to forget the heavenly look on
Grandmother's face when she had kissed her and
clasped the pearls about her neck. Trying most of all to
forget that every time she saw or thought of the pearls
she felt ashamed of herself. She half wished that the
precious things were back in Grandmother's treasure
chest waiting till a time when some one, not herself
perhaps ever, could claim them legitimately.

Doris met her at the head of the stairs, gay in a rose
colored frock of tulle, looking like a lovely rose, her
eyes starry with joy.

"Oh, you darling!" she exclaimed as she saw Constance. "I was just coming up to see if you were ready.
You look just wonderful,—though I did think you'd
wear something bright. But perhaps this severe type
will be best after all, and it surely makes the pearls
stand out. You look just like a million dollars, Con!
Come on! I'm dying to watch his face when he sees
you. And yours too when you see him. He's wearing
that dark, scholarly, brooding look, now, and the girls
are green with jealousy that you've drawn him. He
really is the best looking thing!"

They were on their way downstairs now, and it was
just then she saw him standing by the door in the lower
hall looking up watching for her coming.

She knew him at once even though she had never
seen him before. Knew him even before she noticed
Casper standing by his side. She recognized the dark
brooding look, the glitter of the handsome black eyes

that yet had such a look of sharp worldly wisdom; knew him by the cocksure lift of his chin, the attitude of having come to confer honor, and to appraise. A wave of anger, of resentment swept her, even while she felt herself fascinated by his dark sophistication. Well, it was only for to-night, and she would show him!

So she lifted her patrician chin haughtily and went on downstairs, aware of his approval, his admiration. Yes,—she would show him!

CHAPTER VI

LIKE a young queen she bore herself through the introduction, giving Coulter a mere nod of recognition, and wearing a cool aloofness toward the stranger.

But a strange thing happened. When she lifted her eyes to meet his own flattering gaze there were two faces there before her, just as distinctly as if they had been there in reality. One the dark-eyed escort boring deep into her personality with his too-intimate gaze, the other Seagrave with his steady earnest eyes and sorrowful gaze piercing her soul. Oh, this was outrageous! Seagrave had no right to look at her that way even in a memory. She must be on the verge of a nervous breakdown. How ridiculous!

She passed her hand over her eyes to dispel the vision but there it was again, pale like a mist, but the eyes searched hers.

Wayne was throwing her white cloak about her shoulders now, with a light gay touch on her bare shoulder, and a deep look into her eyes. This was a man of the world indeed, and her intuition taught her he was not her kind. Ordinarily she would have drawn back and resented his forwardness, but those other eyes upon her confused her, angered her. How did Seagrave's eyes dare look at her like that? She impulsively resolved to fling herself under this other influence and see if she could not drive Seagrave's haunting eyes away.

Suddenly she was finding that this man Thurlow Wayne, if she allowed herself to meet his gaze, to yield to his challenge, stirred her more deeply than any man had ever done before. He almost frightened her with the intensity of his gaze, while yet she resented it. It was as Doris had said, there was a strange fascination about the man, which yet in spite of her resolve to yield to him for the evening, repelled her inmost feelings.

Presently they were dancing together, and he held her intimately, closer than she usually allowed, and yet she seemed to have no power to withdraw herself. His handclasp was presuming, she knew, and while she did not exactly return it, she seemed to have given up the right to resent it. There was a strange intoxication in his gaze that was unlike anything she had ever experienced before, and she had a distinct realization that it was not good, that there was nothing high and fine about it, that it appealed directly to her lower nature, to the things of the flesh.

Constance had not been unaware of the things of the flesh all her life, but she had not been tempted by them. So far they had never appealed to her. Her cool soul had not been interested in them. But this man was different. He made wickedness suddenly brilliant, alluring, excusable, more to be desired than anything in life.

And yet what nonsense was this she was thinking? He had done no wickedness, merely flattered her by a gaze that spoke volumes, merely made his touch more vital, more mysteriously interesting than other men she knew. Was it necessarily wrong, ungentlemanly, lacking in respect for her because he showed his deep interest in her at once and seemed to want her to understand that there was a mystical bond between them? That was absurd! Why was she so excited over meeting just another stranger? Why should she think of such things? Oh, she knew! It was those other eyes, those steady grave ones looking at her now from across the room, now from close by, and always that deep sadness in them. It was just her consciousness of that other man, a man just as much a stranger as this one, that made her so uncomfortable, so unable to enter lightly into the gayety of the evening. Never before had she been troubled by thoughts like this. And yet she felt herself yielding to the spell this dark man put upon her, as they glided about the floor in such perfect harmony. Ah! This was ecstacy! Why should one ever be sad?

Something that had always been conscience to her struggled within her, tried to cry out a warning, yet a power greater than her own seemed to be carrying her away beyond its call.

He drew her outside on the wide balcony where a great moon was rising, touching with silver the budding spring world and a silver mist was shimmering down just made for such a time and place. He put a possessive arm about her drawing her, against her own volition, close to him and her heart stood still within her waiting afraid, yet fascinated, her usual poise all gone. He bent his handsome head with the moonlight shimmering on his shining black hair he brought his face down till his hot breath touched her cheek, and his sensuous lips were almost on hers, and she seemed helpless to prevent them. Till suddenly she lifted frightened eyes and there above her she saw the calm stern eyes of Seagrave but he was very far away and vanishing into silver mist and the look in his eyes cut to her soul as nothing had ever done. And then she knew in a flash that she was doing this of herself. That she had willed to yield to this thing, this way of the world that she had always heretofore despised. This was not the sacred thing called love. This man did not know her nor she him. He had shown her no respect, only flattery, only a desire to touch her skin and dominate her spirit This thing that held her in its clutches now was really of the underworld. She had no love for this man. Even now within his embrace she caught a gleam in his dark eyes that frightened her as she had never been frightened before and yet had it not been for those other eyes watching her sadly from afar she would have had no power against this mighty avalanche that seemed to be about to overwhelm her.

Suddenly with a cry she started back and pushed him from her with all her might, struck out at him as he started back astonished, and evading him, slid from his grasp and darted back into the dancing hall again, weaving her way swiftly among the dancers over to the opposite door, and out into the night again across the campus to her dormitory.

She had no thought of consequences. She was angry beyond any indignation that had ever come to her before, angry and frightened, and utterly humiliated. Out in the coolness of the moonlit campus it seemed impossible that she had ever allowed herself to be put into such a situation. She had always despised petting, but she had thought it merely silly, beneath the dignity of a well brought up girl. But now she knew it was not just silly. It was playing with fire. A fire that could blast one's better feelings and leave a scar forever where it had touched, even but lightly.

She was amazed at herself, and ashamed of herself that she had so easily been drawn into a situation where a thing like this had been possible. She had thought herself so far above such things, and now she found to her shame that she was just like every other silly girl led about by feelings!

Blindly she tore across the campus in her little satin dancing pumps, minding not that spring was oozing from the spongy turf, wetting her feet, and menacing the delicate heels.

Half way to the dormitory she passed two of the chambermaids idling along in the moonlight, and realized that her mad race would arouse their curiosity. When she halted and looked back she saw they had already paused to turn their heads and stare.

Then she summoned breath to call: "Maggie, would you mind going over to the dressing room and asking Bella to look after my cloak? I didn't feel well and ran out in a hurry."

"Oh, sure, Miss Courtland, I'll do that right away. Is there anything else I could do for you?"

"Thank you, Maggie, why if you would just ask Bella to send word to Doris, my roommate, you know, that I've gone to bed. Don't let her think she must come back to the room. I don't need anybody. I just need to get to sleep."

Constance hurried up to her room and locked her door. Her heart was beating wildly, and her face was burning. She flung herself headlong upon her bed as she used to do when she was a very little child, and broke into hushed sobs, the tears stinging their unaccustomed way to her eyes and pouring out in a flood. Constance had never been a crying girl. When she was grieved she usually hardened and grew sarcastic rather than to vent her sorrow in tears. But now it was something deeper than grief. It was utter humiliation. She felt as if she were groveling in the dust. She had caught a glimpse of her own soul reflected in those gloating dark eyes of the brooding stranger and she loathed herself as well as him. It was not just anger that he had dared to try to kiss her without her permission. That was something that she had always been quite able to control. She was accustomed to admiration. This was not the first time a man had tried to kiss her. But heretofore she had always seen it coming and warded it off. This time it had come almost at her bidding. Just a little yielding of herself, the barriers thrown down, and she saw the evil thing coiled in her own self.

Startlingly it came to her how she had told Seagrave on the hillside that she was not a sinner and why should she need to be saved. It hadn't even occurred to her that there were the makings of a sinner in one so well born and bred as herself. And now she saw that the thing that makes men and women fall into the depths of degradation, that very same thing in embryo had lain within her own heart and almost caused her to lose what she considered her self-respect.

It was of no use to tell herself that even if it had been consummated it would have been but a kiss and what was a mere kiss? Constance was too honest with herself for that. She knew the power that had led her so far might easily have led farther some day. She knew that if it had not been for that sad-eyed stranger in her memory she would have let that kiss be completed, might even have returned it. Not that a single kiss would be considered to mean so much to-day. It was what that kiss stood for that was so appalling to her. A letting down of her own standards.

It had been no power of herself that had kept her

from it. There had been no victory of her own better self. Perhaps she had no better self. How terrible!

She felt that she had been rescued, snatched from something she would all her life have loathed to remember. Doubtless in her escort's mind it had been merely one more kiss, merely one more girl. He probably made all girls feel they were the one and only. That dark brooding look, that tender pressure that hinted at deep splendid passion. How her whole body revolted at the thought that he had held her close even if only for an instant. How her cheek still burned with the memory of his hot breath. The glitter of his eyes in the moonlight, how it had charmed her like the eyes of a serpent. And to think that nothing in her calm poised self had been able to resist! She had been no better than the lowest girl upon the street whom she had always hitherto despised and spoken of with contempt. Well, she knew herself now for a sinner! Capable of yielding to any sin that reached her in the right subtle way.

Oh, she had always been so proud that she was able to take care of herself! She had boasted of it! And here she had been able to do nothing. It had just been Seagrave who had rescued her.

He had said he would pray for her. That morning standing by her father's gate, he had told her he would pray for her. Perhaps he had been praying now, kneeling by his bedside somewhere in the stillness and darkness breathing a prayer for her!

The thought filled her with a great awe and started the scalding tears again. She felt like a little humble frightened child who hadn't known her danger or her need. All her self-sufficiency was gone. She despised herself.

The Constance of yesterday would have said:

"Oh, such a fuss about a little kiss. What did it matter whether he kissed me or not? Of course I've always hated those things, but what's a kiss more or less? No real harm done."

But the Constance of this evening lay and shuddered because she had seen into her own heart and seen weakness and vileness and sin there. Playing with a principle of right and wrong. That was what it was. Oh, of course the world to-day was doing it all the time and laughing openly about it. But that did not make it any better now. She had seen into her own heart.

Maggie came to the door with the lovely white coat, and a message from Doris that she would come if she was needed, but Constance sent back word that all she needed was rest, and would she please make her excuses? Maggie went away again and quiet and darkness settled down about her.

Constance arose and undressed in the dark, crept about her room giving little gasping sobs, now and then a long shudder of horror at the memory of the evening, an utter despising of herself. It was as if for the first time she had gazed into her own heart which she had always supposed to be white and pure, and found it a nest of filth and creeping things.

She got into her bed and sobbed again into her pillow. She thought of Seagrave praying for her. Had it then been his prayers that had haunted her, held her back? She had thought it was her own nerves, seeing his face following her everywhere that way, reproaching her. But now, suddenly she wondered if prayer did really have a power, an effect? Was it perhaps like the radio, just as sounds were stored up in the air, so perhaps prayers were hovering about on their way to and from God? It filled her with great awe. It made her feel strangely as if God were in her room watching her thoughts.

But at least whatever had done it, she was free now from that feeling that Seagrave was following her. She was still burdened by the thought of her own failure, her own worthlessness, still ashamed of the way she had gotten her pearls, and oppressed by the thought of confessing to Seagrave, but at least he was not haunting her any more. She could look off into the darkness of her room and not see his spectral glance searching her. She had snapped back to normal, but she had left her self-respect and her self-esteem behind somewhere, and could she ever get them back anymore?

At last worn with alternate rage and shame and despair she fell asleep and when Doris came in later she tiptoed about the room and did not disturb her, for which Constance, partly roused, was vaguely grateful. She knew there was a reckoning coming but she did not want to think about it now.

But the next morning it had to come.

Doris was coolly suspicious.

"But, Constance, were you really *sick?*" she asked pointedly. "You seemed perfectly well when we started."

"I had a headache," said Constance evasively, glad to reflect that this was perfectly true.

"But Connie, you never stay away from a good time just for a headache."

"A good time?" said Constance with a touch of her old familiar sarcasm, "I didn't exactly feel that I was having a good time. You know I only went to please you."

"Well, you certainly didn't please me, going off like that. What do you suppose Thurlow Wayne thought of you? Just beating it like that without a word of explanation?"

"I'm afraid I wasn't thinking about his opinion," said Constance, a troubled look in her face. "But didn't you get my message? Maggie promised to give it to you."

"Oh, yes, I got your message. But I knew there must be something back of it. You never are rude like that."

"I'm sorry," said Constance, "but I really had to get away at once. I had to lie down."

Doris swung around on her.

"What did Thurl do? I can't understand it. I was just sure you'd fall for him as soon as you saw him. I thought you'd see how clever and sophisticated he is. I was sure you'd fall for him hard. And I knew he was simply nuts about you just from having seen you in the distance, and then—you *vanish!* What was the matter with him? What do you want for your money?"

"He's probably all right for the people who like him," said Constance, feeling somehow a weight on her tongue. "He's just not the type that I admire that's all!" she finished lamely.

"For goodness sake! What could you ask for more? Handsome as a picture, rich as Croesus, crazy about you, and clever as they come. And you treated him like the dust under your feet! Well, I can tell you he's not used to that. No wonder he said you were like an icicle!"

Constance rose up on one elbow and looked at her roommate earnestly.

"Did he say that, Doris?"

"He certainly did!" said Doris indignantly, "called you a polar star and a lot of other poetic things, but I could see he was mad all over. Of course I excused you, said you weren't feeling well, and a lot of bunk, and that you hadn't wanted to come, but wouldn't let him down and all that. But I could see he was cut clear through and I know something happened. I don't see why you had to develop such an awful hate for him. Now what was it? Confess."

"Nothing really happened at all, Dorrie," Constance spoke quietly, almost humbly, "and I don't really hate him. I think perhaps it was myself I hated. While I was dancing with him, I—just—hated myself. Perhaps you won't understand, and I'm afraid I can't explain, but that's the way it really was."

Doris stared.

"If you aren't the queerest girl!" she said. "And you didn't used to be at all! You used to be a good sport, ready for anything. You never even took such a dislike to Casper Coulter till this last time you went home. If joining the church ruins a person for life then it's to be hoped no more of our class will join. That string of pearls has just ruined your disposition, Connie Courtland. You're getting too good for this earth!" and Doris snapped a string of amber beads about her neck and slammed out of the room and down to breakfast.

But Constance got out of her bed, locked the door and then stood staring across her room in a kind of dazed wonder.

"Then he didn't know!" she said aloud. "He thought I was an icicle. Oh, I'm glad, glad, glad!"

Suddenly the color flowed into her white cheeks, and she put up her hands and covered her face, dropping upon her knees beside the bed, burying her face in the pillow.

She wasn't praying. She didn't really know how. But she felt as if her soul was being bathed in prayer, made clean somehow from a smirch she dreaded, by a prayer, some one else's prayer, not hers. But nevertheless prayer.

All that day she went about quietly, almost humbly, feeling a strange uncertainty in herself. It was as if somehow she had discovered depths in herself that had never been sounded. She even went to church, though there was nothing in the stately service nor the eloquent and intellectual sermon to remind her of anything that had happened at Easter time. Yet she sat during the whole time and tortured herself with thoughts of it, like a man wearing a hair shirt as penance.

Doris, never long to hold a grudge, came out of her sulks and tried to start a little gayety. Constance stayed sweet and gentle but somehow aloof. Doris tried various methods but found Constance still disinterested, absent-minded, and at last with an uneasy stare at her Doris went out of the room to seek more light-hearted companions.

CHAPTER VII

THERE was one outcome of the Saturday night dance for which Constance was grateful. She was no longer obsessed by Seagrave's reproachful eyes. Scorn and indignation at Thurlow Wayne had taken its place. She hated the thought of Thurlow Wayne. Not so much for what he was as because he had made her see into her own heart and shown her only ugliness and sin.

She tried to blame it all on him, but her honest mind would not suffer that, and over and over again in her leisure moments she reënacted that evening, going over just where she had made her mistakes, trying to think just what she should have said and done. Scathing sentences scorched to her lips from a heart hot with annoyance. How she would have enjoyed showing him how she despised him! There was only one thing that kept her from arranging a meeting with him somehow

and doing it and that was that she had learned also to
despise herself.

But the days were very full of duties, and Constance
was a conscientious student and worker. Also because
she was clever and a good executive she had many
burdens heaped upon her willing hands, and she was
glad to have it so. It was easier thus to get back her old
happy ease and self-content.

Now and then a hint of worry about Doris crossed
her mind. For Doris was hurried and excited, and Doris
kept out of her way a good deal. Often she suspected
that Doris was out with Casper Coulter for when she
questioned her there would be only an evasive answer.

"Con isn't like herself," she heard Doris say one day
down in the hall, talking to a group of classmates, just
as Constance approached the stairs above. Doris' voice
was a carrying one, and the halls had many echoes.
"She's really got religion I guess. She's as long-faced
and fussy. It's too bad she couldn't have waited till
after commencement. She's spoiled no end of good
times for me just because she's getting so straight-laced.
She's actually made Thurlow Wayne think she's a regular dumb-bell. I never knew her to be so before in all
the years we've been together."

Constance, stung by the tone and the words both,
turned quickly and walked back to her room, her eyes
full of sudden hurt. Doris! Her friend! Oh, what was
the matter with everything? And it had all started with
Easter Sunday and the pearls. No, it had started with
the shabby stranger with the searching eyes and the
radiant face.

She stood looking out of the window and faraway
over the campus, till suddenly she heard Doris' gay
voice ring out again, in a greeting, and there was a lilt
in her tone that made Constance lean over the window-
sill and look down. Who was it that had stirred Doris'
voice to that joyous note?

She looked and saw it was Casper Coulter again and
her heart sank. Was Doris really interested in him after
all her protestations to the contrary? Oh, she ought to
try to do something to stop that intimacy. Only yesterday she had heard some of the girls telling how drunk

he had been at a week-end party some of them had attended in one of the suburbs.

She watched them an instant the trouble growing in her eyes. The young man took Doris' hands possessively in his own and held them longer than was necessary. He looked deep into her eyes. She could hear Doris' conscious little intimate laugh of understanding. Then they separated, calling a gay word back and forth as Coulter went down the campus path toward the village.

Well, there were only a few days more before commencement, and they would be necessarily full. Perhaps it was better not to anger Doris. Dear Doris, how she loved her! They had had so many gay times together. And surely Doris was only having a little harmless flirtation. Perhaps it would be better just to try to hold her interest and keep her busy in other ways than to make a fuss now. She would soon be far away in California and her mother could look after her admirers. Far be it from Constance to set herself up as a judge in a case like this!

But suddenly she heard Doris herself coming gayly along the hall, singing a popular song, that lilt in her voice still, and her eyes wearing that starry look.

Constance drew away from the window quickly and turned with a smile of welcome.

"Dorrie, I was just wondering where you were. How about trying on that rose silk frock now? I could easily turn up the hem if you still feel it is a little too long. I've just got that paper finished and off my hands at last. Such a nuisance, Professor Hart insisting on my making all those changes at the last minute this way, and now I'm thankful to say we can have some good times together again before it's all over."

There was a flash of pleased surprise in Doris' eyes for an instant and then a sudden withdrawing, apology in her manner.

"Oh, Connie, I'm sorry!" she said hesitantly, "It's awfully good of you to offer, but I've just promised to go out for a drive. I hadn't an idea you would be free. But say, you go with us, won't you? I know Casper won't mind, and I hate to leave you at home this gorgeous day."

"Oh, Dorrie, you're not going out with him again are you?" said Constance impulsively. "Please don't! He really isn't your kind! Come on and let's do something together, this is almost our last Saturday you know. There'll be too much going on next week to have any fun together."

"I know, Connie, but I thought you were all tied up, and it's too late to change now. Casper has gone for his car. It's a new one, Con, a twelve cylinder sport model. It's a wow. I'm the first one to get a ride in it, and I wouldn't miss it for anything. He drove up from New York on purpose to take me out to-day. I promised him three days ago I would go."

"But Doris, I'm afraid of his driving. I really am. It's not just fast or careless. It's dare-devil! It's as if he was out of his mind sometimes. I've seen him driving when he was drunk, Doris, and it's awful. Rose Mellen says—"

"Oh, cut it, Connie! Don't try the preaching act on me. You can't tell me anything that Rose Mellen says. She's jealous. She tried her best to get asked to ride in that car. Come, Connie, be yourself and help me get ready. I was going to ask to borrow your red hat. It's just the thing I need with my new red dress. Do be good. I'm in a terrible hurry. I promised I'd be ready in ten minutes. Aw, come on, Connie, and be a good sport!"

Constance turned with troubled gaze and helped her get ready. After all if that was what Doris wanted out of life what business was it of hers?

She loaned her the red hat, she hunted her gloves, and produced a new pair of silk stockings of the right shade when Doris discovered a run in one of hers at the last minute.

She watched furtively from the windows as the great purring car arrived at the entrance below the window, shiny and luxurious, bright with chromium trimmings. Its top was down and the sunshine glanced from every polished point. There was about it a nonchalant air of tremendous power, and Constance could not help but admire the beautiful thing.

Doris, bright-faced and gayly apologetic for going, kissed her lightly and tripped downstairs. Constance saw the young man help her in. He was good looking, there was no denying that, but the very tilt of his hat denoted recklessness, and a kind of disregard of conventionalities. He wasn't Doris' kind.

Doris looked up and waved a blithe farewell, the car darted off with a roar and became a mere speck in the distance of the road that wound away below the campus.

Constance turned away from the window and looked about her blankly. She had come to a brief spot where there was nothing she actually had to do that minute, and there came the thought that college life was almost over. It would be easy to be melancholy about it, but she didn't intend to give in to any more doldrums. So she caught up an armful of books to be returned to the library and hurried downstairs.

There were plenty of the girls about the campus, gathered in little groups. Three of them invited her to play tennis, a forth summoned her to join a hike, two more begged her to go in town on a shopping trip and help them pick out new dresses.

But Constance did not feel inclined to join any of them. She had a sudden desire to rest herself. She decided to get a good book from the library and just lie down and read, perhaps take a nap and be fresh for the evening. She knew the evening would be a gay one. Several men friends were driving up from New York.

So presently she wended her way to the library, returned her armful of books, and set herself to find the right book wherewith to read herself to sleep.

She had browsed for half an hour from shelf to shelf before she came on the book she wanted, a new novel, a best seller, just out a few weeks before. What luck to find it in! That couldn't have happened if it were not so near to commencement, with so many crowding duties, and a gorgeous day out besides.

She took her book and started for the dormitory, but several classmates idled in just then and they paused to talk together, luxuriating in the fact that there were no quiet rules to be kept in the library today. It was almost another half hour before Constance turned away

from them and started toward the door again, resolved
to get her resting time now at all cost.

But just at that instant a young freshman rushed in
at the door calling for her, her face white and dis-
traught, her eyes wide with panic.

"Is Constance Courtland here?" she called out before
her eyes had accustomed themselves from the out-of-
doors to the dim light of the library.

"Yes?" said Constance with apprehension in her
voice. Her hand flew to her throat involuntarily.
"What's the matter, Nan?"

"Oh, come quick, won't you, It's Doris. She's hurt!
Terribly hurt! The doctor says she can't possibly live
but a few hours and she wants you right away, Constance."

"But how did it happen?" chorused the other girls in
horror.

"They went over the cliff!" said the breathless freshman. "They say Casper Coulter was killed instantly,
and there isn't a particle of hope for Doris!"

The freshman was panting and stopping for breath.
Constance seemed rooted to the floor, her face gone
white and stricken. For an instant her head reeled and
she felt as if she were falling. Then she set her lips hard
and took a deep breath. She must not faint, if this was
fainting. She had never fainted in her life.

"Oh," moaned one of the girls, "I told you he had
been drinking. We saw him on his way down for his
car, and he stopped and kidded with us. I thought then
he wasn't quite himself and his breath was strong of
liquor."

But the freshman had got her breath again and seizing hold of Constance drew her along.

"Come quick!" she said. "They told me to tell you to
hurry. She might not live but a few minutes. No, not to
the dormitory. They have taken her to the hospital!"

Constance's brain began to function at last, and her
heavy feet to move. She was anguished with the need
for haste. She tried to run and seemed to be creeping.

The freshman, Nan Smythe, kept easy pace with her
and talked breathlessly every step of the way.

"They went over the cliff on the river drive! The car

is a wreck in the valley! Casper Coulter was dead when
they picked him up! Doris was under the car! But she
was conscious. They say—"

"Don't!" said Constance. "Oh, don't tell me anything
more or I can't get there!"

The freshman looked at her speculatively. She was
easing her own soul's excitement by telling the tale.

Constance fled along trying to keep pace with her
thoughts. Down there was the drive where they sped
away into the sunlight just a little over an hour ago. She
could see again the flashing of Doris' white hand in
farewell. The glint of the red hat in the sun. She caught
her breath in a deep quick sob, and putting her head
down ran toward the hospital entrance, outdistancing
the freshman.

Breathlessly she followed the white-garbed nurse
who awaited her, through those white halls that had
never meant anything to her before but a haven for a
few day's rest, a case of mumps or measles out of due
time, a twisted ankle with plenty of good company and
flowers and candy. Now the echo in the marble halls
filled her with awe. Death was here somewhere! Death
waited to take Doris, her Doris, away forever!

Pale with horror she arrived at the room where they
had laid the poor broken body, and approached the
bed. And Doris, gay, blithe Doris, cried out in fright
and suffering. Constance scarcely recognized her ago-
nized voice. Doris, who had no friends or relatives
nearer than California, and who turned to her in her
extremity!

"Oh, Connie," she cried out frightsomely, "They say
I'm going to die! They say I've only a few hours at most,
it may be only a few minutes. Connie, you've got to tell
me how to die! You joined the church. You ought to
know what to do. Tell me quick! For the love of
Mercy, help me quick!"

CHAPTER VIII

CONSTANCE with ghastly white face and knees trembling so that she could not stand, dropped down beside the hospital bed and struggled for her usual self-control. She had always prided herself on being able to adapt herself to any circumstances, had always thought she could rise to any crisis. But here was one she could not meet.

There was nothing, absolutely nothing she could do to keep this comrade alive longer. She was up against it. Doris had to leave this earth in a few short hours! How terrible!

It had never occurred to Constance that any such horrible situation could ever face any one whom she knew, and her poise was absolutely shaken, her mind became a blank.

"Try to quiet her," whispered the nurse, "She's been calling for you ever since she was brought here. She said you would know what she ought to do."

"Darling!" murmured Constance from a dry throat, and could think of nothing more.

"Oh, don't waste time," cried out the anguished girl. "Tell me something quick! He said I might go any minute. I heard him. He didn't know I heard him. He thought I was unconscious, but I wasn't. Tell me something quick to do to be safe. What are you going to do when you die?"

Constance had never thought of that before. The question stabbed its way into her own soul. It was as if she were anguished not only for this friend of hers, but for her own self too.

"Do you want me to send for the college chaplain?" she asked frantically at length when she could bear Doris' importunity no longer.

"Not on your life," said Doris, "I've listened to him four years and he never told us how to die. Why would he know any better now? Can't you tell me yourself, Connie? Wasn't there something said the day you joined the church? Oh, Connie, I can't go out like this. Hurry! Hurry! Can't you think of something to tell me? They want to give me dope to dull the pain but I know that'll be the end. I won't have another chance after that. And I'm afraid, Connie, afraid to go to sleep like that and wake up— Where? Connie I'm going to die, right away, pretty soon! Do you realize that? I'm not going to graduate, I'm going to die! I never somehow thought I'd die! Oh what shall I do. You must tell me. Connie!"

Constance desperately struggled for words, thinking back into that Easter Sunday.

"You have to be saved, Dorrie." The strange words struggled to her white lips.

"Saved, but how?"

"You have to be born again," she said snatching at another word from memory.

"How could one do that, Connie? Oh, hurry! Tell me quick! This pain is something awful!"

Constance gripped her hands together in anguish.

"Why, you just believe and it happens." She struggled with the tortuous alien phrases, surprised to find them indelibly stamped on her memory. How had he put it that day, the handsome stranger? Oh, if he were but here now! He could tell her.

"Believe what, Connie?" Doris clutched at Constance's wrist until it hurt her.

"Why, believe God. Oh, I don't know, Dorrie, I don't know just how they say it. But I'm sure there's a way and you needn't be afraid."

"Oh, Con, if you could just find some one who knows the way before it is too late! Oh, isn't there someone, someone? Not any of those preachers at the church where we go! Not the one that talked about sweetness and light, nor the one who preached about finding God in Nature, nor the one who said that about the greatest sin being the sin against your own personality. I want somebody real, Connie. Don't you know anybody, not anybody who is sure about what comes after we die? Listen, Connie, I've been an awful sinner! I never thought so before, but now I know it! I've been thinking of all the things I've done— Oh,

Connie, I can't die this way! Can't you find some one? Isn't there anybody in the whole world that knows about God?"

"Yes!" said Constance, suddenly springing to her feet. "I know one. I'll try to get him. You lie still Doris and just be as quiet as you can. I'll get him somehow, or make him tell me what to tell you."

"I will, Connie, but hurry! Oh, hurry!"

Constance, breathless, flew down the hall to the telephone and asked for Long Distance. Her heart was beating wildly. Never in any stress of her own life had she felt so helpless, so utterly frightened, so frantic. She closed her eyes and tried to think what she should say to the operator. He was Mr. G. Seagrave, and he was in the office of Howarth, Wells and Company. She tried to locate the exact block in which that firm had their offices, and when the operator answered she was ready with her directions.

It seemed an incredible thing that she should so soon hear his voice answering. That he should be there at the end of the wire without delay. It thrilled her strangely across all that distance.

"This is Graham Seagrave speaking!"

Graham, so that was what the G. stood for, said her sub-conscious mind as she caught her breath and tried to speak naturally.

"This is Constance Courtland, Mr. Seagrave," her voice was shaking and sounded unnatural to herself, "This is an S.O.S. for help."

"Yes?" he said with an eagerness in his tone that thrilled her again with deep relief. His voice was just as she remembered it, dependable, strong, ready to help as she had known it would be. That was why she had dared to call him.

"How can I help?"

"My roommate has had a terrible accident. She has but a very few hours to live, though she may go at any minute the doctor says. She is horribly afraid to die. She is begging me to tell her what to do, and I don't know what to say to her. I've tried, but I don't understand it myself—" her voice broke with a quick sob—

"Could you possibly come? I don't know anybody else to ask."

"Of course I'll come. Where are you?"

"At college." She gave brief directions how to find her.

"I'll start at once. I'll get there as soon as I can, but—meantime,—surely there must be some Christian nearer who can help you at once, at least till I get there?"

"I don't know one who talks about it the way you do. They don't any of them *believe* what you do, and I don't know how to quiet her. She is frantic."

"Have you a pencil there?"

"Yes."

"Then write this down: 'John 3:16.' Those are Jesus' own words. Read them to her, and tell her to trust herself to His promise. Good-by, I'm coming, and I'm praying."

Constance turned from the telephone and found that her face was wet with tears. She brushed them away as she hurried down the hall looking at the bit of paper she held in her hand. This would be a Bible reference. She must find a Bible somewhere. The library would be the place to go.

But to her annoyance she found when she reached there that the librarian was not there. No one was there but the old janitor sweeping the front hall. Search as she might she could not find a Bible. It was not in its numbered place. Somebody had likely drawn it out for reference, or perhaps from disuse it had become lost. Anyway she couldn't find it.

"Oh dear!" she said aloud thinking no one was in the great empty room but herself. Of course it was late in the afternoon and so near to commencement that nobody would be consulting the library now. "Now, what shall I do?"

"You want someding?" It was the old janitor who appeared from behind a book alcove, duster in hand.

"Oh, I want to find a Bible, Emil, but you wouldn't know where they keep it. Is the librarian coming back soon?"

"Her gone for de week-end," said Emil, "What you want? Whole Bible? I got Testament right here. That do?" He put his hand into the gingham pocket of his jumper and brought forth a cheap little Testament.

"It's John," said Constance, "Yes, John is the New Testament isn't it? John-three-sixteen."

"Oh, yah! Him! I know him. Gott so luve de worll'—" he opened the little book and there was the verse right before her as if it had been much opened at that place.

Constance seized the book.

"Oh, thank you. I'll bring it back as soon as I can."

"Keep so long as you need," said the old man smiling. "I like lend."

As she hurried back to the hospital Constance marveled that the janitor should be carrying a Testament. He was perhaps the last one to whom she would have thought of applying for a Bible, and perhaps the only one in the building who had one. It seemed a special providence that he should have been there. And he knew the verse! How strange! Were there perhaps more people in the world than she dreamed who lived by the Bible, who knew God? By the look of the light in his face when he had brought out that worn little Testament, she had a feeling that this old man was somehow akin to the man of the hillside who had brought her the flowers. What an odd idea to float through her head.

Before she entered Doris' room again she paused to read the verse Seagrave had given her, and as she opened the door Doris cried out eagerly:

"Did you get some one? Is he coming?"

"Yes, dear," said Constance her voice vibrating with hope. "I got him on the telephone. He's coming just as fast as possible. But it is a long distance to come. You'll have to be patient. He has sent you something to help though. Listen. He said it was the words of Jesus, God's Son, and I was to tell you to trust them utterly."

Doris fixed bright haggard eyes upon her face, eyes that had already begun to have that other-world look, and from which gaunt terror driven by pain looked forth to a world that could no longer help nor satisfy.

"Read!" she commanded with quivering lips.

Constance read:

"For God so loved the world that He gave His only begotten Son, that whosoever believeth in Him should not perish, but have everlasting life."

"Read it again."

Constance read it again, and yet again, and then her eyes catching a word or two of what followed, read on:

"For God sent not His Son into the world to condemn the world; but that the world through Him might be saved."

"What does it mean, Connie?" the bright eyes searched her face, and Constance's heart was wrung. She wanted so much to be of help, and she knew so little. She tried to think what Seagrave had told her in their brief talk on the hillside but it was all vague.

"Just what it says," she answered simply. "At least it sounds that way to me, and that's what he told me to tell you. Just take Him at His word and believe it."

"Read it again!" pleaded the voice that was weak with pain.

So Constance read it again and again, over and over; and the brilliant eyes were fixed on her face, drinking in the words, trying to puzzle some comfort from it.

"If she could only get a bit of sleep," whispered the nurse. But the sharpened senses of the sufferer heard her.

"No!" she said with the fright in her eyes again, "No! I must not sleep till I am ready to go. Oh, won't he come soon?" she cried out in her agony.

"As soon as he can," answered Constance, "but—he said he would be praying!" She said it brightly, as if prayer now would work some charm, as if she herself believed it would, and then wondered at herself. She had been wont to sneer at prayer, some professor in the early days of her scholastic career had once remarked that the only benefit of prayer was its reflex influence upon the one who prayed. But now she held it out as a charm that would relieve.

"Pray!" said Doris, "Oh, I never knew how to pray! I used to say 'Matthew, Mark, Luke and John, bless the bed that I lie on,' but that isn't real praying is it? I wish

I knew how to pray now. Oh, Connie, do you think he really will pray for me?"

"I'm sure he will," said Constance.

An hour dragged by, and then another. Constance looked at her watch and began to calculate the time. If he should catch the next train after he hung up the receiver—which was scarcely likely, there was still a little over three hours before it was due in the nearby city, and then he would have to wait for a local train— or perhaps he would be thoughtful enough to hire a taxi if he couldn't make good connections at once. It was the very soonest she could hope to expect him. Oh, would he be too late? Could Doris hold out till then? She was perceptibly failing now, moment by moment, even to Constance's inexperienced eyes. Would she have it always to remember that Doris died needing comfort that she could not give? Surely, surely as Seagrave had said if she only knew where to look there must be somebody who would know the way of life!

But when she thought of all the people in the college and in the village whom she knew at all there was no one whom she could ask to come here and try to talk to Doris. But stay! There was the janitor. He had a Testament. Would he perhaps know how to pray?

Yet when she tried to imagine him here in this room in his overalls, kneeling beside Doris' bed she didn't know whether it would do or not. She wished she had told Emil about Doris and asked him to pray for her, only she was so unused to talking of such things it had never occurred to her.

Suddenly Doris spoke:

" 'God so loved the world,' " she said slowly, sharply, "Yes, but that's good people, I suppose. I've not been good. I've never thought a thing about God, not since I was a little girl and had a nurse once who tried to teach me to pray and I wouldn't. I guess He would have no use for me after that. It's probably only good people He loves."

"It says the world," said Constance reasoning her way uncertainly, "there are more bad people than good people in the world. It takes them both to make up the world. It must mean both. Listen. You lie still and I'll read it again, and you just try to believe it, the way he sent you word to."

Constance read the words slowly, impressively through again, taking in their wondrous beauty and fullness as she read, wondering why she had never read them before, nor known how much they contained, thinking in her sub-conscious mind that if she ever came through this awful experience she would never be the same care-free girl again. Life could never be the same after this.

And then, just as she was turning the page back to read the verse over again because Doris was less restless when she read, the door opened, and Seagrave stood beside her.

"Oh, you have come!" she quivered, a great joy and relief in her voice. "How could you get here so soon?"

He gave her a fleeting grave smile and said quietly.

"I flew of course," and then he turned toward the bed where Doris' great frightened eyes were watching him.

Constance came closer to her friend.

"This is Mr. Seagrave, Doris. He knows how to tell you what to do."

Seagrave's face lit up with one of his tender smiles.

"Well, little sister," he said tenderly, "they tell me you are going Home to God. What can I do to help?"

"Oh, but it isn't home to me," wailed Doris, "I don't know God."

"But God knows you," said Seagrave gently, "See, it's this way, He's always known you, and He loves you. He sent His Son the Lord Jesus to take your place and pay the penalty of your sins so that you might be free and come Home without a spot of blemish or any such thing."

"How do you know that?" asked Doris in the shrill high voice of one who is near the end.

"God's Word tells me so," said Seagrave, pulling out his little Testament.

"But my college professors say the Bible is just a book written by men," said Doris with a despairing note in her voice.

"How do your college professors tell you you may be saved?" asked Seagrave.

"Oh, they don't!" wailed the girl, "Most of them think this life is all there is."

"Then isn't it better to trust in the only way that gives you hope of everlasting life? Would you rather trust God, or your college professors?"

"Oh, I must trust God. My professors cannot help me. I must believe God!" she cried.

"Then listen!" he said, "these are Jesus' own words: 'Verily, verily, I say unto you, He that heareth my words and believeth on Him that sent me, hath everlasting life, and shall not come into judgment; but is passed from death unto life.'"

The restless eyes were fixed on him earnestly.

"But won't I have to be judged for my sins?" she asked anxiously. "I have always heard that Christians believed that everybody had to stand up and be judged before the world for everything they had ever done while they lived."

"No," said the young man confidently, "Christ says not. If you have heard the word of Christ and believe that the Father sent Him to die for you, you are saved. The question of a believer's sins was settled once for all on the cross, where our Lord Jesus Christ received in His own breast the judgment that was our due. The believer cannot come into judgment for the reason that Christ was judged in our stead. It is true that believers shall appear before Christ to be rewarded for the way they have lived the Christian life after they believed, but that has nothing to do with our sins."

"But don't I have to do anything?"

"Just believe."

The troubled eyes searched his face.

"Please show me how! Quick! The time is getting so short."

"Look!" said Seagrave holding out his little Testament, "Suppose I tell you I want to give you this."

Her eyes were on him eagerly.

"Would you believe me?"

She nodded.

"Then what would you have to do to get it?"

"Just take it?" she answered wonderingly.

"Then just take what Jesus offers, full salvation." He answered smiling. "Will you do it?"

"Oh, I will," she said with the tone of a drowning person catching at a rope flung to him.

"Then we will tell Him so."

The young man was down upon his knees now talking to God. Such a prayer! Constance as she stood at one side, her tears flowing, marveled at the way it brought the little hospital room straight into the presence of God. And Doris was introduced to her Saviour and handed over into loving care, like a lost and frightened guest who had wandered away from the mansion to which she had been invited; nay like a child of the household who had been long alienated from her Father's home. Pleading the claim of God's great promises, pleading the death of Christ on the cross, and His shed blood, Doris was put beyond the shadow of a doubt into safety and security.

Constance watched her friend's face change from terror into strange sweet peace, and then heard to her amazement, Doris' voice, quavering with weakness, yet not frightened any more: "Oh God, I do believe, please forgive me and take me home."

And then she opened her eyes and said softly, her voice suddenly so weak it could hardly be heard.

"Now, I can go. Good-by." Her eyes closed gently, and she drew a soft little breath of a sigh.

The doctor and nurse who had come in unnoticed hurried up. They touched her wrist, listened for her heart beats, but she was gone!

"She is at Home with Christ!" said Seagrave softly. "Isn't it blessed that it does not take time to know God?" and he drew Constance gently from the room.

CHAPTER IX

SEAGRAVE took Constance out into the cool evening air and the stirring of a little breeze revived her. Afterwards she remembered how strange it seemed to see the campus stretching away among the trees just as it always had done. Doris was dead and the world was going on just the same! You could even hear the chorus of an old college song from one of the more distant dormitories. They did not know yet that Doris was gone from it all forever. Constance's head whirled, and she stepped uncertainly.

She was conscious of a strong arm that upheld her, and then Seagrave drew her down to a bench under the trees.

"Rest a minute," he said. "You have been under a heavy strain. Did you have your dinner?"

"Dinner?" she looked up vaguely, hardly aware of the time of day.

"Why, no," she said slowly, and then roused to the situation. "And you? You could not have had time to eat. How wonderful of you to come right away! But I don't understand yet how you got here so soon."

"I have a friend who flies," he explained, "I just happened to catch him on the telephone as he was starting out for Boston,—that is, if anything on this earth just happens. I don't believe it does. If I had waited to come on the train I would not have been here in time."

"She was just staying alive for your coming," said Constance, a tremble coming into her voice and the tears raining down. "Oh, I can never, never thank you enough!"

"Don't try," he said. "I am honored that you called upon me. I thank God that I was allowed to point the way before it was too late. I could ask no higher service."

"Oh, it was wonderful to see the change in her face," said Constance, weeping now quietly. "You don't know what terror she was in!"

He let her talk about it a minute or two judging that it would help her to get adjusted to things, and then he said quietly:

"Now, where shall I take you? Would there be some place nearby where we could go and get a bite to eat together, or would you rather go and lie down and let me send something to your room?"

"Oh, no!" said Constance, shuddering to remember how empty that room would be now with Doris gone, and all Doris' pretty trifles thrown around, her books, her slippers, the hat she did not wear. She caught her breath at the thought. "I will go with you!" she said determinedly. "There is a little tea room. It will be quiet at this hour I think. It is not far. They don't have much but chicken sandwiches and hot soup and ice cream, but that will do, won't it?"

"It sounds fine," said Seagrave giving her a grave smile and helping her to rise.

They walked across the campus arm in arm like old friends, and he managed it so that his strong arm supported her, and she was glad, for she felt inexpressibly weary.

The tea room was a tiny old-fashioned house across the street from the campus, kept by a little old lady in quaint attire, and the food was delicious. Sitting thus and talking while they ate Constance felt somehow comforted and strengthened.

But suddenly, just when they had almost finished eating Constance put her face down into her hands and shuddered, then looked up apologetically, her face white and drawn with anguish.

"Oh," she said, "you must excuse me! You've been so kind. I oughtn't to give way to my feelings. But it all came over me just now unbearably. It seems so awful to think she is dead! Just a few hours ago she was so bright and happy and sweet, and now she is dead!"

"But she isn't dead!" said Seagrave triumphantly.

Constance gave him a strange wondering look.

"What do you call it?" she asked in a kind of a hopeless tone as if she were humoring some theological whim. "Do you think she is merely asleep?"

"Her body is asleep, yes, asleep in Jesus. It is said in the Bible of believers who die that they 'sleep in Jesus,' though I have read that that phrase might be better translated, 'them also who have been put to sleep by Jesus,' just as a mother takes her tired fretful suffering child and quietly soothes it to sleep, so the Lord Jesus puts His beloved people to sleep. And the time will come when He will raise them up again, when He comes for His own. But it is only her body that is asleep, and has to be laid aside for a time. Her spirit is not there. I think we saw it go, did we not?"

Constance gave him another wondering, half comprehending look as she recalled the look on the face of Doris as she drew her last breath.

"Where?" she half formed the words. "You think she is—Somewhere, now? You think she is conscious?"

"I do. I know she is. She certainly accepted Christ as her Saviour and we have Christ's own words that such go immediately to be with Him. He promised even the thief on the cross who begged for mercy, 'To-day thou shalt be with me in Paradise.' And we have several passages where Christ Himself made it plain that those who have departed to be with Him are conscious, even conscious of some things which go on in this world. We are told that there is joy in heaven over one sinner that repenteth."

Constance watched him fascinated with great wistful eyes, and was silent thinking for a moment. Then she said:

"Oh, but it will all be so strange there for her. Nobody there she knows!" and she shuddered again and struggled with her tears.

Seagrave looked at her pityingly.

"Do you think the little newborn baby is lonely and frightened in this world when it looks up into the face of its loving mother? And you must remember that your friend is in the arms of a loving Saviour. His love will not let her be lonely."

The girl sat watching him as he spoke, her face full of longing.

"It all sounds strange," she wailed. "I wish I could see it that way, but I can't. I never heard anybody talk that way before. All I can feel is that she is dead. Gone! Done forever! That's what she and I have been taught and have believed for years."

"But surely you do not think that she believes that now? Surely you saw the change in her face when she accepted salvation?"

"Yes," admitted Constance doubtfully, "it was wonderful. But I can't explain it. I can't understand it!"

"Can you understand a rose when it blooms? Can you explain where life comes from? 'The wind bloweth where it listeth, and thou hearest the sound thereof, but canst not tell whence it cometh, and whither it goeth: so is every one that is born of the Spirit.' You cannot explain it nor understand it until you have experienced it. After that you need no explanation."

She was plainly bewildered over that, and after an instant drew a long breath and sighed deeply, returning to the gloom of death that hung over her like a pall.

"But it is so terrible to think of never seeing her again," she began again. "Even if what you say is true that there is a life somewhere hereafter, it will be a long, long time, ages perhaps before the resurrection day, if there is a resurrection. And one has to die first and lie in the grave." She caught her breath and buried her face in her hands again with another of those long sorrowful shudders that were like suppressed sobs.

"Not necessarily," was the quiet answer.

"Not—necessarily?" She looked up astonished. "What do you mean?"

"I mean that the Lord may come first, before you die, and bring her with Him. That's our precious hope. The word of comfort for believers. And it looks very much as if that coming may not be far off."

"Coming? What can you mean? You mean we all may die soon?" Her eyes were wide with dread.

"No. I mean the Lord may come for His church, His bride, and the promise is that He will also bring with Him 'them that sleep in Jesus.' That takes in your friend I am sure."

"But, I don't understand. You mean Jesus is coming back with all the dead people who have died, to live here again? I never heard of such a thing."

"No, not that. Listen. Don't you know the Lord Jesus just before He was crucified told His disciples that He was going away and that He would come back again for His own? Don't you know that when He ascended into heaven in a cloud angels told his watching disciples that 'This same Jesus would also come in like manner, as they had seen Him depart? Don't you know that Paul wrote about it?"

Constance slowly shook her head.

"I don't know anything about it. I've heard some of those things read in church of course, but I never supposed anybody took any of those things literally. I'm sure none of my friends do."

"Listen, then, these are the words that were meant for comfort at just such a time as this:

"*But I would not have you to be ignorant, brethren, concerning them which are asleep, that ye sorrow not, even as others which have no hope. For if we believe that Jesus died and rose again, even so them also which sleep in Jesus will God bring with Him. ... For the Lord Himself shall descend from heaven with a shout, with the voice of the archangel, and with the trump of God: and the dead in Christ shall rise first: Then we which are alive and remain shall be caught up together with them in the clouds, to meet the Lord in the air: and so shall we ever be with the Lord. Wherefore comfort one another with these words.*"

Seagrave's voice was very clear and tender as he recited these wonderful words, and Constance could not help being thrilled by them.

"And you believe that is all literally true?" she asked, "and that it may happen any time?"

"Any time now. I would like to go into it all more deeply with you some day if you are interested. But meantime, you are very tired. You have been through a terrific strain, and should have rest. I wish you could just rest your heart down on that blessed hope of the true believer and take comfort."

Constance looked up through a veil of tears that she could not seem to control and tried to smile.

"You have been very kind," she said, in an unsteady voice. "Sometime, when I get beyond this awful thing, I'm going to be appalled at myself, I know, for daring to call an utter stranger all these hundreds of miles to a task like this. I know there will never be any way to repay you. Money couldn't do it. But I just couldn't let her go out frightened into the darkness alone without any comfort or hope."

"Of course not," he said, "You honored me by calling upon me, and I shall never cease to be thankful that I had the privilege of leading her to the Saviour. Now please don't ever again suggest any obligation on your part."

"Well," confessed Constance, "I'm grateful to you on my own account. I'm sure I don't know how I'd have lived through that awful hour without you. And there wasn't another soul around here except the old janitor who would have understood how to help." Then she told him of the little Testament the janitor had offered in her need.

His eyes lighted as she told her story.

"God has more children here and there than we realize," said he. "I presume if you had only known where to ask there were others too who would have been glad to point the way of life."

And then suddenly he glanced at his watch.

"I'm sorry," he said in surprise at the time, "but unless I can be of further service to you I'll have to be hurrying away. My man starts back in a little over an hour, and it will take me all of that to get back to the flying field if I'm going with him. And I really ought to go unless there is some pressing reason. Is there anything more I could do to help here?"

"Oh, no," said Constance, wondering why she had such a lost feeling at the thought of his going, "you must go right away of course. I've kept you far too long already. And there isn't anything more to do now of course. The college will look after everything."

Then she remembered her responsibility in bringing him so far.

"But I've made you a lot of expense," she hastened to say. "Of course I'll see to that. If you'll come over to the dormitory and wait in the reception room just a minute I can give you enough to cover it. I just drew some money out of the bank this afternoon." She was embarrassed saying this, but remembering the shabby trousers that Easter morning in church she dared not let him go away without it.

He smiled.

"I had no expense. The flier was a friend of mine you know." And the quiet way in which he put the matter by closed the subject forever, yet without making her feel uncomfortable.

Then suddenly her lip quivered, the tears came again, and she had to put her head down in her hands and weep.

It was very still in the little tea room. There were no other customers present. The old lady had gone about her preparations for the morrow, the lights were soft from shaded pink candles.

Seagrave rose and laid his hand softly upon her bowed head.

"Child, your Father will comfort you if you will let Him."

There was great tenderness in his voice and Constance was deeply stirred. Her shoulders were quivering now.

"It has been dreadful!" she murmured.

"Yes, it must have been," said the sympathetic voice, and then after an instant, "Could I help any if I were to stay longer?"

Constance lifted her head and took firm hold of herself.

"No, you mustn't," she said trying to smile, "I—I'm—all right. I don't know why I act like this. I'm not a weeper, but I just can't tell you how grateful I am for your coming. I shall never never forget it. No, you must not stay. I've taken your whole night now. I've got to snap out of this. I've got to go through this awful commencement somehow."

He gave her another grave smile.

"I wish I could help, but—will it help you any to know that I'll be praying?"

The color flew into her white cheeks.

"I think it will," she said softly. "Since what you have done for Doris, I think it will."

"Bless God for that!" he said. "But say not what I have done. Say what our God has done. We have a great Saviour!"

They walked almost silently to the dormitory entrance, and there at the door he paused.

"I wonder if you would read this little book and let

it comfort you if I were to leave it with you?" he asked, taking out his little soft leather-bound Testament.

"I would love to have it," she said, accepting it eagerly. "Yes, I'll read it."

"Well, I must leave you," he said, and took her hand in one quick close grasp. "I'll be seeing you again, I hope, when you come home."

Constance stood watching him walk rapidly down the elm-shaded path among the flickering shadows where the moonlight sifted through and thought to herself that he was a great man. He was the greatest man she knew. She remembered how he had looked when he was telling Doris the way to heaven, till it almost seemed that she standing by, could see the gate swing wide to let her friend come in. She remembered his voice when he had prayed, and she gave a great shudder of a sob and turned away. Here was a man worthy of all friendship that any girl could give. A man she would rejoice to claim as near and dear, but she knew in her heart that she was unworthy, and the matter of the pearls swung down like a locked gateway between herself and him. If he ever knew what she had done he would want no further friendship with her.

Then with a doubly heavy heart she turned and went up to her desolated room. When she had gathered up Doris' things and put them out of sight she flung herself face down upon her bed and wept her heart out on her pillow.

She was so terribly conscious of that other bed across the room, empty to-night. Conscious of her last conversation with Doris. She had said some bitter scornful things about Casper Coulter. Perhaps if she had been more loving, less sarcastic, she might have won her to stay away from him. Oh, the bitterness of regrets!

If she could only go back a few hours! Perhaps she might have kept her at home from that fateful ride! She had been so occupied with her thesis and her other activities that Doris had been much to herself. Perhaps it was all her fault that Doris had kept up her friendship with Casper.

So, like a penitent, she lacerated her soul with such thoughts.

A member of her class tapped lightly on the door and begged that Constance would come over and sleep with her that night. But Constance thanked her and refused. She said she wanted to be alone.

So over and over the deathbed scene she went, rehearsing every hour of that awful waiting time till Seagrave arrived, feeling again her own sorrow and despair for her friend, feeling again the thrill of his arrival so much sooner than she had hoped he could come! And then hanging on every word he had spoken, the steady tender voice calming the fear of Doris lying there dying—Doris dying—Doris dead now! A long shudder would pass over her body as she remembered. Then those quiet answers to Doris' frightened questions, and at the last her eager acceptance of the offer of salvation, the smile on her lips as she had given them farewell and slipped away!

In a great tide of awe Constance lay hour after hour, going over and over again the whole dreadful afternoon, till finally Seagrave had taken her away into the moonlight and comforted her. Yes, though she was greatly afraid, he had somehow managed a touch of comfort. And his hand upon her head at the last! How like the God he had pictured, he seemed. Christlike! Wasn't that what people called it? Ah! If she could have a friend like that always with her!

And at last she drifted into an uneasy sleep dreaming that Seagrave's hand was upon her head and he was praying for her, for her!

CHAPTER X

THE days that followed were hard terrible days.

Constance had told Seagrave that the college would attend to everything, but she found when she was awakened early in the morning to give information which the college found it did not possess accurately, that the college could not attend to everything.

The telegrams that had been sent soon after the accident brought no response, and a follow-up showed that the telegrams had not been delivered because the family were not at home and the house was closed.

It was Constance who had to go through letters, and rack her memory to finally discover that Doris' family were on a motor trip. It was Constance who had to open the letters that came in for Doris that morning, and at last trace her family's probable whereabouts.

In the absence of any family or close friends it was Constance who had to settle all trying questions, to make decisions, and finally when the stricken family had been reached, it was Constance who was asked by the dean to frame other telegrams and make final arrangements.

Meantime all around her swirled the preparations for commencement, muted somewhat it is true because of the sad death of one of the senior class, but still inexorably going on. And because she was so inextricably mixed up in the many plans for plays and dances and class and sorority doings, there were many more demands upon her time and thought. There was constantly some one tiptoeing to her door and tapping apologetically.

"Connie, I'm so sorry to bother you to-day, I know you're worn out, but this was something quite important and no one else seems to know a thing about it. Do you happen to know what was finally decided about the order of the procession? And can you tell us where to find Lola's costume? Wasn't it to come from somewhere in New York? They said you had ordered it." Or, "Connie, would you mind consulting with us a minute or two about who should take Doris' place in the class play?"

It was all so terrible and so exhausting.

And then suddenly everything was interrupted just a brief solemn hour for a sad pompous service in the chapel, with Doris lying there in her lovely graduating dress amid those banks of expensive, oppressive, gorgeous flowers, with still that lovely smile upon her lips, the smile with which she had said to God, "I do believe! Please forgive me and take me Home." The smile with which she had said, "Now, I can go! Goodby!"

Constance sat there with folded hands and downcast eyes and listened to the stately requiems, the meaningless words of the distinguished speaker who had been asked to assist the presiding clergyman, and thought of Seagrave's tender announcement:

"She is at Home with Christ!"

The clergyman read the story of Dorcas' dying and being brought back to life again, and commented as his concluding words: "We also wish that this our friend could live again and be among us, and she will live again in the good and kindly deeds which she has left behind her. She will live brightly on through the years in the memories of those who loved her."

Constance shuddered.

Not a word of the everlasting Home Doris had closed her eyes expecting to enter. Not a word of the resurrection life that Seagrave had spoken of so confidently. These people did not believe in a life hereafter. Or, if they did, it was some vague, general, misty thing called Life-as-a-whole, no individuality about it. Nothing precious and sweet and comforting.

Oh, was Seagrave mistaken? Were these wise heartless speakers right? Was life a hopeless brief flash, and death a dark despair? Oh, it was piteous! Death! Death made everything different, took the glow from all the things on earth, changed the whole outlook!

But what a pity that there could not have been some one like Seagrave to have said the last words above Doris' lovely dead face. Some one who could have voiced the hope she bore with her out of the world, instead of this dead chaff. She had a feeling that Doris would have hated all this. That she would have wanted some one to tell what comfort she had found in the end. What hope and peace and yes, joy, dying with a smile like that! Those words being said over her were but a hollow mockery. Ah, even if Seagrave had not been right about it, it would have been good to have some of his wonderful words said in the service, some of the truths he had given to Doris which had enabled her to go gloriously into the gloom.

Yes, even if they were not true they would have been more fitting after the way she died.

Ah, if she were worthy, if she had indeed been the Christian that Seagrave thought her when he spoke to her by that communion table on that Easter Day that seemed so long ago, even she might have told something of what had come to Doris at the last. Even now she almost felt as if she must stand up and cry out, as if Doris would have wanted her to. Only her lips were sealed. She knew that she was alien. She did not know the language.

Oh, Death! Death! Death! Why did there have to be a world at all if Death had to be in it? And someday she, Constance Courtland, would have to die too, and what would come to her? She who had mocked the Saviour of the world for a string of pearls.

It was over at last, the solemn procession, her classmates all in deepest black, the class banner draped, the flag at half mast, the terrible hearse bearing Doris away down the drive through the campus, just where she had gone so gayly such a little while before, out through the arched gateway. Doris' little white-clad body started on its long journey to its final resting place, until the resurrection-day—if there was a resurrection.

Coming back from the station where she had insisted upon going, for the last little tribute she could ever pay to her dear friend and roommate, Constance was met by her eager classmates. Already they had flung the glamour of the world over the solemn interval. Already most of the class were going gayly, excitedly on their way, forgetting that death had entered their ranks.

But Constance was not able to forget. Yet the whole gorgeous program of play and panoply and procession swept mercilessly on, and it seemed to Constance as if every step of the way they were trampling over her heart. Rose Mellen taking Doris' place in the play, laughing giddily, unconsciously imitating Doris' very mannerisms, bringing down the house just as Doris had done. Deborah Faust in Doris' place in the class procession, lifting her classic black gown and pirouetting coquettishly when some of her men friends happened to pass, when none of the powers-that-be were noticing, casting bright glances toward visiting strangers. It all hurt Constance. Everything going on as if nothing had happened. Just a black band hastily added to the programs after Doris' name, that was all the notice or memory most of them had now. The commencement which had meant so much to Doris was going gayly on without her, and up in heaven,—if there was a heaven,—Doris was entering upon a new life, a life that would never end!

Constance packed all Doris' things to send to her sister in California. Doris' lovely coral dance frock, the green chiffon for the class tea, the presents that had come, unopened, the books and photographs. The little slippers, shining silver, in which she was to have danced. And Doris was gone to a world now where these things did not count. She needed them no longer!

Commencement day came at last and dragged its slow harrowing length along. Constance's father and mother came and Frank too, and brought her gifts. Ruddy Van Arden was there and brought gorgeous roses. Even the little grandmother in a new gray silk and a little gray malines bonnet of quaint pattern, sat there in the audience watching her with proud eyes, and Constance had to wear her pearls! She could not disappoint those keen dark eyes that had come all these miles in the family limousine to watch her on her graduation day. But as she clasped them about her neck she shivered, as if they were the price of her soul. Poor pretty things! It was not their fault, she thought, as she looked at them wistfully.

There came a box to her at the last minute just as she was dressed to go to the auditorium, that brought tears to her eyes and a glow to her heart. For when she opened it there were masses of heavenly blue forget-me-nots, against a background of lilies of the valley, every tiny flower a blue reminding of hepaticas, and every little waxen lily bell reminding of a pearl. Graham Seagrave's card was on the top.

She wore a lovely knot of the blue and white flowers and left Ruddy Van's gorgeous roses lying in the wash bowl. But all during the commencement exercises she was thinking as she looked down at the little flowers, that as soon as she got home she would summon Graham Seagrave to audience, and make a clean confession. He would not be interested in her anymore of course, but at least she would stand honestly before him and her own conscience. Yet she took that day the much needed comfort from his flowers she was wearing, and from his little Testament which she had wrapped carefully in tissue paper and stowed in the tiny pearl-beaded bag she carried.

There had been no time to read the Testament as yet. To tell the truth she had almost feared to begin to read lest it would master her self-control and carry her back to that death-bed scene, the first death she had ever witnessed.

But commencement was over at last, and then came the rush of good-bys, of packing and last things, of getting off her trunks and boxes; so many things that had accumulated during her college years. It seemed to her that she was being rushed through the hours like a meteor to whom a resting place would never come, just going round and round the universe at high speed, her heart aching, her body tense, her throat full of tears.

In the midst of it all came Ruddy Van Arden taking it for granted that she was to drive home in his car with him. Constance was aghast. She looked around fearsomely for her own family, lest they, taking it for granted that she was to ride with Ruddy, might already have departed without her. She was reassured when she saw her father standing nearby talking with the dean. She drew a long breath. She couldn't possibly stand Ruddy to-day. Somehow he seemed years behind her in experience, a mere child, who would not understand her as she was to-day. Death seemed to her to have made such a difference.

She had just been up to her desolate room to make sure that nothing was left behind, and had come on one of Doris' little worn out blue satin mules trimmed with foolish pink ostrich feathers and bits of rosebuds, tucked back in a dark corner of the closet out of sight. The silly trifle had brought the tears to her eyes, a great lump to her throat, a kind of vague terror to her whole being.

"Oh, I couldn't, Ruddy, really I couldn't!" she hastened to say in alarm, "You know this is my grandmother's first trip up here to see me—my commencement—she has counted on it for a long time. I must go back home with her and the family. It's her only commencement trip you know." She tried to smile lightly.

"It's my only commencement too," gloomed Ruddy, "and I've been counting on it too. Been saving up all my times out to get this time free to come up and take you home! And you never even wore my flowers! Just wore some other fella's rotten little weeds."

"Oh, I'm sorry, Ruddy, but you know the roses are so gorgeous. I couldn't wear them all and I didn't want to separate them. You were a peach to send them to me, and I was all kinds of proud to receive them. The girls were crazy about them. I'm taking them home in the spray just as they are—" She reflected that he must not know that the roses were still in the deserted wash bowl, forgotten, until he spoke— "I think if I put them in the box and sprinkle them they will keep fresh till I get home. I want to show them to everybody, you know."

She wondered if she would be able to find the box. She must run right back to her room before the maids got there and carried off the roses.

"Well there isn't a reason in the world why you can't ride home with me," begged Ruddy slightly mollified, "Then I could look after sprinkling the flowers on the way."

"Ruddy, really, I couldn't do it. I'm riding with Grandmother!" she said firmly, and then grew silent over the reflection that here she was making her grandmother an excuse again for having her own way. Wasn't this just what she had done about the pearls? Was she inherently dishonest with herself and everybody else? But, oh, she couldn't ride with Ruddy today!

She got rid of him at last, promising to go to the country club with him some night the next week, and then rushed back to her room to rescue the poor forgotten roses.

She was ready to drop with fatigue when at last she climbed into the limousine beside her pleased little grandmother. She wanted nothing so much as to put her head back, close her eyes, and let the tears pour down her face. But she managed to sit up and receive all the family congratulations, answer all the family questions, tell in detail the life history of every one of the members of her class, identifying the one with black hair, blue eyes, and a dimple; the one with red hair; and the one who walked so well. Then they plied her with questions about the accident, exclaimed, said it was dreadful that Constance had to be there alone with her, and that the college authorities ought not to have allowed her to go through anything so dreadful right on the eve of her graduation. It was mainly her mother who talked, though her father sometimes added his word, and Constance, though she loved her mother, shrank inexpressibly from these criticisms.

"Oh, I wouldn't have missed being with her, Mother," she said at last with a quiver of her lip, and her grandmother patted her hand and said:

"That was quite right, Constance, to stick to your friend when she was all alone and in trouble."

"But Mother," spoke up Constance's mother, "she was likely under anesthetics and didn't realize who was there. There really was no need for Connie to stay there and get all harrowed up. A young girl has to think a little of her looks at a time like a commencement. It isn't as if it was just a party or something like that. One only has one commencement you know. Connie really looks ghastly. I noticed it the minute I laid eyes on her. Really, Connie, I think such devotion was utterly uncalled for. It seems to me that some of the other girls might have stayed with her, at least part of the time. Didn't any of them offer?"

Then Frank quite amazingly took a part in the conversation.

"Aw, cut it out, can't ya, Mums? Don't ya see Con's all in? Fer heaven's sake talk about something cheerful!"

Constance gave him a surprised feeble little smile, and received a big comradely wink in return by way of the little mirror over his head.

They stopped soon after that at a hotel for the night that the grandmother might not have too hard a jour-

ney, and Ruddy Van Arden turned up while they were
eating dinner, just as Constance had been wearily sure
he would do. But after a brief chat in the hotel parlor she begged off from a moving picture he suggested,
and pleading a headache slipped off to her room and
went to bed, glad to get a bit of quiet darkness where
it didn't matter whether a tear slipped out unbidden
or not. Constance had just about reached the limit of
her strength.

But even when she was lying in her bed she could
not sleep. Her mind was in a tumult. The old ways
and the new were meeting and she could not see ahead.
The zest had been strangely taken out of life. Was it
all Doris' sudden tragic death that had done it or was
it the disturbing stranger and his strange confident
talk of another world, his radiant smile, his eyes
lighted with a joy she had never seen before in human
eyes? She could not tell.

She decided at last that she must snap out of this
and do it quickly or life that was opening up before
her would be a flat failure. But she was further convinced that she would not be able to snap out of it
until she had seen Seagrave and made her full confession. Then the look she was sure she would see in
his eyes when he heard that she had desecrated a sacred
sacrament for a string of pearls would cure her. She
would be an outcast in his eyes, and would have to get
back into her own world again and get to work enjoying herself.

She spent the last few minutes before she fell asleep
in planning how she would summon Seagrave to an
interview as soon as she got home, and just what she
would say to him.

CHAPTER XI

CONSTANCE was much relieved the next morning to
find that Ruddy Van Arden, still sullen from his de-
feat of the evening before, had left the hotel some two

hours before the rest of them had arisen, and must be well on his way home by this time.

It was also a pleasant surprise to find that her brother had maneuvered a change of seats and that she was to ride in front with him while her father and mother would be in the back. Somehow there was a gentle deference in her young brother's attitude toward her ever since he had come to commencement that was exceedingly restful. She did not understand it, but it was nice and pleasant, so she accepted and enjoyed it. He was being what she had always dreamed an older brother might have been, though he was more than two years younger than she was.

He helped her into the seat, disposed of the bags and her coat comfortably, arranged the windows to please her, and treated her exactly as if she were a visiting lady. Constance rewarded him with a grateful smile as he took his place at the wheel, and when they were well under way so that his voice was covered by the sound of the motor he said gruffly:

"Say, Kid, you've got more sense than I thought you had!"

Constance looked up astonished at the commendation in his voice, touched with a sudden impulse to tears in her throat. She couldn't understand herself. Crying had never been in her line before. She studied his face for a moment till she was sure of herself, and then said in light tone:

"How come?"

He whizzed past a great moving van that was taking too slow a gait on the highway to please him, before he answered.

"How come yourself?" he retorted. "I don't know what made you do it, but I certainly was proud of my sister giving that Ruddy Van the go-by! I didn't think you had any interest in your family any more now you've got the pearls, but it seems I was mistaken."

"Oh, that!" said Constance, adopting his own vernacular, "I couldn't be bothered with Ruddy Van. What's the use of having a perfectly good family come to your commencement if you don't go home with them once in a lifetime?"

"I'll say!" said Frank.

There was a long pause and then he added:

" 'f' you knew the kind of girls he plays around with when you aren't here you wouldn't ever go with him. All painted up, and mascara on their eyelashes like black dew! They're a mess!"

Constance considered this for a moment and then asked gravely:

"And you don't think I ought to go with him to save him from them, Brother?"

"I should say *not!*" said the boy indignantly. "If you'd once see them you'd say so too. Any fella that likes that kind of girl to play around with when he hasn't got any better has no business coming round my sister!"

There was a manly ring to his voice that made Constance look at him in new surprise. She was touched with his vehemence and his evident desire to protect her. After a moment she said:

"Thanks for the tip, Buddy, I'll watch my step."

Frank was evidently deeply touched with the way she had taken it. It would seem as if the brotherly advice had been a great effort for him and he was relieved at the way she accepted it for he hastened to change the subject.

"Gee! See those young colts over there! That sorrel one is just like the polo pony Bill Howarth rides. Some horse!"

Late in the afternoon as they were nearing home there had been a long silence. Grandmother and Father were dozing in the back seat, and Mother was placidly planning schemes of her own. Frank suddenly spoke again, musingly.

"I like yer other boy friend fine!" he growled in a tone that would never reach to the back seat.

Constance's heart gave a queer little leap that surprised her, but she sat with calm exterior apparently undisturbed.

"Boy friend?" she managed to ask quite casually, "Have I a boy friend? I've been away from home so long I scarcely know any of the boys at home anymore."

"Say, come off! I ain't so dumb as I may seem. When a man gets you up to take a walk at sun-up, and loads you up with fillylou-blue-weeds, and then sends you forgetmenots—and you leave seven-dollar-a-dozen-roses in yer room and wear the blue weeds, things aren't so cool as you try to make 'em appear. I guess I got eyes in my head all right, and I'm just saying I like your boy friend, see?"

"Oh, you mean the tall stranger that came to church Easter Sunday, don't you? What was his name. Seagrave?"

"You've said it. Graham Seagrave! I thought you weren't quite so forgetful as all that. You see I took the trouble to look him up. I didn't want another poor fish like Ruddy coming around after my sister, and I thought there was nothing like taking precautions early, so I made it my business to investigate. And he's all right!"

"That's awfully kind of you, I'm sure," said Constance putting a little amusement into her tone, although she felt strangely touched at her brother's interest, and definitely pleased at his commendation of Seagrave.

"Well, he's all right," said Frank again earnestly, "Bill Howarth tells me his dad thinks he's great. They wouldn't have sent him to Europe so suddenly on important business if they hadn't had all kinds of confidence in his judgment."

"Oh," said Constance, trying to make her tone sound only mildly interested, though her heart felt suddenly heavy, "They've sent him to Europe have they?"

Frank gave her a searching glance.

"Say! Didn't he let you know?" he queried. "But maybe he didn't have time yet. He just sailed day before yesterday. Only had an hour to make the boat. You know Mr. Howarth himself was going, had his passage all engaged and everything, and then just at the last minute he got a telegram his brother out west was dying and he had to go west. Mr. Wells is sick in bed, and there wasn't anybody else in the firm they could very well spare so they sent Seagrave. I guess it was a lucky shake for him. He's going to stay six weeks and do a lot of traveling. Gee! I wish I had his chance to see all the places he'll get to! He's a lucky devil! But he wouldn't have got it if he hadn't been the right kind. Bill says his father would have had to give up going to his brother if he hadn't felt Seagrave was the right sort, for the business was awfully important and meant a lot to the firm."

Constance found her heart sinking. Six weeks! Then she would have to carry her burden all that time!

"That sounds interesting!" she managed to say with a voice that seemed to herself very small and far away.

"He's going to bring me one of the balls they use over in England for that game they call bowles. Ever hear of it? We were talking about it one night when I was over with Bill and he said he'd get us each one. He's going to look up the regular rules for us and we're going to try to start it over here. It'll be something new."

"That's kind of him," said Constance feeling a strange elation. "You know him then pretty well, don't you? Better than I do, I guess."

"Well, he's a crackerjack tennis player. He played with our bunch all last Saturday afternoon. Say, he's got some serve! It's just about impossible t'return it. Ever play with him?" he asked scanning his sister's profile keenly.

"Oh no," said Constance, reflecting that when she got done her confession she would lose her last chance of ever having that experience. "Oh no," she said again quickly, "I really know him very little indeed, although you seem to have made a lot out of that little. By the way, you haven't said a word about Mary Esther Cowles. Are you as fond of her as ever?"

Frank's face went down several notches and a cloud came over his expression.

"Aw, I'm off her for life. She's getting nutty. She dolls up with paint on her face, and makes her lips so red they stand out like a sore thumb. She's had her hair cut a new way and she wears earrings like the glass chandeliers down at the old Masonic Hall. She used to be sensible, but now she goes around with that Elmer Baldwin in his red sports roadster, and last week she let him take her up to that road house on the Pike. I'm disgusted. When you got home at Easter and ran around with Ruddy so much I decided I was done with women. But I'm getting a little hope again since you turned Ruddy down."

Suddenly Constance began to laugh. She laughed almost hysterically, in little nervous catches, and then she patted her brother's arm tenderly, and nestled her cheek against his shoulder.

"Oh, you're a cherub, Brother!" she said affectionately, "I never did care so much for Mary Esther myself. Her eyes are too light a blue."

"I don't see what's the matter with her eyes!" growled Frank inconsistently.

"Oh, well," soothed Constance, "if you really feel that way then why don't you get some other girl and take her around somewhere? If Mary Esther really likes you best she'll probably take notice."

"Who'd I go with?" growled the boy.

"Well, there is that little Dillie Fairchild next door. She's rather stunning looking I thought when I was at home Easter, with those cute little short dark curls and her great big pansy-eyes. I used to wonder why you didn't like her. She's really a sweet little thing you know."

"She's nothing but a kid!" said the boy very indignantly.

"She isn't any more of a kid than you are," said Constance. "She was in the third grade when you were, and just because you skipped a grade when she had the scarlet fever doesn't make her much younger. Why don't you take her to the tennis tournament? Doesn't that come off pretty soon?"

"Yeah."

"Well, if I were you I'd ask her to go. It would at least show Mary Esther that she wasn't the only girl in town. And incidentally I believe you'd have a good time with Dillie."

"Yeah?" said Frank in an enigmatic tone, and thereafter drove silently into the dusk with an inscrutable look of thoughtfulness on his young face, while Constance on her part settled back into her own

thoughts, and speedily forgot Dillie Fairchild and Mary
Esther Cowles alike, feeling her heart sinking back
again under that burden that had oppressed her ever
since Seagrave had left her at the college on the night
that Doris died. If she only could get right with him,
even though it meant he would respect her no longer,
she felt she might somehow climb back into her old free
and easy life where questions of right and wrong had
not oppressed her.

She considered the matter of writing a confession and
decided it would place her in an even worse light than
if she told him. It would make it appear that she cared
too much for his opinion, for after all he was a comparative stranger. Though come what might she would
never, after their experience at Doris' death bed and the
intimate little supper in the tea room beyond the campus, feel that he was a stranger. They had somehow
come so very near to real vital things that night that she
could never again in her heart call him a stranger.

But stranger or friend, she shrank inexpressibly from
trying to write out a picture of her true self and what
she had done. No, she would have to tell him if she
ever had the opportunity.

Still, there were the forgetmenots and lilies. She must
somehow thank him for those. She could not let that
attention pass unnoticed.

She tried to formulate a note of thanks, her mind
racing fast ahead of her intentions, and planning how
she might also get in her confession. But her soul
writhed away from that thought again. No, she must
bear her own depression until a time came when she
could get it off her mind by word of mouth. Perhaps it
might even wear off as the days went by and she settled
again into a normal life. Though she knew very well it
would not. She knew that somehow the tall Christian
stranger had taken deep hold on her, and she felt she
must be right before him, must come clean, though it
might lose her any further friendship with him forever.

At this point in her thoughts her brother spoke
again.

"Thanks for the idea, Con, I'll think it over. Dillie is
a cute little kid. She's got a peach of a smile, and she

can catch a ball like a boy. They say she's a crackerjack tennis player too, and last winter she was captain of the girls' basketball team."

"Is that right?" said Constance summoning her thoughts from afar. "Well, I should think she'd be a pretty good partner for a time or two at least. Try it out, Brother!"

"Gee! I b'lieve I will!" said the brother as he turned the car in at their own drive and drew up before the door with a flourish.

Constance looked up at her father's house with a new interest. She had come home now after all her years of school and college life, to stay, at least as far as she knew. This was different from the other home-comings at Christmas and Easter and summer vacations. She was done with school life and home life would begin again. She wished she were not coming back to it with this dark heavy cloud of Doris' death, like a pall that cast a gloom over everything; also this new enlightenment about herself that took away the old happy carefree self-satisfaction, and made her see her own imperfections where she had never suspected them before. What was it in the meeting of just one stranger a time or two that could so upset her life? She remembered also with a stab of mortification her experience with Thurlow Wayne. Well perhaps that too was due to Seagrave's influence. She had thought her philosophy so modern, so altogether up to date and satisfying. And now here it was all upset, everything topsyturvy. Well, she hadn't time to think about it now. Grandmother was tired and they must get out and unpack and eat their supper.

So she summoned a cheerfulness she was far from feeling and made herself useful; gathering the small hand luggage together; identifying the larger suitcases; telling Frank where each belonged; helping her grandmother up the steps; giving an old-time greeting to the family servants who bustled out to meet them; helping her father to give directions about her own trunks which had been sent by express two days before.

And it did seem good to get home. After she had helped to get her grandmother to bed and brought up the tempting tray, lingering to coax her to eat, and to hear the satisfaction the old lady expressed in the commencement exercises she had witnessed, some degree of peace seemed to come to her. She wondered if somehow there might not be a way in which she could atone for her unworthiness, to make herself better by acts of kindliness? Perhaps after all if she devoted herself to her grandmother, did the things she wanted her to do, church-work or something that would please her, it might be that she would never feel it necessary to tell that tall stranger with those pure keen eyes how she had sold herself to the Lord for a string of pearls. Yes, that was it! Work out her own salvation somehow! Make herself good so that she didn't have anything to confess, so that she was in reality what she had professed to be? Could she do that?

The thought brought a relief from the gloom that had oppressed her all the way home. At dinner she was her old cheerful self, and told them all how nice it was to be at home again, and to know she did not have to go away. She was rewarded by a flash of a smile from her brother, as if he were glad too.

Was Frank at last growing up, and were they going to prove to be comrades after all these years of separation? Of course he was young yet, but she could not but feel a warm bond between them since what he had said about Seagrave that afternoon.

After dinner there was an exciting hour looking over the improvements and changes that had been made in her own room since she was home at Easter. A new bedroom suite, or rather a very old one, brought down from the attic by Grandmother and done over, a relic of Grandmother's childhood, rare old mahogany smooth as satin with wonderful markings, and lines of distinction! A new rug from Father and Mother, a delightful new tiled bathroom opening from her own room; new closet room with built-in wardrobe compartments, and shoe-drawers. Built-in lockers softly cushioned in the wide windows. Why, it was nothing short of a delight to put away the things from her suitcase, and the morrow when her trunks would arrive looked full of new interest.

Yet after she had put the things away, and got into the new bed with its luxurious fittings, laid her tired head upon the pillow, back like a flash came the whole problem of the stranger upon her. Then she had to live over again that awful day when Doris died and he had come to her rescue in her great need. Hour after hour she lay trying to frame a note to thank him for the flowers. And always there was that tantalizing possibility that she might also tell him all about herself in it and end the matter once and for all right away before it could go any further, for she felt more than ever sure that that would be the result if she should tell him just what a hypocrite she had been.

So she tossed, and thought, and cried a little into her pillow, until the small hours of the night.

About that time, far out on the ocean a ship plowed forward over the bright moonlit waves, and one alone upon the forward deck looked up to God and prayed for her, that she might find and know the Lord Jesus as her own personal Saviour.

CHAPTER XII

CONSTANCE was up early the the next morning in spite of her long vigil in the night. Somehow her restless mind would not let her sleep. She had that note to Seagrave on her thoughts and must get it written. It ought to go at once. He must not think her indifferent to his flowers.

She thought she had the words that she would write all arranged and learned by heart, but when she came to the writing other words kept stealing in, that old confession persisting. So she finally yielded and wrote it out just to see how it would look on paper. Then with a shiver of dislike she tore it into little bits and started out again.

When she heard the sound of the breakfast gong she was no nearer to a note of thanks than she had been when she first started, and she had torn up several sheets of her best monogrammed note paper.

After breakfast she tried again, destroying more note paper, still dissatisfied. It was almost time for lunch when her mother tapped at the door and asked her to come down to the garden. She wanted to consult her about some flowers she was having moved.

"I'll be there in just a minute or two, Mother dear!" she called.

Then she sat down at her desk again in desperation and dashed off a brief note of thanks, the phrases coming clear cut from her heart, and added a line requesting an interview as soon as convenient on his return home as she had something she wanted to tell him. Determinedly she put it in an envelope and sealed it, addressing it care of Howarth, Wells and Company. There! She had done it. She would run right down and slip it in the post box at the corner. Then she couldn't recall it and have it all to do over again. It was a great relief to have it done at last. It would be forwarded to him somewhere on his journey, and she need worry no more till he got back. She had taken the first step toward confession. She had committed herself to tell him something, and now she would have to tell it. Now that there was nothing further to be done until his return. Perhaps this ridiculous obsession would leave her for the time and she would be able to get back into normal living and have a good time.

So she ran down to the mail box, slipped her letter in with a click, and back to the garden where her mother was awaiting her.

All that day her heart was a little lighter because of the letter which she knew had started on its way; and by dint of keeping herself well occupied and always around with the family she was able to forget for a little while the tragedy which had so filled the last week of her college days.

Her trunks and boxes arrived and had to be unpacked. She enjoyed putting her things away, though she was constantly coming on something that reminded her of Doris. For one cannot live in the same room with another girl four years and not have every little article they have shared in common, bring back experiences, grave and gay.

But her mother and grandmother came back and
forth into her room, and Frank dropped in now and
then to look over her photographs and question about
who was who in her class, and the day got itself comfortably away.

Ruddy was sulking. He did not appear in the evening as she had rather dreaded lest he would. She was
not in a mood for her former gay playmate. She was
glad of the family gathered together in the little summer
house in the garden behind the house after dinner.
Even Grandmother was there in a special chair that
Frank brought out for her, soft with cushions.

They sat and watched the garden grow dusky with
evening, watched the colors blossom in the sky and
fade. Mother talked about the changes she was making
in the flower beds, Father discussed the possibility of
getting a new car, Grandmother told about her own
garden long ago when she was a child, and Frank
played about with his dog and came to rest occasionally
at his sister's side with his hand on the dog's head. It
was just a happy home-coming time and Constance was
glad in it. She felt like a little girl once more without
grown-up problems to decide, the little girl she used to
be before she went away to college and learned to
doubt; before she had ever come into the presence of
death and knew what it was to be afraid of the future.

Then when the dew began to fall they picked up
Grandmother, chair and all, she on one side, Frank on
the other, and carried her into the house. Afterward
Frank got out a new picture puzzle and the two sat
over it till it was completed; a great beautiful hunting
scene, with dogs and horses and red hunting-coats scattered over a lovely landscape.

It was late when Constance went up to her room
with a little-girl content in her heart.

But when she turned on the light there was Doris'
photograph on her desk where she had placed it, and
there before it lay the little soft leather Testament that
Seagrave had given her, and which she had not read as
yet. Then the whole terrible tragedy rushed over her
again, and Doris' pictured eyes looked at her sorrowfully, while Doris' voice seemed speaking to her:

"What are you going to do when you die?"

Well, what was she?

Suddenly the imminence of death came back to her in full force again. Death was always just around the corner and one never knew when it might strike. One must be ready! But how could one be ready?

As if it were a life-line lying ready to hand, Constance reached out and took up the little Testament, dropping down in a deep upholstered chair and snapping on a reading lamp. She had promised to read this, and it likely held some solution to her problems, yet she was afraid of it, exceeding fearful of an arraignment she might find within those pages.

It was to John three sixteen that the pages fell open of themselves. How strange! She remembered that old Emil's book had done the same. Was there something peculiar in the binding of Testaments that made them open always to that verse? Was it the middle of the book or something? No, it was only about a third of it. Did the other third open naturally like that? She closed the book and tried it. No, it must be opening from habit. The owner had turned much to that spot. Had he read it to other dying ones?

Constance began to read and discovered that she knew the words. They were deep graven on her mind. She closed her eyes and repeated them to herself, and the whole panorama of Doris' accident moved before her consciousness, every word, every little incident, including the fright and terror in Doris' eyes, and then that inexplicable peace that entered her face before she died. And once more Constance had to face that thought of death for herself.

She went back to the beginning of the chapter and read it through. And there was that verse, marked heavily, about being born again, that Seagrave had read on the hilltop that first morning of their acquaintance.

She fluttered the leaves through remembering how the little book had looked in its former owner's hand as he turned the pages so familiarly and seemed to know just where to find what he wanted. Why, there were many marked verses! How interesting! It would give her a key, as it were, to his habits of thinking to see what verses he had picked out to mark. Here was one, quite a long passage marked with a single line at the side, and the verse at the beginning and end each heavily underlined with blue pencil:

"Be ye not unequally yoked together with unbelievers;"

She stopped, startled. She was an unbeliever. Yes, really, even though she was a member of the same church with him, in reality she was an unbeliever. That was what she had tried to tell him on the hillside. He had not understood. Ah! But when she told him about the pearls he would thoroughly understand.

"For what fellowship hath righteousness with unrighteousness?" asked the rest of the verse, "and what communion hath light with darkness?"

The verse stabbed her with its truth. Of course, she had known it from the first. He was righteousness and she unrighteousness. In God's eyes, if there was a God, and she now began to feel there was—she would be counted unrighteous. He was light and she was darkness. It was quite true, and somehow it hurt her.

She read on through the bracketed verses, vaguely understanding the separation line carried through them, and then the other underlined verse made its appeal; she almost felt as if it were spoken directly to herself:

"Wherefore come out from among them, and be ye separate, saith the Lord, and touch not the unclean thing; and I will receive you."

Yes, but at what price! Coming out and being separate! Was she willing to do that? Forego the world with all its brightness when she was just for the first time in her life in a position to fully enjoy it? The world to which she had looked forward?

She drew a quick annoyed breath and turned over to another marked place:

"I am crucified with Christ: nevertheless I live; yet not I, but Christ liveth in me: and the life which I now live in the flesh I live by the faith of the Son of God, who loved me, and gave Himself for me."

Crucified with Christ! She shuddered. Was that what Seagrave felt he was? The pleasures of the world, didn't they draw him at all? What a waste it seemed of a splendid fine life to be like that! Why, that was fanatical, peculiar! Yet he did not seem fanatical. Rather he seemed an unusually strong character with something great behind his belief. Oh, she wished he were here to tell her what all this meant. Of course, one had to die sometime, yet she was young—so young.

But Doris had been young too. Doris had been a year younger than herself. Youth had not saved her.

She tried to tell herself that that was an unusual happening, an accident. After all there were not so many accidents. It was not likely that she would die young. And she wanted those years of brightness on earth. She wanted them so very much!

Yet it had been good to have a man like Seagrave near when death came. She shuddered again to think what death would have meant to Doris if Seagrave had not come and talked with her and prayed. Oh, it had been a real something, what he had brought, and she could not help a yearning to have it for herself, only— she did not want to be crucified with Christ. She did not want to shut out all the fun and gayety.

She closed the little book and got into bed, but her thoughts were still filled with the words she had read, and when she woke in the morning it was with a feeling of gloom upon her, a burden of death and—yes, sin— upon her. She simply must snap out of this! She must do something to forget her gloom. She had promised Seagrave to read his little book, and she had read it—well of course he didn't mean just read it once. She would be fair. She would keep her promise and read it every day from now on, she would read it every morning, and then she would have the whole day to forget it in.

So she sat down and read a chapter, choosing it at random, mainly because the page did not seem to have anything marked in it, for she was afraid of any more of his marked verses. They probed too deep.

She read through the first twelve verses complaisantly, her mind turning over meanwhile what she should do that morning, and then when she turned the page she started, for there were a lot of verses marked, and they stood out amazingly: "But I would not have you to be ignorant, brethren, concerning them which are asleep, that ye sorrow not, even as others which have no hope. For if we believe that Jesus died and rose again, even so them also which sleep in Jesus will God bring with Him."

The very words that Seagrave had quoted to her in that memorable talk in the tea room, when he had told her that the Lord was coming back again and would raise and bring the bodies of those that sleep in Jesus.

Ah! That would be Doris! She was asleep in Jesus. Nothing else would describe that look she wore when she closed her eyes and left them for the other world. Nothing else would describe the look she wore in her casket. And God was going to bring her back again! Constance had a sudden conviction that it was all true, that she believed it. She was startled at that. She read on curiously, eager to know what it all meant, wishing Seagrave were here to explain more. Of course she had heard this passage before at occasional funerals, though she had never gone to one if she could help it. But the words hadn't meant a thing. Just picture language, poetry to soften a hard hour.

She read on through the description of that wonderful meeting of God's own in the air, the church of Christ called home, till she came to those strange words: "Wherefore comfort one another with these words," and she wished she knew how to get the comfort that the words seemed to imply, but they meant nothing to her but alarm, a dread of something uncanny that she did not understand. The only comfort connected with those words was the memory of Seagrave's hand upon her head.

She sighed deeply as she closed the little book, laid it down almost impatiently, half wishing she had not read it, yet knowing that the memory of what she had read would cling to her through the day unless she did something strenuous to obliterate it from her mind.

She hurried downstairs with an air of joyousness upon her which she was far from feeling, determined to dispel this cloud that hung over her.

Frank was swinging glumly in the hammock on one

end of the porch looking over toward the Fairchild place.

"What's become of Dillie?" his sister asked him, "Did you succeed in making a contact there?"

"Dillie's gone to her aunt's for a visit," he said gloomily. "She won't be home till to-morrow." He spoke as if all the universe must halt until Dillie returned to her home.

"Oh, well, that won't be long. How about some tennis this morning? Like to play me?"

"Oh, gee! At the country club? Say, that's great, only— Aw gee! We'll just get started and Ruddy or some other dumb egg'll come along and you'll go off again."

His tone was deep dejection. It was his first week of vacation and he felt that it was beginning like a failure.

"Say, what do you think I am? A quitter?" his sister inquired gayly. "No, sir. I'm engaged to play you all the morning or till you want to stop. And we won't take anybody else in unless it's some one you pick. However I'd rather play singles if you don't mind."

"Don't mind!" said Frank springing up with alacrity, "Where'd you get that? Don't you s'pose I've heard about your tennis scores? But I didn't suppose you'd stoop to play with a mere brother."

"A mere brother is a good thing sometimes," said Constance with a sisterly grin. "Come on and let's get breakfast over so we can have a choice of courts before the angry mob arrives."

"O.K. with me!" said Frank with a light in his eyes.

So they played tennis at the country club all the morning, developing such good form that the benches about the court became filled with observers, and more than one young man, old friend or former schoolmate, or neighbor, ventured between sets to petition Constance for her company; but Constance gayly refused every one.

"My brother and I are trying each other out after a long separation," she laughingly told every one. "It's a singles contest, and we'll be at it all morning."

She could see the sparkle of admiration growing in her young brother's eyes, and she wondered why it had never occurred to her before to get acquainted with him and try to have something in common between them. He played well, and after his first few self-conscious games began smashing the balls across the net like a professional. Her admiration for his quickness and exactness grew, and the audience on the benches was moved to occasional applause.

They finished with a dip into the pool, and drove home just in time for lunch with keen appetites, both sides voting the morning a success.

"Now," said Constance as they entered the house, "How about driving out this afternoon to that nursery Mother's been talking about and getting her plants and shrubs for her? We can take the old car and fill it full."

"O.K. with me!" said Frank joyously, "I'm not dated up for anything. Bill Howarth is down to the shore till Monday."

"Well, I thought we might as well enjoy each other's company while we had the chance," smiled Constance, "After Dillie gets back I don't suppose I'll see much of you. I have a hunch she's going to be a pretty good pal."

"Oh, I don't know about that," said Frank offishly, "she's only a kid yet you know."

"Oh, I know," said Constance, "but she used to be pretty good at tennis even when she was twelve years old. I remember her playing with her uncle all that summer he was here."

"That's so," said Frank excitedly, "I don't suppose we could play on the country club courts though. They usually act kind of high-hat if any of the younger people take the courts."

"Oh, we'll get Dad to fix that up for you," said Constance.

"Say, you're some sister!" said Frank, wholly won over now. "Tell you what. Dillie'n I'll practice up and play you an' Seagrave when he gets home. What?"

Constance's face flamed scarlet to her great annoyance, but she tried to laugh it off.

"Sure, I'll play you, but of course I can't answer for Mr. Seagrave," and she caught a little breath of a sigh and smothered it. When she got done telling Seagrave

what she had to tell him he wouldn't want to play
tennis with her, she felt certain of that. And she was
the more certain since she had read that Bible verse
which he had marked, about being separated from the
world. He wasn't one who made friends with unbelievers and unrighteous people, except to try and help
them, as he had done for Doris.

Constance was surprised that afternoon at what a
good time one could have with a mere brother. Somehow all the rankling and criticism that had grown up
through the years since she had left home and gone to
school seemed rooted out and swept away. They had a
merry time and came home laden with many plants and
shrubs, and spent the time between dinner and dark
setting them out in the garden under their mother's
direction.

"Now," said Constance, drawing a long breath, and
feverishly wondering what she could do next to keep
from that intensive thinking that had seemed to seize
her at the slightest unoccupied moment ever since Doris' death, "now, what shall we do this evening? This is
our day and we must finish it off in a regular way. Shall
we do another picture, or would you like to get your
guitar and play duets?"

"Both!" said the eager brother, "Say, you're great! I
wouldn't need anybody else if I had you. But of course
it can't last. Ruddy or some other poor fish'll come
around and you'll be off."

"And you'd get good and tired of just me," laughed
Constance. "You just aren't used to me, that's all. But
I'm glad we've had this nice time together. And we
must keep it up whenever we have a chance," she
added with a promise in her eyes.

So they played until they were tired, played all the
old songs from High School, that Constance used to
know, all the new jazzy ones of modern days, a lot of
college songs, popular things from radio programs, and
then dropped into a sacred tune or two for Grandmother who came down from her room to listen, and sat
smiling, well pleased.

Constance, drumming away at accompaniments of
things she had never heard and never hoped to hear

again, smiled to herself. She was really pleasing Grandmother, and Frank, and in fact the whole family, for they sat around adoringly and seemed too happy to think of bedtime. Perhaps things like this would somehow atone for that joining the church just to get the pearls. Perhaps by the time Seagrave came home she would feel it was quite all right not to tell him at all. She would keep up this good work. It made her feel quite righteous and self-satisfied.

And then she went up to her room and there was the little book lying on her desk drawing her irresistibly to open and read again.

CHAPTER XIII

IT WAS remarkable what a hold that little book got on Constance. She was almost afraid to go up to her room at night because she knew inevitably she would read that book; afraid to wake up in the morning because there was the book again, and she had made a kind of compact with her conscience that she would read it night and morning. She was making a virtue of it, building up good works to atone for the past hypocrisy.

On the other hand she was filling her days and evenings just as full as she could be, far into the small hours, to keep from having to think, for the little book was slowly, steadily getting her. She had begun to know that she was a sinner! Not just to fear it, but to know it.

The Bible had never been an unknown book to her. She had been sent to Sunday School when a child, had gone to church regularly until she went away to school, had been taught many Bible stories at her grandmother's knee, but never had the old truths of sin and death and salvation through the atoning blood been made very plain to her until that memorable night when she heard Seagrave explain it all to Doris in those few breathless moments while Death tarried at the door to take her.

Oh, she had known these things in a general way, but not in any way that touched herself at all, so that when she came under the influence of unbelief it had done its withering work quickly, and what little truth had been implanted in her heart when young had soon died out. But now, just reading that book, and hearing an echo of the clear believing voice that had spoken some of those words into dying ears, seemed to bring her to a strange new knowledge of God. She hadn't as yet much knowledge of what it was all about. The plan of salvation was but vague, the reason for it vaguer, but somehow what she gleaned from the little book was more disturbing than she cared to own even to herself, and to antidote it she plunged inconsistently into the world with all her might.

She had kept her word and worked things so that Frank and Dillie had an entrée into the country club, although the younger set were as a rule frowned upon and discouraged from taking their recreation there. But as soon as her brother was fairly launched on a safe little friendship with Dillie, a sweet shy capable little girl of fine instincts, Constance got herself a throng of friends and began to amuse herself.

It is true that what she did was not often amusing to her, was seldom as interesting as she had hoped it would be, but it filled her days to exhaustion, so that at night she could fall asleep in spite of disturbing scripture faithfully read with eyes that blinked with sleepiness. But somehow she managed to get through time, with longer and longer intervals of thinking about Doris' death; or planning what she would say when Seagrave came home. After a little, one night, she acknowledged quite frankly to herself that she was just marking time till Seagrave came home. After she had made her confession, and perhaps been able to offer a few good works to offset her evil, then she would be relieved and could plunge in and be as mad as anybody.

But now, even though she tried hard, and sometimes almost let herself go to lengths she had never allowed before, she could not seem to get the consent of herself to be anything but conservative. She always insisted on going home a little earlier than the rest of the revellers did, and gave smug virtuous excuses where erstwhile she would not have cared what people thought of her so she felt she was in the way she had chosen for herself.

It was one afternoon about four o'clock that she drove home earlier than usual to snatch a bit of a nap, for the evening promised to be a long one, and she was unusually tired.

She found a visitor in the living room, too late discovered to be escaped from.

"Oh, here she is now," she heard her mother say, as she attempted to slide up the stairs without being seen.

So there was nothing for it but to go into the living room as pleasantly as she could and greet the caller. And then it was only Miss Harriet Howe, a maiden lady of uncertain age whom Constance had never quite liked. She had a sweet subdued air about her, a little too humble perhaps, and eyes that were eager but not quite keen. Kind loving eyes, but not as discerning as they might be. She never dressed well either and Constance had always wondered why somebody had never suggested to her to fashion her garments a little less antiquely. Of course she was poor but one didn't have to be frumpy if one was poor. One could do something about it. She was a teacher of girls in the Sunday School. Constance had just escaped having to go into her class once. She was considered quite spiritual and it was rumored that she often gave surprisingly to missions. Constance could not understand a woman who gave a five dollar bill to a missionary collection and wore the same old queer hat to church for three years in succession.

Constance sat down on the edge of her chair, poised ready for flight after she had greeted the unwelcome guest, and waited. Why had this woman come to see her? She was not wont to come to their house. This must be a special call, probably to ask her to train some girls for a pageant or something.

"My dear," said Harriet Howe eagerly, "I'm so glad to find you in. I've had it on my heart to come to you for several days. I didn't know when you were due to arrive home, so I've just taken the chance that I'd find you here and come. I do hope I'm not hindering you at an inconvenient time."

Constance looked at her watch as if time were a great consideration in her life.

"Oh, no," she said hesitantly, "I can spare you a few minutes before I have to go."

"Well, then I'll talk fast. It won't take long," said the little woman with a quick catch of her breath. "You see it means so much to me."

"Yes?" said Constance unencouragingly. She did not want to be bored with getting up bazaars and pageants and things just now, not in company with this dowdy woman anyway. She would be utterly impossible to work with from an artistic standpoint.

"It's about my Sunday School class!" said Harriet wistfully, and she spoke the word class almost with a caress. One could see by the light in her eyes that that class meant everything to the lonely homely elderly woman.

"You see—" she gathered breath with an effort as if she were about to run an unpleasant race but meant to do it conscientiously, "You see—I'm getting a little too old for them!" She stated the fact rapidly, as one might give a sudden jerk to a loose tooth to get it over with quickly and have it out.

"At least," she added with a nervous laugh, "I've been suspecting for a long time—that is fearing a little— that they had outgrown me and my methods of teaching. I had some reason to feel that another teacher, perhaps a younger, better looking one, might be more to their liking. And last week I found the superintendent agreed with me. That is—" she lifted honest eyes, "he frankly told me so before I even had a chance to ask him about it, though I was considering doing so."

"Oh," said Constance pityingly, sorry for the woman in spite of her dislike.

"Well, then, so I told him I would pray over it, that probably he was right," she went on sorrowfully, swallowing hard to keep a brave front. "And so, I made it a subject of prayer all last week, and the Lord showed me that I ought to give up the class."

Her lip quivered and her glance went down briefly,

then up again, and the submissive smile trembled out
again.

"You see I love that class. I've had them for twelve
years, ever since they came out of the Beginner's room.
I had them in the Junior Department and then when
they were promoted they sent me up to the big room
with my class, so you see they're almost like my own
children."

Constance was watching the transfiguration of the
plain homely face when she spoke of her girls, and
marveling that a thing like a Sunday School class could
become the sole interest of a life. Suddenly her heart
was full of pity for this withered, faded, lonely old
maiden with her few interests in life and her few con-
tacts with society, about to lay down the most precious
thing that life held for her.

"Oh, Miss Howe!" Constance said impulsively, "I
don't think you ought to give up your class if you feel
that way about them. If they knew I'm sure they would
say they wanted you to stay."

"No! No!" said the little woman quickly but firmly,
"They wouldn't! They want a new teacher! They really
do! I put it up to them last Sunday. I told them I'd
been thinking that I'd been teaching a long time, and
probably needed a rest, and that I felt it would likely
be good for them to have a new teacher, a bright young
pretty thing that could bring them new ideas, and,
and—sort of new interest. And they owned it would be
nice to have a change. Well they didn't exactly say it in
so many words, but you can tell you know. If you love
somebody you can always tell whether they are kind of
tired of you or not."

"Oh, Miss Howe!" protested Constance again, this
time indignantly, "they ought to be ashamed!"

"No! Oh, no, I don't feel that way about it. I don't
hold it against them. They are young things, and I'm
an old-fashioned body. It isn't their fault. It's natural
for them to want something new. You know some of
them are only a little over sixteen, some of the girls who
came in after we went into the senior department. They
really aren't to blame. And I truly feel that it is the
Lord's will that I give that class up—"

She paused to wipe away a gentle tear that had slipped out unaware.

"And what I came to say is," she went on after a minute, "I think the Lord has laid it on my heart to ask you to take the class."

"Oh, I couldn't teach a class!" said Constance aghast. "I'm not that kind. It's utterly out of my line."

"Oh, but the Lord'll teach you how," said the homely old castaway, smiling through her tears. "I've had that all out with the Lord. He's made me see that He can guide you just how to teach, and there's nobody I know that is so sweet and pretty and kind as you are. I've watched you ever since you were a little girl in the Primary, and I used to wish so I might have you in my class. Do you know, I've always included you in my prayer list when I prayed for my girls; and when you joined the church at Easter I just felt it was in answer to my prayer. And I thanked the Lord, oh, how I thanked Him, that you had come! You've always been to me just like one of my girls, though of course I haven't known you very well and couldn't do anything for you but pray. Once I thought they were going to give you to me, and I was so disappointed when you were put in another class. But the Lord showed me I was being selfish and wanting all the pretty girls in my class, so I was content after that. But I've always loved you, and now I see the reason why. God was getting you ready to take my class when He found it was time for me to give it up, and He knew if I gave it to somebody I loved it wouldn't be near as hard for me."

Constance was ashamed and appalled. She watched the little brave smiling creature and felt a rising admiration, almost a kind of awe before the sweetness of this humble servant of the Lord.

And suddenly she saw in this despised plain woman's eyes a look that reminded her of the light in the eyes of the tall stranger who had talked to her of spiritual things. Were they all alike, these followers of God? Was it somehow a family likeness people got when they were really born again? As she thought of it she remembered the look in Doris' dying eyes. Actually, Doris too had caught that light of exaltation just before she closed her

eyes. Constance gazed at her with awe and embarrassment and then suddenly she roused herself to protest.

"Oh, my dear Miss Howe!" she said gathering words
in a tumult, "It's awfully sweet and dear of you to feel
that way about me, and I only wish I had known it
sooner. I would have liked to do something in return.
I would have been glad to have been in your class if it
would have given you pleasure."

"It's all right, dearie," said Miss Howe smiling happily! "The Lord showed me long ago that it was all
right. He wanted you to help Miss Burk in her
class. She needed you I'm sure, and I'm sure she loved
you and enjoyed you quite as much as I did."

This was a new angle to Constance. She could only
stare at Harriet Howe and feel tremendously sorry for
her.

"But really, Miss Howe," she said again, "I think it's
all wrong you having to give up a class that means so
much to you. The girls ought to be ashamed of themselves letting you think they don't want you. They're
just thoughtless I suppose and don't realize how rude
they're being. Would you like me to talk to them? I'd
just enjoy setting them straight. I know I can make
them understand."

"No, dearie," said Miss Howe shaking her gray head
and shutting her lips firmly, "It's all settled. The Lord
has shown me I'm not to teach them anymore. I
wouldn't feel like doing it now even if they did ask me
to. I can see it isn't wise. No, I'll just find a little spot
perhaps as a helper in the Primary class, or if there
isn't any place there, perhaps as assistant to the Librarian, though I'd rather be telling the story of salvation because I love it; or there's just a possibility they
may want me down at the mission where it doesn't
matter whether one is old and out of date—"

"Oh, don't, Miss Howe," said Constance sharply,
feeling as if she should cry herself now. "It's perfectly
wicked of those girls—"

"No, no, dearie, they've been lovely, you mustn't
think that. They all said they wanted me to stay after
we'd talked about it, they explained they'd had engagements and been out late to parties was why they didn't

come very often, but I knew in my heart it wasn't very interesting to them, and that was the real reason, though they maybe didn't know it. They wanted to be nice. But now, listen, dearie. What I came here to say was that they and I and the superintendent all want you to take the class. We feel it is just a Godsend having you come home at this time. The girls were delighted about it when I told them I was going to ask you to take my place. They have all promised to be there next Sunday to welcome you, and they say they will be regular at School every week."

"But really, Miss Howe, I couldn't think of doing such a thing! I never taught a Sunday School class in my life. I wouldn't know what to say!" broke in Constance in consternation.

"Oh, yes, you could, Connie," interrupted her mother, "You'd be a splendid teacher. And how it would please your grandmother! It's what she's been looking forward to, your coming home and taking your place in the church work the way all the family has always done. You'd soon learn how to teach. It's something that comes easy. I used to teach myself before my children came. I didn't always have so much time to study the lesson of course, but when I didn't I just took a good story book and read to the class. They always like that and it passes the time."

"Oh, but there are wonderful lesson helps," said Miss Howe looking a little troubled at the idea of a story book in her beloved class. "I'm sure she wouldn't be troubled with lack of time to prepare, and I'm sure she'd be a wonderful influence now she's a church member. I'm expecting to see them all Christians when you get to teaching them, dearie. Some day we'll see you with all your class gathered into the fold, all standing up together to confess the Lord. That will be a glad day, for I shall be sitting there in the church giving thanks, and being so happy that I had a little part in laying the foundation for what you are going to do. Paul plants and Apollos waters you know, and God gives the increase. I'll just be happy in the wonderful work you are doing."

Constance gathered herself once more to protest.

"But Miss Howe, you don't understand. I'm not like what you think at all. I'm not a teacher, and I'm not a wonderful person the way a teacher ought to be. It really would be quite impossible!"

Then little gentle Miss Howe settled down to the battle in earnest. She was quite convinced that her Lord and Master had picked out Constance Courtland to take her Sunday School class and had sent her like a prophet of old to confer the duty upon her, and she did not intend that anything should go amiss. She had come like Elisha to anoint Saul, with her cruse of oil ready, and the words of blessing on her lips, and she would not be dissuaded nor turned aside from her purpose. She set gently to work to prove it all over again to the girl.

And then Constance's mother took a hand.

"Really, Connie, you're making an awful fuss about a little thing. Why isn't that the easiest and best way you could select to do church work? You don't care for singing solos, nor making chocolate cakes for bazaars, and you know you never would be willing to go out on the every-member canvass. And of course you've got to do something. Now you're a member of the church you've got to do your bit. It doesn't take your time during the week, and only about an hour and a half on Sunday. It isn't as if Sunday School were in the afternoon or even after the morning service as some have it. It's early, half past nine you know, and when it's over you have the rest of the day before you. I should think it was about your best plan just to take the class and then you could feel you were doing your part and wouldn't have to worry about anything else."

Then occurred a diversion in the form of the stately little grandmother, arrayed in soft gray foulard silk, a sweet little lace frill at throat and wrists, and after she had greeted the caller she took her hand in the discussion.

"I'm just telling your granddaughter that she has been elected to teach my class that I'm giving up," explained Miss Howe convincingly.

"That's just what I'd hoped you would do, Constance," said her grandmother approvingly, "You're

just about the age that I was when I took my first
Sunday School class, and I taught forty-five years in all
before I gave up my last Bible class, a little less than
ten years ago. I hope you'll have such a record, my
dear. It's the best way a young woman can devote
herself to the church,—teaching others the right way,"
and Grandmother brought her sweet stern lips together
firmly. It seemed almost like a foregone conclusion.

Constance longed to cry out the truth, how she knew
nothing to teach, didn't want to teach, wouldn't teach;
how she wasn't even a Christian at all. That would
have stopped them! They wouldn't have wanted her to
teach if they knew she doubted the Bible, and didn't
know God, nor believe in the church, nor anything.

But her lips were sealed. She couldn't tell them that.
She couldn't let her grandmother know right before this
stranger, this sweet-eyed homely stranger, that she had
been a hypocrite the day she took those solemn vows
upon herself, that she did not even respect the vows she
had made, had no intention of keeping them when she
made them, was only doing it for a string of pearls.

There! There were those pearls again barring her
way, keeping her from telling the honest truth and
appearing in no disguise. And she was a weak coward
that she dared not tell the truth.

Once she even opened her lips to speak, and then she
saw in quick vision the stricken look that would come
into the beloved grandmother's eyes if she did. The
horrified indignant, disgusted look that would come
into her mother's eyes. The scathing words she would
speak, yes, even before a caller, if she thought her
daughter had so transgressed the laws of decency and
churchly etiquette.

Almost panic stricken at last because she could never
confess the real reason, the only reason that would
make them desist, and unable to just roughly refuse and
walk out of the room, she finally promised to think it
over, though she still insisted that she would not do it.
And then she had the agony of sitting there and hearing
her mother and grandmother and Miss Howe plan it all
out for her, how she would be on hand next Sunday
and meet the girls at the close of the lesson, sort of get

acquainted with them, and arrange things for the next week.

"Connie could have them here for pleasant little evenings you know," suggested her mother graciously, "Invite some of their boy-friends, and a few, just a very few of your own most intimate friends, dear," she turned to the unwilling daughter, "and really show those girls a good time."

Constance shut her lips tight and said nothing. Would this thing never end? Of course she didn't intend to teach that class under any consideration, but she saw it could not be refused successfully in their presence. She would have to write a note of refusal later so that it couldn't make any fuss. Just a final refusal. That would be the right way.

So she let them talk, let Miss Howe tell each girl's history and home life in detail, and listened in spite of herself; and finally, at five minutes to six the good woman finished her harangue and took herself away beaming because she thought that she had accomplished her mission.

Constance, too vexed to trust herself to speak about the matter, took herself up to her room to dress, with a tacit agreement upon her to teach a Sunday School class!

And her grandmother actually expected her to look forward with pleasure to forty years of teaching a Sunday School class! Poor little grandmother!

Yet strangely enough as she looked back down the stairs and saw that grandmother, off her guard, standing at the front door silhouetted against the late afternoon of a lovely summer day, there was a smile upon her relaxed lips, and a look in her eyes that reminded her of the look in Seagrave's face, the look in the eyes of the homely little maiden lady when she talked about the Lord. Could it be possible that Grandmother also, knew the Lord, in that strange unworldly intimate way? Was it possible that she cared so very much that her granddaughter should be doing church work?

Then another thought came to her mind. She had been seeking some way to atone her own hypocrisy. Was not this perhaps the very opportunity? Could she get away with teaching religion to a class of girls only two or three years younger than herself?

And would this be a way to win back Seagrave's respect after she had told him the truth about herself? Or would it only be walking another far step into more hypocrisy?

CHAPTER XIV

MEANTIME Dillie Fairchild had come home and a friendship had been established tentatively between herself and Frank Courtland.

It had been most casual in its early stages. Frank's room was on the Fairchild side of the house, and he had a good view from his window of the Fairchild grounds. He knew exactly when Dillie arrived and went up the walk to her home, and he happened (?) to be out in his own grounds searching for a tennis ball which he had been bouncing back and forth against the side of the house.

It was opportune that he should have discovered it just at the moment that Dillie alighted from the taxi with her suitcase and hat box.

He let her pay the taxi driver, and pick up her baggage as the driver seemed to be in a hurry, before he appeared to notice her arrival. Then he caught up his ball and called out most casually,

"Hello, Dillie! Been away? Here, let me carry those in for you."

He sprang across the low hedge and bounded over to the walk.

"Oh, that's all right," said Dillie, astonished at the unusual attention from a neighbor who had never seemed to notice her before, "I can carry them in. They are not heavy."

He was by her side however, and had seized the luggage with an easy grace that made her stand back and admire.

"Oh, thank you," she said, "But I'm quite used to carrying things. That driver wanted to take them in but I knew he had a woman waiting for him down at the station and I wouldn't let him."

"Well I'm glad I'm here!" said Frank graciously in the tone Mary Esther had always demanded of him, a grown-up tone, very polite. "You oughtn't to carry such heavy things."

Dillie laughed.

"Why they aren't a bit heavy, but it's kind of you to carry them."

Suddenly the subject seemed to be exhausted. They walked several steps before another one presented itself.

"My, it's good to get home!" said Dillie looking up at her home adoringly. "I feel as though I'd been away a year."

"I thought it seemed terribly lonesome around your house for the last few days," said Frank gallantly. "Have a good time?"

"Oh, wonderful!" said Dillie with a soft flush in her cheeks and her eyes shining. "I have five cousins and they were all home."

"Oh!" said Frank, "Boys or girls?"

"Both!" said Dillie. "Three girls and two boys, only the youngest is only a baby, about three years old. The oldest cousin is a boy too. He's about your age. You'd like him!"

"Oh!" said Frank, wondering if he would. That one boy cousin somehow seemed a bit annoying. He didn't want any lingering friendships to get in the way of his experiment in friendshiping with Dillie.

"Been playing tennis a lot?" he asked looking down at the tennis racket neatly strapped on to the suitcase he was carrying.

"Oh yes, every day. Ronald, my oldest cousin is a champion in his college. They have a wonderful court and we played just all the time."

"Gee! That must have been great!" said Frank without enthusiasm. "How about you and me having a set pretty soon?"

"Why, I'd love it," said Dilly eagerly, "But our court is in awful condition. The weeds have sprung up all over it. Father said he'd have it put in order but the man was so busy this spring he hadn't got around to it before I left. I don't know whether he has yet or not, but it won't be like my cousin's court."

"What about playing at the country club?" asked Frank with a large air.

"The country club? Oh, could we? I thought they didn't let the younger people play there?"

"Well, I can. I'll be glad to take you over. When will you go? This afternoon?"

"Why, I guess so, unless Mother has planned something else for me."

"Awwright. What time? Two o'clock be all right?"

"Oh, I should think so. Suppose you come in a minute and see if Mother has any other plans."

So Frank carried Dillie's baggage into the house and up to her pretty room, with her mother standing at the head of the stairs smilingly thanking him. He gave a shy glance about on the dainty appointments, pink things on the bureau and dressing table, pink drapery on the bed and at the windows. It looked like a flower garden. Her home seemed pleasant, at least the rooms of which he could get a glimpse. The background of Dillie, although he had known it from a distance nearly all his life, suddenly took on new interest to him. He felt that a girl from a happy home like that was a nice girl to know. He rather liked it that Dillie asked her mother before she made dates with boys. He knew Mary Esther did not. Mary Esther had often sneaked off to go with him to a ball game when her mother had told her to stay at home and practice her music lesson. Also Mary Esther carried a silly vanity case and stopped on the sidewalk to pencil her lips redly, and scrub her face over with powder. Frank had always felt embarrassed when she did that. It didn't seem quite nice. Yet on the other hand the house that Mary Esther's father lived in was much larger and grander than Dillie's home, and Mary Esther was much more sophisticated than Dillie. She had begun to smoke. He had never quite liked that. His sister did not smoke and neither did his mother. He wondered if Dillie's mother smoked. He looked at Dillie and decided that she hadn't ever tried it yet. Well he would find out. He liked Dillie.

So he stood watching while Dillie kissed her mother, and asked about the tennis game, and then he went away with Dillie's mother's smile upon him and a feeling of something clean and fine in his heart, he wasn't just sure what it was.

Dillie came out at exactly two o'clock in a little green dress with a snood of soft green silk knotted about her short dark curls to keep them out of her eyes. She was swinging her racket and skipping down the steps happily like a child, and Frank wondered why he had never noticed before how pretty she was. She was surprisingly at her ease too. She could always think of something interesting to talk about. She chatted all the way to the country club about her journey, and he was able to explain to her several things she seemed not to understand. It was nice having a girl who wanted you to tell her things, and seemed interested. Not just to be always fooling, and getting off smart sayings on each other. A fellow liked to have a girl look up to him. It made him feel he ought to be more worthwhile. Mary Esther was always making fun of somebody, either him or somebody else, or else trying to get something out of him. Sometimes his allowance had been greatly overdrawn trying to satisfy Mary Esther's appetite for sodas and sundaes at the corner drug store.

He asked Dillie if she would like to stop and get something. Of course it was the expected thing to do—that is the other girls expected it. But Dillie said: "Oh, don't let's waste time in the drug store, unless you want something. I'm not thirsty are you? Not yet anyway. I'm just crazy to try those lovely country club courts. I've heard they are wonderful this year."

He apologized for not having a car to take her because his mother had one and his sister the other; but Dillie said she liked to walk, and they stepped out in rhythm and kept step. It was great. Dillie was as good as a boy. She was a real sport. Yet she was pretty, prettier than any of the other girls he had been with. Queer, Connie had known how that would be. He wished he could see Mary Esther, that is he wished Mary Esther could see him. She would see that he didn't miss her in the least.

And then they swung into the gate of the country club and there came Mary Esther!

But before either of them had seen Mary Esther they had spied together a little baby robin sitting hunched up in the drive and a big blue sports car all glittering in chromium coming toward it at a fine pace.

Both at once they swooped down upon the tiny frightened creature, and gathered it tenderly, their hands cupped together to scoop it in, and drew back to the grass, while Mary Esther stood with a disgruntled youth on the other side waiting for the car to pass.

Then Mary Esther saw her erstwhile devoted attendant so utterly absorbed in another girl and a silly bird that he did not even notice she was there. That was something that she had never thought could happen. And she could not at first identify the girl because of the silken snood and the falling dark curls.

The car passed and the two of them were still absorbed. They had the bird on one of their rackets now and were examining its wing and planning what to do with it. Mary Esther simply couldn't go by and not have Frank see her at all, so she spoke.

"H'llo, old thing!" she called listlessly.

Frank lifted his head with a frown at the interruption.

"Oh. Hello!" he said carelessly and bent his head to the broken wing again.

Dillie also lifted her head and glanced across with a fleeting smile of recognition. They were not intimates these two girls. But there was nothing of rancor in Dillie's smile. She was just absorbed in the bird.

"Oh, is that you, little Dillie?" said Mary Esther disagreeably.

Dillie looked up with a twinkle.

"Yes, it's me, Big Mary Esther!" she answered with a good-natured grin.

Then Mary Esther marched on with her head up in the air and Frank and Dillie walked on down the driveway to put the bird in the hands of the caretaker at the club. They talked entirely about the bird. They did not mention the little passage with Mary Esther.

But when they had seen the bird in a safe and

comfortable box reposing on a neat bed of dried grass with a few crumbs to the good beside it and a tin top to an oil can filled with water beside it, and had started toward the tennis courts Frank drew a deep breath and looked at his companion, growing admiration in his eyes.

"H'm! 'Little Dillie!'," he said contemptuously, "I don't see as you're so awfully little!"

Dillie only laughed.

"Say, that was some answer you gave her!" he said again. "I guess she won't call you that again."

Then after a pause he added.

"It's nice to be little. It's nicer to be little than big."

There was a pause and then Dillie spoke, her face suddenly serious.

"I oughtn't to have said it I suppose. It came out quick before I stopped to think. Mother says I'm always doing that."

"Why shouldn't you have said it?" demanded the boy, "She deserved it."

"Yes," said Dillie slowly, thoughtfully, "but it wasn't very Christian of me."

Frank eyed her curiously. It appeared then that there were realms above petty meannesses and retaliations, and Dillie Fairchild moved in those realms. Henceforth Frank Courtland would never again look up to Mary Esther no matter how much more sophisticated she might become, for he had had a vision of something higher.

But soon all this was forgotten in the delights of tennis. The court was perfect, the day was rare, the two players were well matched. Each stimulated the other to do his best, and many a seasoned player paused to give an admiring glance at the two promising youngsters.

They played until late in the afternoon, the long slant rays of the sun were lying low on court and turf, ladies were beginning to appear on the distant club-house porch in delicate afternoon attire after the strenuous play of the day.

"Wantta take a swim?" asked Frank eyeing the pool where a few late swimmers were still sporting.

"I guess not to-night thank you," said Dillie. "I

didn't bring my bathing suit, and besides, isn't it getting awfully late?"

"Well, there's time enough for a bite to eat anyway," said Frank. "That won't take long."

So they went in step across the grass and over to the clubhouse where late afternoon tea was in progress, and there at the far end of the porch they saw Mary Esther with her grumpy escort. Frank steered Dillie away to the other end and they ordered a sundae.

They had just finished when a familiar voice called out behind them:

"Hello, old thing! Mind if we bring chairs and sit down here beside you children."

"Help yourself!" said Frank rising quickly, "We're just leaving. All set, Dillie?"

Dillie sprang up, Frank picked up the rackets, and they started away, his hand just slipped inside the turn of Dillie's elbow, keeping them together in perfect step, and so they walked away across the smooth turf, and out the big club gateway to the road, while baffled Mary Esther sat amazed and watched them.

About seven o'clock Mary Esther called up the Courtland house on the telepone.

"That you, Frank? I'll let ya take me out to a picture tanight if you wantta."

"Thanks awfully, Mary Esther," said Frank in his most grown-up tone, "but I've got a date."

Meantime Constance had plunged into a wild orgy of social engagements. Her promise to Ruddy Van Arden had taken her to an affair at the club at which a number of young people new to the neighborhood were present. There was one especially, a man a little older than the men who were Constance's friends, who sought her out more than once during the evening, and seemed to be determined to absorb a good deal of her time. He asked her to play golf the next morning, to ride with him in the afternoon, and to dine with a few of his friends from a nearby city a few days later. His attention could not but flatter her. He was a man of the world with an interesting personality and fascinating manners. He had just fallen heir to a beautiful estate in the neighborhood that had been in the hands of caretakers for several years while its elderly owners traveled, and he was preparing to make it entirely up-to-date in every way, a charming place for house parties and social affairs on a large scale. The swimming pool he was building was on a far larger scale than any in that vicinity, also he was planning to keep polo ponies, and lay out a private golf course. He was certainly a man whom it would be a social advantage to know, and just now when Constance was troubled in her mind and trying frantically to fill her thoughts to the exclusion of all serious matters, he seemed the very one she needed. She was not slow to accept his various invitations, glad of the chance to be constantly on the go, and also to have a good excuse to get rid of Ruddy Van who sulked his days through and drank his nights through in other and perhaps more questionable company.

Constance had a passing thought now and then that perhaps Delancey Whittemore was no more what her brother would desire as a companion for her than Ruddy Van, but at least he was exciting, and that was what she wanted more than anything else just now.

Not that even her wildest attempts to be gay and busy every minute completely exorcised the memories, that crowded upon her the instant she was alone. It seemed that Doris' death was something she never would shake off. Sometimes when she was laughing and gay at some evening affair Doris' face with the terror in her eyes would look out at her from the throng of people, and she would hear her wild voice saying "What are you going to do when you die?" Then she would start, and catch her breath, and take on that faraway look. She wondered if people noticed it sometimes?

Then at other times she would see that last light of peace in her friend's face, the utter rest and trust, and find an inexpressible longing in her own heart to get that same peace for herself.

She was wearing her pearls now, almost every night. She had felt she must get over that silly feeling about them. It pleased her grandmother to see them. Yet

every time she put them about her neck she shivered
a little.

And then there was that Sunday School class! She
had been duly introduced that first Sunday and was
virtually bound to take it over. Not that the teaching of
it worried her particularly. Miss Howe had promised to
bring her a book that would have everything in it she
needed to know about the lesson and she would merely
have to read it over to get a good idea of it. Miss Howe
was sure it would not take much of her valuable time.

"And if there should come a question that you are
not quite certain of, why just ask Dillie Fairchild to
answer it," Miss Howe had smiled. "Dillie always
knows her lesson perfectly, and she's a wise little thing.
You'll love her."

Yes, Constance thought she would love Dillie, but
not in her Sunday School class. It hadn't occurred to
her that there would be young people in the class that
she would come into contact with at other times than in
the church. She had had a vision of a class that needed
uplifting in a lovely way. But Dillie! Why Dillie was a
charming child. Dillie, her choice for Frank's girl
friend! That too was a little hampering. She would have
to study her lesson more thoroughly if Dillie were in
the class. Still, that didn't bother her so much, the idea
of study, for she was bright and liked to study things.
But the class itself seemed somehow only another
hypocrisy on her part, and some day Seagrave of the
keen kind eyes was coming home and going to look
straight through her when she told about the pearls,
and she wasn't so sure as she thought about it whether
taking that class was going to atone for her own superficial attitude or not. It might only make things worse.

So Constance in spite of all her gayety was not
happy, and was constantly seeking more excitement in
the hope of relief from her restlessness.

Delancey Whittemore more than any of the others
seemed able to fill her days with excitement and
interest.

Perhaps there was something in the fact that all the
other girls were crazy about him and were jealous of

her for having interested him more than any one else in
their circle. And Constance of course was flattered.

For one thing he had an air of mystery about him
which flung a mantle of romance about him. And then
no one seemed to know much of his history. It was said
that he had traveled much, and could on occasion tell
strange stories of his experiences. He talked well, too,
and seemed always at his ease. He intrigued Constance.
Sometimes treating her as if she were an old friend of
years' standing whom he might at any moment take
into his confidence, a friend to whom he could talk or
not as the whim seized him. And perhaps this was a
relief to Constance who often in his company found her
own thoughts straying to matters of her own life while
he seemed to be musing on profound problems, his eyes
great dark pools of what might be sorrow, or remorse.

Yet there were other times when he startlingly reminded her of Thurlow Wayne, that same thrilling
look into her eyes, that same electric touch as he
helped her into his car, or danced with her; and when
he was like that a strange fright seemed to possess her,
and she drew herself away from him, and answered him
coldly. She did not like him when he was like that.
He reminded her too keenly how she had once despised herself, and just now she was attempting to
whitewash over all her sins and become flawless in her
own eyes so that when Seagrave should return she
would not feel it incumbent upon her to confess.

But Whittemore never forced himself upon her. He
seemed to sense her coolness and became himself at
once so formal that she presently forgot he had been
anything else, began to think it was all her imagination,
told herself that she was getting hyper-sensitive since
Doris' death. Probably it had been a case of mere
nerves even the night she went to the dance with Thurlow Wayne. Then she would fling herself into gayeties
with renewed fervor and there grew up a comradely
fellowship with Whittemore which pleased her more
and more as he took her into his confidence, and asked
her help in the metamorphosing of his estate. What girl
does not enjoy having her whims carried out in marble
and landscape and furnishings with unlimited money to

make it possible? So Constance more and more became involved in the scheme of things at the Whittemore place.

The days passed on one after another, and no word came from Seagrave. Sometimes she counted the hours when she might hope to have a reply to her note, and then told herself how foolish she was, and sought to forget the hour and the day. What was Seagrave to her? A few forgetmenots, what were they? She had thanked him, that was all that was necessary. And maybe, by the time he came home she would have so successfully forgotten him and his preachments that the matter of the pearls would no longer worry her.

Delancey Whittemore was most attentive. He came to the country club every day, and often he came to the house after her. She wondered that Frank did not notice and remark; but Frank was helping Dillie make a landscape garden now, studying colors and forms of beds. He was over at the Fairchild place every waking minute.

So Constance went her gay way unmolested through the week. She got up early to find something interesting to tell her girls on Sunday morning, and then frequently played golf all Sunday afternoon, after the manner of the pagans round about her, and thought nothing of it. She was rather amused and pleased to find that her Sunday School class was not such a drag after all. They were sweet pretty things and looked adoringly at her. They simply swarmed out to receive her and tell her how delighted they were to have a new teacher and to have that new teacher herself. Constance, flattered, smiled at them all and told them what rare times they were going to have together. She suggested a possible tea or something gay in the near future. Then she went her way into the bright new week, and told herself she was getting on famously.

Delancey Whittemore had evolved a pageant that was to be held on his estate as soon as ever it was in shape to receive guests. He had put the house into the hands of an interior decorator, and he frequently took Constance out there to approve and suggest. More flat-

tery. Constance found herself drawn farther and farther
into his schemes.

He had traveled abroad a great deal. He was fascinating to talk to. He had hunted lions, been to Siberia,
and flown over frozen seas; he had dabbled in art and
letters and knew great people; among them many noto-
rious people; or at least he said he did.

Then before his house was ready for guests he gave a
little affair at the country club. Quite an exclusive affair
he said he wanted it to be, yet he gave Constance carte
blanche to invite whom she would.

Constance, happening to arrive late at lunch one day
about the time her brother came in from planting Fairchild delphiniums and madonna lilies so they would
make a heavenly picture in the corner of Dillie's garden, and feeling especially gracious toward him,
thought to grant a large favor.

"How would you like to take Dillie up to the country
club to-morrow night, Frank?" she asked. "There's
going to be a lovely exclusive little dance in the East
room, and I can get you tickets if you'd enjoy it. Mr.
Whittemore told me I might ask who I liked."

Frank looked up without enthusiasm.

"Thanks awfully, Connie," he said with an air of
absorption in something else, "but I guess you don't
need to bother. You see Dillie and I don't dance."

"You don't dance!" said Constance in amazement.
"What do you mean? You both went to dancing
school!"

"Dillie never did," said Frank decidedly. "Her dad
didn't care for it, and she thinks the same about it as he
does now she's grown up. She thinks it isn't a good
thing for a Christian to do. And I don't know but she's
right. Must say I don't want my girl going around in
some man's arms. Anyway we talked it over and we
don't dance, see? Just as much obliged, Connie, though.
Well, s'long. I gotta get back and finish planting those
lily bulbs."

Constance stared after him as he went whistling out
of the house. What had come over her gay young
brother? Talking about what "Christians" ought to do?
Saying "we" didn't dance. Why, two weeks ago, or

three at the most, he would have jumped at the chance
to take Mary Esther to the country club to a private
dance! She marveled and looked out of the window
thoughtfully. Strangely enough it came into her mind
just then to wonder what Seagrave thought about
worldly amusements. The question had never been
presented to her mind before. Well, what did it matter
anyway? Life was a terror anywhere you looked unless
you just whirled on and tried to forget. "What are you
going to do when you have to die? What are you going
to do when you have to die?" The question had become
a fearful refrain that chanted over and over in her
brain.

And then when she went upstairs that night what
should she find in the little Testament which had become in some sort a fetish to her, but the verses about
coming out from the world and being separate, and she
threw the book down and herself on her bed and buried
her face in the pillow. She wasn't their sort, Seagrave
and Grandmother, and Dillie! She was just herself.
How could she be grave and get ready to die? Maybe
she wouldn't die for years and years. She must have a
good time while she could.

So she went to bed and tried to sleep, but even in her
dreams she saw first Doris and then Seagrave, and
woke at early dawn unrested. Her heart was not at
peace.

CHAPTER XV

A MOST unexpected thing happened the next day. There
came a haggard-eyed, sorrowful father and mother
from California who wanted to know every minutest
detail of Doris' last hours. They had taken a room in
the city in a hotel and they hired a taxi and drove out
to find their daughter's roommate the first morning they
arrived.

Constance met them with consternation. Must she go
over all that awful time again and put it into words that

would not cut too deep for the sorrowing family to hear? How could she soften the hard details?

But she found that was impossible. The mother watched her like a hawk and seemed to detect every sentence that was meant to cover up suffering or fright on the part of Doris. She would pierce Constance with a keen question, and equivocation was of no use. She seemed to know by intuition just how Doris must have felt. Perhaps she had lain at death's door herself, and remembered.

"Wasn't she wild with fright at the thought of dying?" asked the mother in a high quavering voice. "Oh my poor little girl! She was always so afraid of death. She never wanted to go to a funeral if she could help it. She just simply wouldn't. She said it made her physically ill."

Constance found that short of actually lying, there was no way to escape without telling the whole truth. So she began to tell the story just as it had happened, and the mother sat and sobbed softly, while the father fixed a stern unseeing glance out of the window across the room, now and then wiping his eyes.

It was a terrible ordeal for Constance. She found her heart aching for the two, her own tears flowing in spite of herself, and her whole heart crying out to be able to comfort them. It was as if Doris somehow had put them in her care to comfort.

There was only one kind of comfort she could give, and because she did not have it as her own she shrank inexpressibly from even trying to tell about it. She found herself longing for Seagrave again. If he were only here these two sad hearts could be comforted about their only child. If they could but have watched the fright die out of her eyes, and the look of peace come! If they could have seen the smile as she said, "Now I can go!" it would surely ease their pain. And there would be something that Seagrave could give them for themselves; a hope. She knew that in her soul. But as she did not own it for her own how could she pass it on to them? She thought of a verse marked heavily in Seagrave's little Testament, that she had read that morning. It had not made its meaning very clear when she had read it, but now it seemed to start out in her memory with sudden clarity. "That I may know Him, and the power of His resurrection—" there was more to it than that, but it was gone from her mind. Still this was the thing that would make comfort possible to these people, to know Christ, and the power that He brought with Him when He rose from the tomb. Dimly she perceived, and understood that it was something she had not, something she was not willing to have because it entailed something else which she was unwilling to give. But anyhow she did not have this something by experience and how could she be expected to tell it to others. And yet there was upon her strongly the necessity to do so.

Then astonishingly she found herself telling in detail the story of that terrible afternoon, going over conscientiously every harrowing word, how Doris had begged for some one to tell her how to die, and how she in her desperation had remembered a certain young man at home whom she happened to know was very spiritually minded, and had dared to call him on long distance and summon him; and he had come.

Doris' father took out his fountain pen and note book and wanted to get the young man's name and address and go to see him at once. He was most disappointed to hear that he was in Europe and would not be home for perhaps three or four weeks. "Then I think, if you don't mind, we shall have to ask you to tell us in detail just what he said to our daughter," said the father. "I feel that it is imperative that my wife have some ease of mind. She has suffered greatly all these days of our journey. It seems as if she just must know Doris' state of mind before she died."

Constance did mind very much. There was nothing short of dying herself that she thought she would not rather do. She tried to edge out of it, to say that she was not sure that she could recall everything that had been said. Yet she knew that was not true. Every word, every syllable that Seagrave had uttered, every fleeting expression on the dying face of her friend was graven on her heart in letters of fiery anguish. She had gone over it and over it in the night time. She would never be able to forget it.

So presently she found herself telling it, forgetting herself and just making vivid the scene. How Seagrave had given her a Bible verse to read, she even told of hunting for the Bible and having to borrow Emil's Testament, and the father stopped her to get old Emil's address. He said he would like to buy that Testament of him if he would sell it. It would be a comfort to have the book that helped their precious child to die.

Constance marveled at herself, her unaccustomed lips speaking such things, telling of matters of the spirit, unembarrassed because she was so overwhelmed with the need of her visitors. She told how she had read those verses over and over to soothe her dying friend. She even repeated the verses twice over for the father and mother who took note of the reference and fairly hung upon her words. She was amazed at her own fluency. And now that she was started it seemed somehow a relief to tell somebody about it. Perhaps after this she would not have to keep going over and over that awful experience.

Presently she found herself to her own amazement telling the way of salvation just as Seagrave had told it, unconsciously using his very words, and her little audience of two hanging on her story, drinking it in, wiping their flowing tears away, relaxing just a little the agony and tension in their faces.

She hurried on to the end, telling of the light that dawned in Doris' eyes at the last; of her surrender and prayer; and then of her last words "Now I can go. Good-by!" and she pictured the peace in Doris' face, earnestly, tenderly with a vividness that carried blessed conviction to the hearts of her eager listeners.

When she had finished it was very still in the room save for the soft sobbing of Doris' mother. Constance sat there embarrassed at what she had done. She realized that the story she had told had not been of her own will. Something outside of herself had carried her along, passing on the story to those who needed it so greatly. She would not have chosen to tell it. She was half frightened that she had. A great shyness was de-

scending upon her, and to add to it she suddenly heard
a book drop to the floor in the library just behind the
heavy curtains that shut it away from the living room.
Was some one in there? Who could it be? Her mother
had gone out on an errand. Her grandmother was up in
her own room she was sure, for she was not feeling well
this morning. Frank of course was away on his own
pursuits, and her father was in the city. It must have
been a maid of course, but now that she had come
down to earth again and realized how strange any
member of her family would think it for her to be
talking of such solemn things she felt most uncomfortable.

Suddenly Doris' mother arose and came over to her,
putting both her arms about her and stooping, kissed
her on the forehead.

"My dear," she said softly, "I cannot thank you
enough! What you have told me has greatly comforted
me. I did not know my daughter was interested in
religious things. That is what has worried me ever since
the news came. You see I was brought up in a church
and I've always been troubled that Doris wasn't interested in it. But I should have been so much better
satisfied if I had known that she had a Christian roommate."

"Oh," said Constance raising a protesting hand,
"You don't understand! It wasn't I who did anything—"

And Constance felt the mantle of hypocrisy drop
down upon her shoulders once more. Ever since that
awful day when she had joined the church for a string
of pearls people would persist in believing her better
than she was. It was like a curse upon her. Her eyes
filled with despairing tears. And Doris' mother went
right on in spite of her protest:

"My dear, don't say a thing. I understand. Of course
the young man you sent for was marvelous, and I am
deeply grateful to him, always shall be, but it was you
really who were the comfort to her. She must have
known what a Christian you were or she would never
have asked you to help her in her distress. It is the
daily life that counts you know, my dear, and I'm sure
she loved and honored you. She often wrote about you.

She loved you very much. Oh, Miss Courtland, you have been wonderful to my darling! Wonderful!"

But Constance rose now in deep distress.

"Oh, please don't say that—" she protested, "I'm not—anything at all. I never have been much of a Christian! I— You— You don't understand. I don't want to pose as something I am not."

"It's quite all right, my dear," said the sorrowing mother. "You are very sweetly humble about it, but I thank God that my child had a Christian roommate and that she knew what to do for my darling when she was dying!" and the mother buried her face in her handkerchief and sobbed quietly.

Then up rose the father.

"I'm not able to express my deep gratitude," he said huskily. "I've never been much of a Christian myself, but my mother was one, and I'm glad my little girl died believing. I can't thank you enough for having given us this blessed picture of Doris' last moments. I too thank God that you are a Christian. You know, nobody but a truly consecrated person could have told that story in just that way. It has comforted us greatly. I don't know how to talk about religious matters very well. I'm just a plain man of the world. But when I see a real Christian like you I bow before her, and I cannot express my thanks as I would like for what you did for our little girl."

It was of no use to make further protest. They would not listen. They insisted that Constance was an angel of light, a wonderful young woman, the most wonderful Christian they had ever met!

When they took themselves away at last Constance stood in the doorway and watched them drive off with a terrible sinking at her heart. Here she was a hypocrite again, posing as a great Christian, when she knew she was nothing in the world but a great sinner! Oh, what should she do? How should she get out from under this awful weight of spirituality that everybody seemed determined to put upon her? It was getting more than she could bear. She felt as if she must run away from home and from everybody she ever knew. She must get away from a reputation which she could not live up to. How

could she have known that that one little act of standing up before a congregation and lightly taking vows
upon her lips was going to have such wide-reaching
consequences?

She remembered once reading a story in history of a
prince who posed as a pauper, and a pauper who took
the prince's place for a time, and when they tried to go
back to their own lives they found they could not make
people believe they were their true selves. Constance
felt that her own case was similar. Everybody would
persist in thinking her a saint. How should she make
them understand that she was not? Would it be necessary for her to do some terrible deed, some wild disrep-
utable thing before she could make them understand?

Then suddenly she sensed that there was some one
else standing near her in the hall, and turning quickly
she saw her brother just behind her, a sweet, solemn
look upon his face.

"Say, Connie, you're great!" he said with a fervency
she had never heard in his voice before, at least not
when speaking of herself. "I hope you won't think I
was eavesdropping. I was in the library all the time,
and I couldn't very well get out without letting everybody know I had heard. You see somebody had locked
the door into the back passageway and there wasn't any
way to get out without going through the living room. I
was in there drawing an outline for Dillie of where we
had planted each kind of flower so she could have it to
keep; and when those folks came I thought they had
only come to call for a minute, so I just kept still and
went on working. Then when you began to tell all
about that accident it was too late to get out."

Constance's cheeks flamed crimson. So Frank had
heard her all the way through!

"Oh, that's all right, it was nothing." She tried to
laugh and failed utterly, "I had to do all I could to help
the poor things." She endeavored to make her voice
sound casual but failed in that also. There was the
sound of a sob in her throat.

"You poor kid!" said her brother, deep sympathy in
his eyes. "I didn't know you had to go through all that.
But I just think it was great how you were such a good

sport and stayed beside your roommate. I thought it was awfully fine of you to know what to do, and to keep reading that Bible verse to her. I'm afraid I'd have skipped out! Connie, I didn't know you had it in you to talk to people like that. I've always been thinking you were just a crazy kid, interested in the fellows and the country club and all like that. I didn't know you ever thought about religion. But I've gotta hand it to you, and I guess I owe you an apology. I always supposed you just joined church ta get those pearls of Grand's but I see I was wrong and I'm sorry about all the things I said, Kid. You're the real thing and no mistake!"

"Oh, Frank, don't!" said Constance shivering. "I'm not. I'm just a sinner and a hypocrite! I'm so ashamed!"

Her face was red with shame and her eyes were filled with tears. She bowed her head and covered her face with her hands.

Suddenly Frank, half shame-faced, laid his hand on her head.

"You're a great kid!" he said solemnly. "I respect you, Connie. I mean it. I honestly do. I guess maybe religion is a good thing. I never thought about dying before, but you need it when you come to die, don't you? Maybe I'll get me some some day too. I never thought religion had much to do with men before. I thought a guy that was religious was a sis, but if that man Seagrave is like that I'm for it. He's a great guy. Say wasn't that great of him to come up there and help you, and it was just the night before he had ta sail, did you know that? He musta been all kinds of busy."

Constance lifted her head at that.

"The night before he sailed?" she said. "Are you sure?"

"Yeah, I'm sure. I figured it all out while you were talking in there. You see Sam Howarth and I drove him ta the wharf."

Then suddenly upon the scene arrived Delancey Whittemore in a priceless new sports car, bringing up around the curved driveway to the door with an "I-have-arrived" air that was both insolent and perfect.

"Who's that poor fish?" growled Frank stepping back into the shadow of the portière.

"Mercy!" said Constance catching a glimpse of the handsome well-groomed face, "I've an engagement with him for luncheon at the club and I forgot all about it. You meet him, won't you, Buddie, and tell him I'll be down in a minute? That's a dear! No, I can't see him looking this way," she protested as she saw refusal in her brother's eyes, "See, dear, my eyes are all red. Go tell him, that's a dear!" and she flew up the stairs.

Frank looked up after her in dismay, and then his expression hardened, his lips set with an elderly manner he could assume on occasion, and he went out to look over another of his sister's suitors. He reflected as he went that he just could not see why a girl wanted so many men underfoot. One girl was enough for him, especially if it was Dillie. However, since Constance preferred that way he would have to take the consequences. But why, for Pete's sake, when she knew a fellow like Seagrave, couldn't she just rest at that without looking further?

In this mood he went frowning out to meet Whittemore, who regarded him from a superior altitude and tried to patronize him.

But Frank was not in a mood to be patronized. He invited the caller in, said his sister would be down soon, and when Whittemore declined to come in and said he would just sit in the car and smoke Frank sauntered out and patronized Whittemore's car. Incidentally too he studied its owner, sizing him up according to a special boy code he had, measuring him with Seagrave in his mind.

Constance made a rapid toilet and presently came down cool and collected, with a forced smile. But Frank looked at her critically and saw still that dewy look of recent tears about her lashes.

"Take care of yourself, sister!" he said almost tenderly, and gave her a meaningful look.

"Why should she?" laughed Whittemore with a half sneer on his handsome lips, "I'm here to do that."

"Oh, yeah?" remarked Frank comically.

Constance looked from one to the other of the two

young men and wondered as she was driven away if there had been a passage at arms between them, and whether Frank had really intended that look of almost warning he had given her.

CHAPTER XVI

FRANK stood looking after them as they drove away, his young brows drawn in a deep frown.

"I'll have to look that guy up," he remarked to himself in a low tone, "I don't like his mug. I wonder what she wants to monkey with him for?"

Then he went into the house to finish the elaborate plan he was making for Dillie's garden. Dillie was gone to assist at a festivity her mother was giving to her mission band in the church parlors or Frank would certainly have been with her. But meanwhile he had a great many things to think about.

For instance, who would have supposed his sister was religious? How well she told that story. There was a great blister on Dillie's garden plan where a tear had fallen unawares from his own eye while listening to that story.

It must be awful to have death suddenly walk into your life and only leave you a few minutes to get ready. It was great that Constance had a head on her and got hold of Seagrave to make that girl die happy. Good night! Suppose he got in a jam like that and had to die suddenly! What would he do?

He drew a ruled line down the garden path where the delphiniums and lilies were supposed to grow, and whistled through his teeth.

That was a great little verse Constance recited to that girl before Seagrave got there. That was John three sixteen. Frank had learned that when he was in the Primary class. He hadn't gone to Sunday School now for seven or eight years. He quit when they tried to run in a new teacher on the class that none of them liked. All the class quit. He hadn't been since. Of course Grand made a terrible row about it and appealed to

Mother and Dad. But he had overheard Mother telling Grand that she mustn't say anything about it; that he would get over it and come back of his own accord some day; that you couldn't manage boys the way you could girls. And he had let it go at that. He had not gone back.

Well, of course if one were going to die maybe it would be as well to know a few verses to be handy when needed, but then he wasn't going to die for a long time, why worry? Only of course if one could be a Christian like Seagrave, well that wouldn't be so bad. He wondered what made Seagrave that way?

Then his mind wandered back to Whittemore. Whittemore, Whittemore! Where had he heard that name? Oh, that was the name of the people that had the old Wilson estate out on the pike, the place with a twelve-foot hedge of hemlock, and inside that a young forest all around so you couldn't see the house. Snobs! People that hid away like that, he thought. If they had a nice house why didn't they want people to enjoy it?

Well, he must look that guy up and see if he was fit company for Connie. Dad didn't seem to realize what kind of brutes were running around these days. He seemed to just trust everybody.

So Frank finished his map and then sauntered downtown to hang around a certain drug store where he could always learn a bit about everybody. All he had to do was buy a soda and then keep his ears open.

But what he learned that day of Delancey Whittemore absorbed him so that he did not notice when a party of boys and girls came in until they were fully upon him, and then suddenly a jazzy sweater was flung across his shoulder the sleeve striking him full in the face and the lazy drawl of Mary Esther cried out:

"Hello, old thing, feeding yer face? Blow me to a soda, darling? I'm simply dying of thirst and I'm broke."

"Sorry!" said Frank rising in haste and restoring the sweater ceremoniously, "So'm I. I gotta beat it. S'long!"

A loud chorus of laughter from Mary Esther's gang followed him as he stalked out of the drug store and down the street to the church where he had promised to

meet Dillie and help her escort the youngest of the
mission band to their homes. But as he went he did
some thinking.

Was Mary Esther always going to hang around and
take it for granted that he belonged to her? Suppose
now that Dillie had been with him when Mary Esther
talked to him like that! He must take some steps to put
Mary Esther right where she belonged.

Yet even as he thought it he wondered whether that
would be possible? Whether or not Mary Esther would
not take all possible occasions to insult and annoy him
just because she was piqued? Well, let her go. It was a
cinch he couldn't stop her, and after all it was his fault.
He had been a fool ever to go with a girl like Mary
Esther. He knew it now. Perhaps he had always known
it even when he was most crazy about her. That was it,
he had been crazy about her. There ought to be some
way for the brakes to be put on a fellow when he got
crazy like that and stop him from being a fool. He
guessed a fellow never did quite get rid of something he
was ashamed of, did he? It was always cropping up. He
thought of the one time he had taken Mary Esther out
in his father's car against his father's express command.
He hadn't been found out. Nothing had happened to
the car. He hadn't done it again. But there was a
memory. Mary Esther had insisted on having the car
parked in a lane and snuggling up to him with her head
on his shoulder. Mushy stuff! He hadn't cared for it at
the time. His mother had brought him up to be clean-
minded, and it didn't seem quite nice to him. But he
had to be a sport, didn't he, and do the thing a girl
expected? There had been a kiss and he was ashamed
of it. He hadn't been given to that sort of thing, it
seemed silly. There had been no thrill in kissing Mary
Esther. He had come as near to disliking her that night
as he could, while he was still rather crazy about going
with her. He rubbed his lips hard at the memory of it.
Some day he would have to tell Dillie about that kiss
perhaps, and it wasn't going to be a pleasant experience, because Dillie wasn't that kind. Dillie gave no
liberties. That is, one took no liberties with Dillie. Dillie
had been kept sweet and clean. He wished he had never

seen Mary Esther. Did one ever get quite clear of the
Mary Esthers?

Then he remembered the rumor he had heard about
that fish-faced Whittemore. He'd got to follow that up
and see if it was true. If it was, there must be some way
to make Connie understand she must cut him out. Gee!
Suppose she wouldn't listen? He was younger than she
was of course. She might be angry. She'd been mighty
sweet lately, but no telling how she would act if he
attempted to get into her affairs. Well, and no telling
whether what he had to tell would make any difference
with her if she should happen to get crazy about the
man. Life was like that, Frank had observed. People got
out of their heads about somebody now and then and
you couldn't do anything with them. Then they were
sorry afterwards. Seemed as if there must be some
ballast or something somewhere that one could have to
keep one from doing fool things!

Then suddenly he was at the church and there was
Dillie in a pink organdie with a swarm of cute little
kiddies around her. Gee, wasn't Dillie sweet! When you
saw her like that wasn't she sweet? Nobody would look
at girls like Mary Esther if there were girls like Dillie
around, thought Frank. But then girls like Dillie didn't
stick around everywhere to be had for the asking. They
weren't always on the landscape like the Mary Esther
kind. You had to go and find the Dillies of life. Discover them and win them. Frank liked that. It made them
more worthwhile than just to get a girl from the other
fellows because you happened to be able to buy her
more sodas or have a better car to ride her in.

So Frank lifted a small tired baby with a sticky fist
full of colored paper favors, and rode her on his shoulder to her home, while Dillie led two other sticky ones,
stained with ice cream but smiling, and several other
larger ones tagged on behind.

Frank liked it. He didn't care if they did meet Mary
Esther and her crew! Let them stare! He was having a
good time.

But to-morrow he had to hunt up the Whittemore
pedigree and take care of his sister!

So Frank and Dillie took the last happy sticky child

to its home, and then sauntered back through the long shadows of the late afternoon perfectly content with each other's company. They slammed through a set of tennis before dinner on Dillie's court which Frank was gradually whipping into fine shape, bolted their dinners, and Frank returned to the Fairchild house for an evening of ping pong.

Sauntering home under the bright summer stars Frank planned out his campaign for the morrow. Dillie was going to the city shopping with her mother in the morning so he would have the time uninterrupted. He would go to the court house first and look up some records, and then hunt up Joe Rafferty who used to live on the old Johnson estate, was stable boy or something to the Johnsons and knew the history of everybody for miles around, all back through the years. It might not be a bad idea to drop around and look the improvements over at the old house. He had heard there was a groom there taking care of the horses of the new owner. He ought to be able to drop a word or two of enlightenment. Then there was a village a few miles north that had been connected with that first rumor he heard in the drug store. If he could get Dad's car he would rustle around there for awhile and see what he could bring to light. It ought to be dead easy.

And when he remembered Constance telling that story to Doris' people he reflected that it ought to be easy to make her understand about Whittemore, provided he really had the facts. A girl who could talk that way wouldn't stand for a guy like Whittemore, not if she knew what he was!

So Frank arose with alacrity quite early the next morning and started out on his tour as detective.

It might have amused his elders mightily if they could have watched the indifferent way he went about it, sauntering into places and buying a paper, or a bag of peanuts. Asking a casual question or two, following out a clew with the quickness of a rat terrier on the scent, yet never seeming to be anything but an idle youth on a day's pleasure.

Strangely enough his father had consented to his taking the car for the morning, which made it possible for him to cover more ground to the hour than he had expected, and just before the two o'clock train came in, on which he expected Dillie to arrive from the city, he came driving into his home town well satisfied with his morning's work. He was reflecting that the few brief entries he had set down in his grubby note book, now reposing in his pocket, ought to be proof enough to his sister of the warning he would give her when the right time came. If they weren't he would take her over to the County Seat, and the village over the state line, and let her see and hear for herself.

So he drove up to the station with a flourish just as the train came in, and was there ready to carry the parcels for Dillie and her mother and take them home in the car. It made him very proud to be able to do that. And it added not a little to his pleasure that they should pass Mary Esther performing the unusual duty of carrying a basket home from the market with not a single swain in sight. Frank gave her a mere gesture toward his hatless head as he flew by with his hair blowing wildly. It didn't even occur to him to stop and take her in. Poor Mary Esther! But Dillie hadn't seen her. Dillie was telling Frank about a cute little dog they had seen in the window of a pet shop in the city. Sparkling little Dillie! How pretty she looked in that dark blue frock with the fluffy white sleeves, and the small blue hat with the bit of a scarlet wing down next her dark curls. He wondered how he had ever thought Mary Esther was worth looking at.

Dillie was all eager to play tennis after her morning in the stuffy city, and they played till dinner time. Mrs. Fairchild invited Frank to stay to dinner so they could finish their tennis set before it got dark, and then Frank came in again. Dillie had bought a wonderful new picture puzzle of seven hundred pieces and they spent the evening putting it together. Frank forgot all about his brotherly anxieties and had a good time.

The last thing he thought of as he laid his happy head upon his pillow that night was that he must try and get hold of Constance in the morning and work it around to tell her what he knew about Whittemore. He couldn't be quite easy in his mind till he got that all fixed up. Then he disposed himself to deep sleep!

But Frank did not waken early as he had expected to do, and Constance went off to the club as soon as she had finished an early breakfast to keep an engagement with Whittemore for eighteen holes of golf before the sun got too high for comfort, for it promised to be a warm day.

So Frank slept on like the seven sleepers. He did not hear an outcry in the hall, nor anxious hurrying footsteps up the stairs. Not until his mother came into his room and shook him did he waken, and with startled eyes still filled with sleep take in vaguely her agitation.

"Get up quick, Frank, and go for the doctor! Your grandmother is very sick, dying perhaps, and the doctor's car has broken down. I told him you'd be there for him right away. Hurry!"

"Good night!" said Frank tumbling out of bed instantly, "Grand! Not Grand sick!"

With the technique acquired in going to fires in the middle of the night Frank dressed in three or four motions and was on his way downstairs in a flash, swinging on his coat as he ran. A moment later the car shot out the driveway and down the street like a speck in the distance.

Yet it seemed to the boy as he flashed along the highway as if he were merely crawling. Grand! If anything should happen to Grand what would they all do? Death! It had never occurred to him that death would enter their household, at least not for many years ahead.

Of course Grand was ready. There wouldn't be any question about that. It wouldn't be like that scene at Doris' bedside that Connie told about. A quick memory came of sitting at his grandmother's feet on a little bright stool learning to spell out words from her big-print Testament, her frail warm hand upon his curly head. Grand knew the way to die. Oh, sure! She knew the way to Heaven! But Good night! If Grand were in Heaven then everything about life would be changed! They would have to be thinking about Heaven continu-

ally, get sort of Heaven-conscious. It would be bound
to make a difference of course. A fellow couldn't just go
on living his own way and never thinking about dying
after that! One of the family in Heaven!

A bright tear dimmed his vision and a tight constriction came in his throat. He drove ahead with a solemn
look on his stern young face and brought up at the curb
where the doctor stood waiting for him, like a flying
Mercury, scarcely halting long enough in his passage to
get the doctor into the car. Grand was dying perhaps!
Nothing else mattered but to get the doctor to her at
once.

He answered the doctor's questions grimly, breathlessly, speeding over the two miles to home and
brought up at the door with a great sob in his throat.
Perhaps even now she was gone!

He parked the car and followed the doctor into the
house, listening in the hall fearfully. His mother came
half way down the stairs to meet the doctor, that frightened non-committal look on her face. They went up to
Grand's room, and Frank, slowly, hesitantly followed,
terrified of what might have happened.

He went and stood at Grand's door, looking in. A
nurse was already there in a white uniform. He recognized her as one who had been staying across the road
taking care of a child who had broken her leg. Mother
must have telephoned for her after he left.

He could see Grand's little lovely old face there on
the pillow, looking like a frail white flower. Her silver
hair which always was so perfectly groomed and pinned
severely about her small shapely head, lay out on the
pillow now in lovely curls, silver curls. He hadn't seen
them that way since he was a little bit of a kid and was
parked in Grand's bed mornings sometimes while she
finished dressing. But the curls weren't silver then, just
brown with threads of white here and there. The soft
curls gave her face an ethereal look as if she were
already something not of earth, some being of another
world, too delicate and sweet for this world. Frank felt
that awful choking in his throat again, the mist in his
eyes. His heart cried out with inexpressible longing to

have Grand open her eyes and break this awful spell of death that seemed spread upon the room, as if a breath might take her away at any instant.

Then his mother tiptoed to him and whispered. There were tears on her cheeks too. She did not try to hide them. Perhaps, even, she did not know they were there.

"Go quick and find Constance!" she whispered. "Her grandmother has asked for her. The doctor says she ought to come quickly."

Frank gave one more anguished yearning look toward that ethereal face on the pillow and turned to go.

"And Dad?" he asked.

His mother shook her head.

"You needn't go for him. Some one is bringing him from town in a car. He ought to be here soon."

Frank dashed silently down the stairs again, his heart heavy with anguish. They thought then, the doctor and his mother, that she was not going to get well! She might even be gone when he got back!

But before he reached the car his mother called softly from the front window:

"Wait, Frank, the doctor wants you to get this prescription filled and bring it back quick before you go for your sister."

Tensely he turned and caught the paper that fluttered down through the morning sunshine. It was a relief to have even that much to do for Grand.

He was back at the house again with the medicine in an incredibly short time, his big anxious eyes appearing at his grandmother's door, searching the white face on the pillow for an answer to his anxiety.

His mother came and took the bottle from him. The strained look was not quite so apparent on her face he thought.

"The doctor thinks she is rallying a little," she whispered reassuringly, "But he says Connie ought to get here as soon as possible."

Ah! The weight dropped down upon his heart again. Grand! Dear little white Grand!

He turned and dashed out to the car again. Oh, why did he have to leave now and go after Connie? Why wasn't Connie here?

CHAPTER XVII

FRANK, driving at a furious rate came whirling down the drive to the country club. He brought the car to an abrupt stop, left the engine running and sprang out.

"My sister here?" he asked a couple of girls who sat tending golf bags as they waited for their tardy partners.

"Why," said one girl, "she just came in from the eighteenth hole."

Frank looked around distractedly.

"Which way did she go?" he demanded savagely.

"She was talking to Carolyn Coxe a few minutes ago," said the other girl. "I think Carolyn just went up to the dressing room. I'll call her."

A moment later Carolyn appeared with the information that Constance had gone with Delancey Whittemore up to his estate.

"It's something about the pageant for the house warming, or the decorations, or else maybe the lighting. That's it, the lighting. I heard Delancey say that he wanted Connie to see if she thought the lights were being put high enough over the pool for the swimming scene."

With a black look, and a murmured thanks Frank sprang into his car and was off again, his engine drowning the last part of Carolyn Coxe's explanation.

"I wonder what's up?" said Carolyn to the two idlers. "He acts as if something had happened."

"Oh, he's just that way," said one of the other girls. "He's just a kid. Boys that age are always that way. I've got a kid brother and he's a pest. He simply is. I suppose he'll grow out of it some day. But it's awful while it lasts."

"He's a stunning looking boy," said the other girl who was younger herself.

"Oh yes, in a way. He's too smart-Aleck for me, and I don't like the way his lips shut as if he were a stone wall and you couldn't move him an inch."

"That's character!" said Carolyn Coxe as she hurried back to get ready for a swim.

Frank's heart was pounding wildly as he drove along. His sister gone off with that bounder! Why hadn't he done something sooner? Perhaps people knew she was off up there alone with him! Didn't girls have any sense at all?

He almost forgot the errand that had brought him out hunting her in such frantic haste as he boiled with anger at Constance for taking up with such a man.

He broke all the laws of traffic as he hurled his car along through town, turned corners on one wheel, took hair-breadth escapes one after the other in quick succession, and whirled on out toward the Whittemore estate.

Into the sacred "snobbish" precincts beyond the high hedge and the young forest he turned, dashed past them all and hurtled round the drive to the great house, nearly pulled the ancient bell from its socket in his fury, demanded of the servant who opened the door to know where his sister might be, and was at last directed to an eminence a little above and behind the great mansion, where stood Constance with Whittemore. She was pointing down to a level below her where a lovely blue-tiled pool glittered in the morning sunlight, and where several workmen, presumably electricians, were at work. Connie was directing them. His sister was on this rotter's property directing how things should be, just as if she had some right there! His young soul nearly exploded within him.

He dashed up the hill his face white with panic:

"Constance!" he called and his voice sounded strangely stern like his father's when he was roused to severity with his children.

"Why, Frank!" said Constance turning around, "What is the matter? How did you happen to come here?"

"How'd you happen, you'd better say!" he barked,

all out of breath. "I've hunted the earth over for you. Come on quick! Mother wants ya right away!"

"Here, you young upstart, cut that out!" interrupted Whittemore. "You can't come here and order your sister around!"

But Constance saw beyond her brother's gruff words and something in his eyes frightened her.

"What is the matter, Frank dear? Has something happened?"

"It's Grand," said Frank huskily, choking over the words as he suddenly remembered the unhappy errand. "She's been taken awfully sick. It's her heart!"

"Oh!" said Constance with that sudden rush of terror at the thought of Death stepping near again. "We must go right away. Where is the car? Hurry!"

"But you can't go yet, Connie," interposed Whittemore. "These men have come all the way out here to get your directions and the time is short. If they have to wire this over again there won't be any time to spare. You'll simply have to wait a few minutes and get this into their heads or the whole color scheme will be a mess."

"Oh, what difference does a color scheme make now when my grandmother may be dying?" said Constance throwing out her hands wildly.

"But, my dear Constance," said the man approaching her imperiously. "It won't take long. I insist that you stop just long enough to make Mr. Ensign understand what you were trying to tell him. You really don't need to get into a panic. You probably can't save your grandmother's life even if you do go at once, and a few minutes more or less can make no difference in the outcome."

But Constance was already hurrying down the hill toward the car.

"But really, Connie, you're leaving me in an awful hole!" he called.

"Too bad about you!" called Frank back. "They'll probably bury you in a hole some day."

"Oh, Frank, don't talk so!" said his sister with a catch in her breath, and then called back coldly, "You'll have to excuse me, Mr. Whittemore, I wish you would get Carolyn Coxe. She will plan it for you. I'm definitely out of this! I really have to go at once."

Panting, out of breath, her eyes wide with fear, Constance climbed into the car, and Frank was almost instantly beside her with his foot on the starter.

But Whittemore had followed them and was calling imperatively, motioning them to wait.

Frank however sent the car shooting forward with a bound.

"Don't you answer that rotter, Con," he ordered as if he were several years her senior. "Where'd you pick him up anyway? He isn't fit for you to wipe your shoes on."

"Frank! How terribly you talk!" said his sister. "You mustn't be so excited that you lose your sense of decency. You mustn't be rude to people!"

"Sense of decency!" snorted Frank stepping on the gas and grimly noticing in the little mirror that the owner of the estate had given up the pursuit. "You're the one that needs to hang on to a sense of decency, going with a rotten egg like that!"

"Why Frank! I never heard you talk so about any one before!"

"No, I guess not!" said Frank grimly. "But I know what I'm talking about all right. And it's time you knew what he is too. Has any one told you anything about him I'd like to know?"

"Why, I was introduced to him by the Fishers, and he's a distant relative of the Wards, I understand."

"Well, they didn't tell you did they that his first wife is living in California with her two children, and his second one in Boston, and his third is down in Reno getting a divorce from him right now? And he has a lotta other children living around in schools and with grandfathers and things. Did they tell ya that?" he looked at her fiercely, the blue of his eyes almost black with his excitement. "If that isn't enough to turn you against him for a playmate you aren't the sister I thought you were."

Constance sat back with a stunned look.

"Frank!" she exclaimed. "That can't be so."

"Well it is so. If you want proof I'll take you over to

the next county and show you some of his recorded marriage licenses."

"How did you find out?" She looked at him aghast.

"Well, I found out all right and I can prove it to you. I hoped you'd have sense enough to see what he was without my telling you. Gee! How a girl can run around with a two-timer like that when you've got a perfectly good friend like Seagrave I don't see! If you really care for this poor fish I'm off you for life."

Then Constance came to her senses.

"Care?" she said. "Why should I care for him or them or any one. For pity's sake get that out of your head. I was only helping him get ready for a big party, but I hate the thought of it now. It's nothing to me if he has a dozen wives all over the United States. Let's forget it. And as for Mr. Seagrave, get him out of your head too. He's a bare acquaintance and nothing more. Now don't let us speak of them anymore. Tell me about Grandmother? How is she, and when did it happen?"

Frank drew a long breath of relief. He had done his duty at least and she hadn't tried to argue about it. Great Scott! That was a relief. Then the larger trouble loomed again. Grand was desperately sick.

"Why, she was just taken about three quarters of an hour ago," he said, his voice softening into gentleness. "I don't really know so much about it. Mother called me and said go quick for the doctor, and then she had Martha phone for Dad, and when I came back with Doc Waters she told me to go quick for you. She said Grand had asked where you were."

"Oh, she isn't dying, is she?" Constance asked with a sob in her voice.

"Well, Doc said she was a little better," soothed Frank. "But he said you oughtta get there, for she seemed so anxious to see you. But he told me to tell you she mustn't talk."

Constance sat back and tried to relax. She closed her eyes for an instant and tried to take a deep breath. Here it was all over again, Death, come to menace her, coming nearer now, into her very home. Would Grandmother feel afraid? Would she know she was dying?

She couldn't think of her grandmother as afraid, yet it seemed so awful for the little sprightly woman who had firmly, sometimes sternly managed them, all through her long placid life, to be met and vanquished now by Death. She couldn't think of Grandmother and Death together somehow. Oh, Grandmother mustn't die. At least not just yet. Somehow before Grandmother died she must atone for the way she had got those pearls. Oh, if Seagrave were at home now she would go on her hands and knees if necessary, and ask him to pray that her grandmother might get well and live long enough for her to atone for cheating her that way about the pearls. But Seagrave was not there and this time she could not summon him by airplane. She must do her own praying!

"Oh God," her frightened heart cried out, "please! Please help!"

Death! Death! Death! Was she to be pursued by this adversary the rest of her life, because of that one act of making false vows on a beautiful Easter Sunday morning?

They had reached the house now and Constance had the door open ready to step out even before the car stopped. She tossed off her hat as she ran up the stairs and appeared at her grandmother's door with wildly beating heart and panting breath.

A linen-clad nurse slipped out of the door and down the hall to the bath room with a thermometer in a glass of water in her hand. Mother came to the door with a finger on her lip and drew Constance into her own room across the hall from Grandmother's. There was an air of sudden hush and awe upon the house. Constance looked at her mother and tried to read the truth in the drawn smile that she turned toward her.

"She's just a little better," she soothed. "She was almost gone! If it hadn't been for Maggie who saw her fall and caught her, we would have been too late the doctor thinks. Maggie was making up her bed and saw her in the mirror of the bureau suddenly put her hand to her heart and turn very white and then just slip down, and she whirled around and caught her before she reached the floor."

Then the nurse appeared.

"The doctor says Miss Courtland may come in very quietly and sit by the bed but she mustn't speak. No, wait, Miss Courtland, till you get your breath. She mustn't be excited. Just take her hand if she seems to want it, and smile at her. Don't let her talk. Yes," in answer to an anxious look of Constance's mother, "I think she is resting easier now, and it seems as though the immediate danger is passed. But she'll have to be kept very quiet."

So Constance in a little soft white silk dress that would not rustle passed into the sick room like a wan wraith and took up her place in a low chair by Grandmother's bed.

The old lady seemed to be sleeping when she entered, but as Constance sat down she opened her eyes and smiled. Constance gathered the frail little patrician hand into her own and the slim old fingers just slightly pressed hers, showing that the old lady was glad of the beloved contact.

Hour after hour Constance sat there with that small frail roseleaf of a hand in her own young warm one, and hour after hour the minutes ticked out thoughts for her, pictures of another bedside scene, words from a little book she had read and read until it had beaten its way into her soul never to be erased.

She watched the delicate wax-like features, cut sharply against the dusk of the afternoon as the day began to wane, watched the slow faint breath come and go, struggled to keep back the tears that smarted to flow, watched sometimes with bated breath because it seemed as if the other breath had stopped. Sometimes a gray look would come over the beloved face and she would make a frantic silent little motion for the nurse to come and look.

The nurse would come and touch the brow, listen, lay a practiced finger on the wrist, then wave an infinitesimal signal that there was no new cause for fear, and the afternoon slowly changed into the evening.

Constance would not leave her except when the doctor insisted that she should eat something. She was afraid to miss a word, a last smile perhaps.

Once, late in the evening, the invalid roused and opened her eyes, looked toward her granddaughter with a faraway light in her eyes, a strange, pleased surprise of a light.

"Why, I saw my Saviour then," she said in a clear voice, looking straight at Constance, a look of wonder and deep pleasure, "and your grandfather was right there by His side!"

Then she closed her eyes again and slipped off into another sweet deep sleep.

Constance sat in fear and watched, expecting to see that change of death come over her face, as it had to Doris' at the end, pondering, wondering. Why, then, Grandmother had that something too that the others had, that joy and peace. The peace that Seagrave wore in his eyes, that the old man Emil had shown when he pulled out his Testament and offered it, that had come to Doris before she went away. Grandmother had it too. It was something real and tangible. In spite of Grandmother's funny little conventional ways, and insistence upon forms and ceremonies, Grandmother seemed to know God Himself, to have known Him well enough to recognize Him in the dream or vision or whatever it was that she saw.

A great longing possessed Constance to have that something for herself too, but a weight oppressed her heart. She had taken false vows upon her. Likely she had committed the thing she used to hear ministers sometimes preach about as the unpardonable sin. Seagrave had seemed to think she had done a dreadful thing in just taking those vows without actually knowing much about them or believing them, and he hadn't known the half of her heinous offense. He hadn't known she did it for a string of matched pearls.

Perhaps if she had gone and talked with Grandmother before she was taken sick, told her just how selfish and wrong she had been and given her back the pearls—let her send them to her cousin Norma—there might have been a way for her soul to come clean so that she too might be saved and find peace and joy in living or dying as these all seemed to have.

So she sat waiting, expecting the shadow of the death

angel to fall upon that beloved flower-like face at any minute.

Quite unexpectedly the nurse touched her softly on the shoulder and she started and looked up, expecting to be told that the change had come without her recognizing it.

But no, the nurse whispered softly:

"She is much better. She will sleep all night now. The doctor says you had better go to bed and get a good night's rest so that you can be with her in the morning if she wants you. I will call you at once if you should be needed in the night, but I don't think you will be. The doctor says she has rallied most unexpectedly this last hour. Now go and get a good rest."

As in a dream Constance slipped out of the room and to her own bed throwing herself down upon it, her heart breaking with the joy and tears of sudden relief.

Oh, God had been good! Perhaps there would yet be a chance to somehow make amends for what she had done! So she fell asleep.

Meantime down in the front hall Frank was keeping watch, answering a muffled door bell, taking in boxes of flowers for his sister from Whittemore, Ruddy Van Arden and others, answering anxious enquiries and offers of help from friends and neighbors. He had the pleasure of telling Whittemore, who had called twice, "where to get off" as he expressed it to himself, though he had couched his conversation in polite firm language, making it very clear that his sister would not be able to participate in any fiesta, either that evening or the next, and probably not all that week.

So Whittemore left his box of expensive gardenias and took himself away. Frank sat down with satisfaction and glared at his shoes. He thought over the story he had heard his sister tell the other day when he sat in the library while Doris' father and mother were calling; thought about that unknown Doris' death. Would Grand be dead by to-morrow perhaps? Would she look like herself lying in a narrow place among flowers, or would her face seem like a vacant house with all the window blinds closed and the occupant moved out forever?

Life! How queer it was! Death, how inevitable! Why was one put here to live just a while, death always at the end?

Was Grand sorry to die? Did she know how ill she was?

So he sat manlike and bore his pain alone, just a boy whom nobody realized was suffering.

Once in the evening he answered the soft whirr of the muffled telephone, and a voice clanged drawlingly over the wire.

"Hello, old thing! The gang are going out on a whoopee party, wantta go? Ef ya do we'll stop by."

"Nothing doing!" said the boy and slid the receiver down with a click.

Frank stole into the darkened living room after a while and tried to rest his aching head, looked out through the window and watched the lights in the Fairchild home twinkle softly among the trees. The light in Dillie's room went out. A few minutes later there came a soft tap at the door and when he opened it there stood Sarah Ann, the maid from Fairchild's, with a note in her hand addressed to him.

After Sarah Ann had gone away across the lawn to the opening in the hedge he took the note to the dining room light and read it where nobody would interrupt him. It read:

Dear Frank:

I am asking our Heavenly Father to let your dear grandmother get well if it please Him, or if not to make you happy about it. But I think—I hope—He will let her get well. You pray too.

Your friend,

Dillie

So Frank locked the front door and the back door, looked after the many window fastenings, and then stole up to his room. In the dark he knelt down with his face turned toward Dillie's home, his heart looking up to heaven, and perhaps for the first time since he was a little child, he really prayed to God.

CHAPTER XVIII

THERE followed a couple of weeks of anxiety, when life took on a different aspect and all normal activities were hushed to their lowest terms.

Two nurses instead of one were installed, a day nurse and a night nurse, and the family grew accustomed to tiptoeing about and conversing in whispers.

Pageants, festivals, the country club, all were forgotten, even golf and tennis were a thing of the past. Dillie and Frank took sober walks in the country lanes at times when Grandmother was resting and improving. Constance could not be persuaded to leave the house. She hovered near the sick room even when she was not actually in it, until the doctor and her mother grew anxious about her. Yet even then they could not get her to go out farther than into the garden for a few minutes. She had a nervous fear upon her that while she was gone her only opportunity might come to confess to her grandmother about the pearls.

She read her little Testament a good deal, but in such a feverish way that it brought her no comfort. All the verses seemed either warnings, or hopeless for her, because she felt she was forever outside all the blessedness of things offered there so freely. She had mocked God with her false vows. Even Seagrave had said something like that to her that morning on the hillside among the blue flowers.

She grew pale and thin. Her mother and the doctor offered a tonic but it could not reach her soul.

She thought of Seagrave now only as a faraway dream, like her thought of God. He was gone out of her life forever likely, had never really been in it except as one who had perhaps been sent from God to bring her to a knowledge of her own careless giddy sinful life.

Oh, if her grandmother would only get well perhaps somehow she could begin again, give back the pearls and make a fresh start. She sometimes even considered whether it might not be required of her to stand up before the church and confess what meaningless vows she had made asking them to release her and forgive her. The whole thing had become an obsession with her. Sometimes she threw herself down on her knees and tried to pray. But her lips had been unprayerful so many years that they refused to utter the longings of her heart. All she could stammer out was a feeble frantic petition for her grandmother to get well.

Slowly but surely the frail ethereal little woman was getting her hold on life again. They wouldn't let her talk much and when she did speak a few words her voice was weak and trembling, but she was gaining strength every day and she could smile almost like herself again. She could even press a hand feebly when one of the family came softly in to kiss her and bring a flower or something good to tempt her to eat.

Since her repeated refusals to join them even for an hour or two the young people of the neighborhood, and the country club, had ceased to depend upon Constance. They simply could not understand such devotion. That grandmother had two nurses didn't she? And a doctor? And a whole household of people to look after her? She was only a grandmother anyway! There wasn't any sense in Constance making a martyr of herself! So they reasoned, and said as much to Constance when they could get speech of her. But Constance froze when they suggested such ideas, and the next time excused herself from seeing them. So they just dropped her, made a few caustic remarks about her, and calmly left her out of their calculations. If she ever got over this "phase" as they called it, she would be welcomed back of course, but at present she was hopeless, impossible! One couldn't carry on festivities and mark time for funerals that held off and didn't mature.

After repeated attempts to draw Constance back Whittemore had solaced himself with Carolyn Coxe, and the rumor that he seemed altogether satisfied with the change was wafted even into the dim light of the sickroom where Constance sat reading sweet old-time books of a beloved past to the placid little old lady.

But Constance, if she ever thought of Whittemore in

these days, had only scorn for him. She remembered his impressive attentions to herself, the tender way in which he had pressed her hand, the eloquence of his eyes that searched deep into her own. He had almost stirred her own emotions sometimes. She recalled the possessive way in which he had treated her before everybody, as if there was an understanding between them of a much closer friendship than people saw, his arm about her on the slightest occasion, the intimate way in which he had held her when she danced with him. The memory of it all made her cheeks burn. And he a twice-divorced man, not even divorced yet this third time! How dared he insult her? Yet it had in a sense been her own fault. She had allowed his familiarities, questioned them perhaps, and worried a little about them, because it was her nature to be aloof. She did not like to be treated lightly. Yet she had not protested. It had been a little like her one brief experience with Thurlow Wayne, only Whittemore was more subtle. He had gone like a whirlwind, carried her with him laughingly, not as if it mattered much, and she had been all too ready to plunge into gayeties and forget the serious things of life. She had been mad with a desire not to have time to think, and she had lent herself to his carelessness, his lightness, his impertinence.

How degraded she felt as she sat hour after hour in the dim shadows of the sickroom and thought things over, how utterly unworthy of a friendship with a young man like Seagrave. Well, that was over at least. No answer had come from him. He had probably forgotten her. The flowers at commencement had been merely a polite gesture. Her answer had reached him in some far journey and he had not thought it worthwhile even to respond. And of course it hadn't been necessary. She had only asked him to give her opportunity to tell him something when he came home, but now she knew with sudden pain that she had counted on a letter from him and her heart was sore that none had come.

Foolish! Crazy! Why should he write to her? He had no interest in her aside from her salvation of course. He was not her kind, and she never could be his. He knew enough of her to understand that, even though he did not know all. It would be enough for him that she had been the kind of girl who would have taken sacred vows without a thought! That would stamp her at once to him as a trivial creature, of light nature, who might be saved of course, but would never be a strong true character. He would not want such a girl for a friend. He was likely trying to make her understand all this by his silence.

And she had striven in that first meeting of theirs to emphasize this very idea. Oh, it was her own fault, and she had no one but herself to blame!

Constance was very quiet in these days, timorously thankful that her grandmother was getting well. Oh, she would never be really strong again perhaps, would always have to be cared for like a fragile flower, always kept from excitement. But she was still with them for a while longer at least.

There came a day when Grandmother was sitting up in a big easy chair and seemed stronger than she had been since her illness. She had taken a little walk across her room leaning on Constance's arm, and now was back in her chair again, "And not a bit tired," she said with a smile.

Constance dropped down at her feet on the little footstool and rested her tired head lightly against the silken lap of the old lady, closing her eyes and drawing a deep breath.

"Oh, Grandmother, I'm so thankful you are truly better," she sighed.

The old lady put out a fragile roseleaf hand and laid it on her head.

"Poor child!" she said with an unwonted tenderness in her usually reserved tones. "You take things so hard! I've been watching you. We're closemouthed, you and I, but we take things hard inside. But it would have been all right child if I had gone then you know. My time has come and I'm ready to go when God calls me."

"Yes, I know," said Constance with a trembling breath, remembering that wonderful look in her grandmother's face when she woke and said she had seen her Saviour. "But, oh, Grand, we couldn't spare you!"

"Dear child!"

"And besides—" Constance caught her breath and stopped short.

"Besides what, little girl?" The gentle hand patted her head again.

"Oh, just something I want to talk over with you when you get real strong again."

"I'm strong!" said the chipper old lady sitting up smartly in her chair. "Tell me now, child. There's no time like the present you know. It's the only time we're sure of."

"Yes, but you might get excited and too tired," said Constance. "It isn't important—to any one but me, and it will keep." She tried to smile but it was like a wan ray of sunshine.

"Fiddlesticks!" said the little lady with her old sprightly manner. "It'll excite me much more to have this thing going on. You don't suppose I haven't seen there was something wrong with you, do you? Out with it, child, and have it over. I'll promise not to get excited over any little thing that belongs to this old earth. I've been too near the other side to feel they matter so much anymore. Come, tell me quick, child! I knew you had a burden."

"But maybe you won't think this thing belongs just to earth, Grandmother," said Constance with a troubled look.

"Well, if it belongs to heaven it's all right somehow, or can be made so. Come. Out with it. You're a dear good girl and I want nothing between us. We haven't any time left for clouds between us."

"But that's it, Grandmother, I'm not good," said Constance lifting her sorrowful eyes. "Not as good as you think, that is."

"None of us are good!" said the old lady crisply. "What have you done, Connie?"

"Well, Grandmother, I didn't join the church because I wanted to, last Easter, I didn't even join it to please you, though I was glad it did that. I joined because I wanted to get those matched pearls! And now

I'm just afraid this will make you sick again, but I had to tell you!" and Constance's head went down in her two hands again, her cheek resting lightly against her grandmother's knee.

Softly the warm roseleaf hand came down upon her head with its gentle touch like a blessing.

"Well, child, I've been suspecting as much for a long time so you needn't worry lest you've shocked me. I've got eyes in my head and I could see you were more interested in the world than in the church. But I began to look back, and I thought it was perhaps as much my own fault as yours. I shouldn't have put those pearls into the matter at all. I meant to give them to you anyway. I always intended them for you. But it did give me great pleasure to have you have them and wear them first at your first communion as I wore mine. Still, I see now I shouldn't have done it, or at least I shouldn't have let you know anything about it."

"But Grandmother, I'm so ashamed!" wailed Constance like a little child, putting her head down in her grandmother's lap under the soft comforting hand.

"Well, little girl, it's always a good sign to be ashamed when you've done something wrong. It's not till we begin to see ourselves that we get ashamed, and you've got to see yourself before you can set things right. So, now, child, what are you going to do about it?"

Constance was still for a minute, the big tears stealing out from under her lashes and rolling down her cheeks till Grandmother's fine soft handkerchief wiped them off. Then the girl spoke again:

"I'm going to give you back the pearls, Grandmother, and let you give them to Cousin Norma."

"No," said Grandmother after a moment, "the pearls are yours. I've given Norma their equivalent in something she wanted more than pearls, the money to go abroad and study. You'll have to work out the cure without giving back the pearls, child. I don't want the pearls. I have always wanted you to have them ever since you came into the world. I planned to give them to you the night you were born. And even if you were to punish yourself by giving them back, or not wearing them, that would not undo the thing you did. Because, child, it wasn't me nor the pearls you sinned against, it was God. You trifled with His holy things. You've got to make it right with Him somehow. I'm glad you came to me and were honest. It's taken a great load off my mind to think you have found yourself out. But you haven't really gone to the root of the matter yet until you've made it right with God."

It was very still in the room. Far away over toward the country club a meadow lark trilled out a long sweet note, and a little breeze came in at the window and cooled Constance's hot brow, blowing back the tendrils of gold hair. Grandmother just laid her hand softly on the bowed head again and waited.

At last Constance raised her head and asked tremulously:

"Do you think I should get up before the congregation and publicly state that I did not mean what I promised? Should I try to undo it somehow?"

"No," said the old lady thoughtfully, "I don't see how that would do any good, unless you wanted to publicly testify that you had come to a different way of thinking. But even that would be something that would come afterwards. And it is not always best to confess your wrong before the world unless the world has a right to know, or you can help somebody by it. There is something that must come first, and that is to make it right with God."

After a much longer silence Constance asked huskily,

"How could one make it right with God, Grand?"

The old lady was slow in answering, with a shy reserve about her as if she were treading upon too holy ground to speak freely.

"There is prayer," she said solemnly. "Have you taken it to God yet, Connie?"

Constance shook her head.

"I'm not sure I would dare," she said softly.

"There's nothing to fear, child. He'll search you, of course. But that's the only way to get right. Make a clean breast of it and don't hold anything back even to yourself. I remember when your mother was a little girl she had eaten some fruit that I had told her not to touch. She didn't seem to know I knew it. I waited for days for her to come and confess but she went right on as gayly as ever. It didn't seem to bother her, except at night I noticed that she didn't like to have the light out, and she always begged me to sit by her till she fell asleep. But at last one night I left her alone in the dark, and then she got to crying. I came in and she told me that the eye of God was looking down on her, seeing how naughty she had been. And then she told me what she had done. I remember how I gathered her in my arms after she had confessed, and how she snuggled down in my neck and went to sleep. We don't need to be afraid of our Father, child, if we really want to get right with Him."

Then in marched the nurse.

"This dear lady is sitting up too long. I'm surprised at you, Miss Courtland! She must get right to bed."

Constance, dewy eyed, and somewhat comforted, arose in haste and helped to get the patient back into bed. As she stooped over her to smooth the sheet across her shoulders, she pressed a quick furtive kiss upon her forehead and whispered:

"Thank you, Grand, it's so good to know you forgive me."

Grandmother said fervently, "Of course, child!"

Thus closed the most intimate talk that had ever passed between these two in all the years of Constance's life, and Constance tiptoed out and left her to sleep, feeling that the experience had been wonderful, a break in the long years of reticence and formality. It might close in to-morrow again and the wall of reserve rise as gray and high as ever, yet there would always be this afternoon to remember, always a bond between them. For a few short minutes she had seen into her grandmother's heart, and had a vision of her own relation to God. It was not merely sentimentality that had kept the pearls for her first communion day. It was a real faith in God and her Saviour that had made her long to seal such a moment for her loved grandchild with the most precious thing she owned.

Constance in her room alone reading her Testament,

thinking as always when she read, of Seagrave, remembered telling him something to the effect that Grandmother didn't know what it was all about, that she thought if one stood up in the church and took vows that did the trick. But now she had found out that Grandmother did know what it was about, that she had a real living faith, and neither was she so gullible as she might have seemed, for she had seen right through her granddaughter's sham and she had probably been deeply dismayed to find out how superficial she was.

Then suddenly in startled thought she sat up and stared at the verses about being separated from the world. Did that mean herself? Is that what it would mean if she did what Grandmother wanted her to do, went and made it right with God? Was she willing to do that? Or would the world be like another string of pearls that would keep her from making good the vows she had uttered?

After a long time she turned out her light and knelt down beside her bed in the moonlight waiting for an audience with a God whom she had insulted, waiting with her heart beating in a frightened way at what she was about to do. At last she said in a broken whisper:

"Oh God, I'm sorry and ashamed. If there's any way for me to make it right please show me, even if you want me to be separate from the world."

That night Constance had the first full rest she had enjoyed since her grandmother was taken sick.

CHAPTER XIX

THE next morning the house was in a perfect whirl. Frank announced that he was going to a week-end conference and everybody had to help him get ready. The plan seemed to have developed overnight.

"A conference?" said his mother. "What kind of conference? Why should you be going to a conference?"

"Why it's a young people's conference. A Bible Conference. It's for the young people of this district, and they're mostly all delegates from different churches around here. Dillie's a delegate from her church, and if you pay your way you can go even if you aren't a delegate, and I'm going. I havta have two sheets and a pair of blankets, and some clean shirts, and my bathing suit. Towels too. Will ya get them for me? I'll take that old football bag."

"Why, how long are you going to stay?" asked the bewildered mother. "Isn't there a hotel or something? Why do you have to take sheets?"

"Oh, it's a kind of a camp," said the impatient youth. "Didn't I tell ya? They live in log cabins, sort of dormitories, with a lot of cots in each one and a man ta look out fer each dorm. Dillie's mother is a chaperone for the girls. That's how I got a chance ta go. They have meetings and athletics and a swell time. It only lasts from Friday till Monday. It doesn't cost much. Say, are ya going ta get me some blankets? No I don't want a suitcase for them. I'll just tie them up in a brown paper. That's the way the others do. Bill Howarth is going. He went last year. He says it's great. He says they had a swell time. They've got a crackerjack athlete along and a lotta swell speakers."

In growing amazement Frank's family danced attendance upon his commands, were duly scandalized when he refused to take his best clothes along for Sunday, demurred at the old sweater he elected to wear, produced more towels and shirts and sheets than he could be persuaded to take along, and in every way hovered about him with hindrances and suggestions till his departure.

Constance drove him with Dillie and her mother in the Courtland car to the rendezvous where they were to meet the bus that would take them to the camp. Dillie's mother was sweet and young-looking with a peace in her eyes that reminded Constance of the look in Seagrave's eyes. She wondered if the same cause made all these people have that look of utter content as if they had a source of strength beyond the ordinary. Perhaps she wouldn't have noticed this a few weeks or months earlier, but now her attention had been called to that look in some eyes, and she was growing quick to detect it. Was Dillie's mother also one of those peculiar people who knew God?

When they drew up at the rendezvous Constance had a new experience. A large bus heavily placarded with "PELHAM GROVE YOUNG PEOPLE'S BIBLE CONFERENCE" was drawn up in front of a church. Young people were arriving from every direction, from trolleys and private cars and on foot, all piling into the bus. The bus driver was good-naturedly busy disposing large canvas duffle bags and brown paper bundles in a rack on the roof of the bus, and everybody was talking and laughing and getting introduced to everybody else.

They were nice-looking young people, but they were not dressed up. Most of them wore plain garments and sweaters that had seen better days, but they had happy faces full of anticipation.

Presently another bus drew up beside the first, labeled "SOUTH DISTRICT DELEGATION" and underneath in smaller letters a magic phrase that Constance never would forget, "John three sixteen." Why! That was the verse she had read to Doris when she was dying! And these boys and girls were flaunting it on a banner! What possible connection could it have with a week-end camping trip?

And while the thought was passing through her mind, even before the driver had parked his bus to suit him by the curb, the young people who crowded it to capacity broke forth into song, every word as clear and distinct as if it were being recited:

A story sweet and wondrous,
Like heavenly music swells;
In chimings clear to all who will hear,
Ring out the gospel bells.
    For God so loved the world
    That He gave His only begotten Son,
    That whosoever believeth in Him,
        Should not perish,
        Should not perish,
        But have everlasting life.

The verse was scarcely ended when a third bus also crowded to overflowing and labeled "NORTH DISTRICT DELEGATION" arrived on the scene. It had come up so quietly during the song that Constance had not noticed it and now it started another song:

Friends all around me are trying to find
What the heart yearns for, by sin undermined;
I have the secret, I know where 'tis found:
Only true pleasures in Jesus abound.
    All that I want is in Jesus,
    He satisfies, joy He supplies;
    Life would be worthless without Him,
    All things in Jesus I find.

Constance listened in amazement, studied the bright young faces leaning out of the bus windows singing with all their might, with as much fervor and eagerness as ever some other young people might have sung the hilarious popular jazz of the hour, or the latest radio favorite. Was it possible that there were young people who had separated themselves from the world and yet had a good time?

But she had no time to think for the first bus which was now more than full burst into song as if in response to the others:

I've found a Friend who is all to me,
His love is ever true;
I love to tell how He lifted me,
    And what His grace can do for you.
    Saved by His power divine,
    Saved to new life sublime!
    Life now is sweet and my joy is complete,
    For I'm saved, saved, SAVED!"

Just at this moment a last comer came running from a trolley, climbed in and the signal was given to start. And then the three bus loads poured the strength of their young voices into the next verse of the same song:

He saves me from every sin and harm,
    Secures my soul each day;

I'm leaning strong on His mighty arm;
I know He'll guide me all the way.

and as they streamed away in a joyous procession in the distance, back came the triumphant words of the chorus:

Saved by His power divine,
Saved to new life sublime!
Life now is sweet and my joy is complete,
For I'm saved, saved, SAVED!

Constance sitting alone in her car watching the vanishing campers, watching the amazed crowds who stood on the sidewalk to stare and listen and wonder, felt a sudden thrill of gratitude that her brother was going away to be three days in such company, and then felt a great loneliness upon herself and a desire to put her head down on the wheel and cry.

Was it really true that there were young people in the world who had chosen a life like that and were as happy as that in it? Could people come out from the world and enjoy it? Yes, there was Seagrave. He seemed happy. He was young. But he was the first one she had ever seen who was like that.

Of course these young people who had just driven away were only boys and girls, not yet out in society, perhaps some of them never would be because of their simple station in life, nevertheless she knew enough of modern high school people to know that they were to-day aping their seniors in every gayety of life. And these had just been normal happy young people, enjoying their outing, yet willing to bring God into it; not only willing but eager about it, for there was no mistaking the thrill in their songs. They were sung from the heart as if the boys and girls meant every word and were trying to broadcast their message to others who did not know about it.

Wistfully she trailed the bus procession for several miles, keeping far enough behind them not to be recognized, yet near enough to catch the echo of their songs.

"I need Jesus!" came the next song through the

crowded highway where people were slowing their cars to turn and look and listen, and Constance's heart echoed the song. Yes, she needed Jesus, but—was she willing to take Him? Grandmother had forgiven her but would He? She had not made it right with God yet. She was not sure she knew how to believe, to just take salvation as a gift and accept it simply as Seagrave had told Doris to do.

Then back from the Bible Conference procession came a new song winging faint and far away, but snatches of words gained clearness even above the sound of traffic:

Would you be free from your burden of sin?
There's power in the blood; power in the blood,
Would you o'er evil a victory win?
There's wonderful power in the blood.
There is power, power, wonder-working power,
In the blood of the Lamb;
There is power, power, wonder-working power,
In the precious blood of the Lamb.

And her heart cried out as she drove,
"Oh, God! Give me that power! Take away my sin! Make me sure of salvation and happy as they are!"

When Constance reached home she went straight to her grandmother's room.

"Where is your brother, my dear?" asked the invalid who had been allowed to sit up as long as she chose that day, and had attained to walking around the room by herself.

"Why he's gone away for the week-end, Grand! Gone to the most extraordinary place. I just can't make it out. Frank willing to go to such a place! But he seemed as happy as a clam to be going."

"What is it, Connie?" The grandmother looked a little anxious. She had heard echoes of arguments about getting her grandson's baggage ready to take and it had apparently worried her.

"Well, it seems to be a sort of glorified camp meeting as far as I can find out," said Constance, and she sat down and told in detail all she had seen and heard,

even remembering some of the words of the songs to
repeat. When she had finished she looked up and
caught a beatific look on her grandmother's face.

"Praise the Lord!" she said softly. "I am being allowed to live to see my grandchildren serving the Lord.
I believe He is answering my prayers before I go! I knew
He would save you both some time but I had begun to
think it would have to be through a lot of tribulation,
and after I was taken. Praise the Lord!"

Constance sat and looked at her grandmother in
amazement. Every day now was revealing new and
unsuspected sides to her character. Fancy Grandmother having been worried all these years about her
and Frank—their salvation! It was a new and strange
thought to Constance. And she had imagined Grandmother as shut within a formal world of ceremonies
and stately habits!

Presently she went up to her room and took down
the Testament. She came on verses that reminded her
dimly of the songs she had heard that afternoon, and
she wished that she might have gone with those high
school children and listened in the background to see
what was said and what they did. She wished she had
somebody to tell her the meaning of some of these
strange verses she read. Grandmother might know in an
old-time way, but there were new vital things that
Seagrave had said that made the truths more compre-
hensible to a modern person.

Then she began to think about her Sunday School
class. What a farce it was, her teaching! What could
she teach them about God and the Bible, she who
knew nothing whatever herself? Well, she must get
rid of that. That at least she could do for them, find
a teacher for them who knew these things. Then they
would stand some chance of getting the joy of those
young people in the buses.

Why had Dillie been the only one of her class to go
on that trip? Didn't the rest know about it? Weren't
they asked? Or didn't they care to go? Perhaps that was
something she could do for them, get them interested in
such things. Only how could she when she didn't know
herself? Well, how could she learn? There must be

some place. Where did all these other people learn? Where had Seagrave found his knowledge? Just in the Bible without any outside help? If he ever came back and gave her a chance she would ask him and then she would go and find out for herself.

Late Sunday night Constance was sitting lonesomely in the hammock on the porch in the dark by herself.

She was thinking how she had come to a sort of standstill in her life, a kind of deadlock with nothing in view. School all done, no plans ahead. She was ready to live now, but strangely she had no zest for living. She might go to Europe as she had planned but she didn't especially want to. Why had all her eagerness to have a good time ebbed away? Was it Doris' death or Grandmother's illness or both, perhaps? She was restless, unhappy, longing for something she didn't know what. Oh, why had her life fizzled out this way just when she had thought it was going to be gorgeous to do just what she pleased? Couldn't one ever do what one pleased and have it work out right?

Then she heard soft distant music, voices, sweet and clear, and looked up sharply thinking she must have fallen asleep and was dreaming. It seemed like angel voices on the soft night air:

Abide with me! Fast falls the eventide!
The darkness deepens, Lord, with me abide:
When other helpers fail, and comforts flee,
Help of the helpless, oh, abide with me!

The voices grew clearer with every phrase, till they were almost before the house, just half way between the Fairchild house and theirs to be exact. She could see one of those big buses. Frank was helping Dillie out and bringing in her things, and now the people in the bus were driving away singing "God be with you till we meet again."

She could see Frank upstairs in the lighted rooms of the Fairchild house putting down the suitcases, smiling at Mrs. Fairchild and saying good-night. Then he came whistling across the lawn and through the hedge, picked up his own things which he had swung over the hedge when he got out of the bus, and came toward the house. But the tune he was whistling was "Lord, abide with me!" Had Frank caught it too? Could that be possible? How pleased Grand would be if it were so!

"Oh, hello, Kid!" was the lad's half embarrassed greeting as he suddenly realized his old familiar surroundings, and began almost to withdraw into his same old shell.

"Well, what kind of a time did you have, Buddie?" she asked moving over to make room for him to sit down beside her in the hammock.

"Swell!" said he eagerly. "Oh boy! It was great! Say, Kid, I wish you'd been along. I do really! You'd have liked it, I'm certain you would. They're a crackerjack gang of kids, and they had a great line of speakers and leaders. It was swell! Simply swell!"

Then he began and told her about it, eagerly, pell-mell, jumbling things all up, fried potatoes and prayers, and how many people got saved; and what a swell teacher they had for the class in Hebrews; and how all the fellows and girls called him "Bill" but not to his face of course, and how they loved him, and would do anything at all for him, simply anything at all! And how he made the Bible a grand book, simply like a story book! And he was funny too sometimes. Why he even told funny stories on himself that made you laugh till you cried, and then suddenly you found you were laughing and crying at your own self, and it hadn't been him at all you were seeing in the verses he was illustrating, but you in your everyday life. He showed you how you forgot God and wanted your own way, and didn't really pray when you thought you were. It was so simply told you couldn't forget it, just had to think about it the next day when you went around. It made you see just what kind of a fool you'd always been about things you'd always thought were all right.

He talked himself out at last and lay back in the hammock thoughtfully remarking:

"Well, I guess I gotta get ta work pretty soon. I don't wantta waste any more of my life the way I've been doing. I've got my eyes part way open at least."

Connie, not knowing exactly what he meant and

hoping to lead him on to show just what was in his mind said:

"I suppose you'll be going to college in the Fall. Have you definitely decided which college?"

"I thought I had—" he answered slowly, and then sat up sharply, "but now I don't know that I'll go, at least not yet." He brought out the last words crisply as if they were a sudden decision.

"Not go?" questioned Constance. "Has Dad persuaded you to go into business instead? I knew he had some notion of that sort a while ago. He thinks a lot of boys waste their time in college doing everything but study."

"No, it's not that," said Frank slowly. "Dad said I might do as I pleased. Said he wanted me to choose my own future, after he had given me a lot of good advice on all sides. But I've got a new idea. I think I'll go to college later, but I'll go to Bible School first."

"Bible School?" said Constance in amaze.

"Yes," said he simply, "Dillie's going and I think I'll go too. I know most folks think it ought to be the other way around and you ought to go to college first. Maybe it ought for some people, but not me. I've never had any real teaching about the way God looks at things. Oh, I know Mother and Grand taught us to say our prayers when we were kids, but this is different. I kind of think I ought to get to know a lot more about the Bible first and get a little real solid anchorage on the true foundation before I go into the world and get to studying what men think about things and get all muddled up. Men's minds can make so many mistakes when they get thinking. I'd like to be able when a new question comes up to know right off the bat what the Bible has said about it so I can keep my bearings and not get switched off."

"But," said Constance in a daze, "I don't understand, Buddie. I never heard you talk like this before."

"Well, I know. I'm different. You see, I've been born again, Connie. I'm looking at things from a different angle from what I did. Up there in the woods you sort of have to get saved or quit. There's no half way spot, and Dillie and I both accepted Christ. And we promised we'd do the Lord's work if He wanted us. That's why, see? I wantta be able ta tell others about it, and I can't waste time on other studying till I know how, see? Why, Dillie and I might even go to the Foreign Mission field or somewhere, and we need to get a lotta Bible knowledge so we can keep it in the back of our minds all through any other studies we'd havta take. And, why, the Bible isn't a bit dull as I supposed it was. It's a swell book! It really is a swell book! No kidding!"

When Constance went up to her room that night she looked at the little Testament with new reverence. It must indeed be a great book when it had been able to catch and hold the attention of her young brother. Frank a missionary in a foreign land! Could anything be more inconceivable? But wouldn't Grand be glad? Would wonders never cease? Her brother with the light of something strange and wonderful in his eyes! Another added to the list of those who understood and turned to God for peace and joy. Seagrave and Doris and Emil and Harriet Howe, and Grandmother, Dillie, and Dillie's mother, and now Frank! What made it? How had it happened? Was there some mysterious law by which it came to some people and not to others?

Then she opened the Testament and read:

"The wind bloweth where it listeth, and thou hearest the sound thereof, but canst not tell whence it cometh, and whither it goeth: so is every one that is born of the Spirit."

The next morning when Constance opened her curtain and looked out on a new day she saw a messenger coming in the gate with a yellow envelope in his hand. With sudden alarm or premonition she sprang down the stairs to open the door. And when she saw it was a radiogram for herself she could scarcely hold the pencil steady enough to sign her name she was so eager to get alone to see what it was.

Of course it might be any one of the three of her college classmates who were gone abroad, and were perhaps cabling her to join them, as they had often talked together of such a possibility. But then it might not be any of them at all, and her heart beat wildly as she started upstairs to her own room.

CHAPTER XX

"This is perfectly ridiculous!" said Constance aloud to herself as she reached the seclusion of her own room and slipped the bolt of the door.

But ridiculous or not she had to own that she was trembling as she dropped into a chair and held the envelope in her hand for an instant, trying to discipline herself into steadiness before opening it. Why, a cablegram was nothing! There were dozens of friends any one of whom might have cabled her to do something for them while they were abroad. What was it she was really expecting that she was so excited? Not Seagrave. Of course he would not cable anything. That was absurd!

And why should she care anyway? Seagrave was nothing to her. A stranger. The significance of his homecoming, if this should be an announcement of that, could not make so much difference to her now. She had confessed to her grandmother and had been forgiven. That was all that was necessary. After all, Seagrave didn't need to know now.

Yet the pounding of her heart told her that she was hoping this was a word from Seagrave, and that she could not bear to open the envelope lest she would be disappointed.

So she tantalized herself still more by coolly hunting for her paper knife under the confusion of letters on her desk. She really must do something about this. She mustn't get notions about that man. Perhaps she would go abroad after all—that is as soon as Grandmother was strong enough to be left—and get this foolishness out of her head.

Then she found the paper cutter and slit the envelope and there was Seagrave's name signed to the message!

The bright color flooded into her cheeks and her heart leaped with a great unbidden bound of joy. Oh,

she was glad, glad, glad! He had answered her letter
after all!

She sank back into her chair again closing her eyes
and drawing a quick breath, and then read the brief
message.

It was dated from his ship.

"Letter just received. Will you go with me to a
meeting I have promised to address the night I reach
home, Thursday, this week?"

Suddenly it seemed to Constance that the world had
begun again just where it left off the night he said
good-by in the moonlight at college.

For a moment she was just dizzily glad, sitting there
and staring at that bit of paper with its few words, and
finding herself engulfed in a great wave of happiness.

It was humiliating for a girl who had always prided
herself on keeping her heart well armored to find that it
had surrendered thus unasked to this violent interest in
a stranger. She tried to steady herself, tried to reason it
out, tried to make herself believe it was wholly her
anxiety to confess to Seagrave and get herself cleared,
but she knew in her heart it was more than that.
She knew that it was something she had never felt for
any one before, this tide of joy that had her in its
grasp. She knew that she cared awfully! That if she had
not received some word from him soon it would have
gone hard on her. And she knew that she would rather
be asked to go anywhere in the world with Seagrave,
than to be invited by any one else to the greatest fete on
earth. Right or wrong, ridiculous or not, it was true. It
would have to be dealt with summarily of course, but
just right now she could do nothing but let this great
joy flow over her, this great relief. She found there were
tears in her eyes and a swelling of laughter in her
throat. Finally she put her face down on the paper and
laughed softly to herself.

Then she read the message again several times, her
heart leaping with every word. He had asked her to go
with him the first night he arrived!

Well, she mustn't think too much of that. Hadn't he
told her he didn't know many people yet? And he had
sailed so soon after they had first met. Still, there had

been plenty of time after she went back to college for him to get to know other girls.

So her mind flashed back and forth, exulting and fearful, till finally she gained a measure of self control and gathering up her message went down to the telephone booth and sent her answer, "I will go." There was a lilt in her voice as she sent the word throbbing over the wire, and the starriness of her eyes was wholly wasted on the dark telephone booth, but she mounted the stairs again afterwards on feet that were as light as wings.

She locked her door again and sat down to have it out with herself. Seriously she called herself to order. This was no way for a sane person to act. Of course she had been through a heavy strain, two strains in fact, and that would probably account for her nerves and notions. And of course it was natural that Seagrave, having been the one who had helped her during that terrible time of Doris' death, should be somewhat idealized by her. But it was high time that she looked facts straight in the face. It would not do to set him on a pedestal this way because when he arrived it wasn't in the least likely that he would measure up to her first impressions of him. Oh, he was religious all right of course. She had come to know there was no doubt about that! He probably was an unusual young man in many ways, and it was undoubtedly true that he knew a great deal of his Bible and really lived up to his faith in a conscientious way. One could not look at the purity of his face without being sure of that. Then, too, she had the testimony of what Frank had told her about his standing with the firm for which he worked. All that was undoubtedly proof of his good character.

But she had to remember that he was just a plain young man, and that her first impression of his dress had been that it was shabby. Not that clothes mattered so much, only as they were an indication of one's background. But he had a good job and had likely shed his shabbiness by now. In fact her remembrance of him when he came to college was that he was immaculately tailored, although of course she couldn't remember his attire. All she could remember were his words, and the light in his eyes. And probably because of her distress she had exaggerated that. She must prepare herself to be disappointed in him when she saw him in the light of everyday living. Not everybody who could talk like an angel was likely to be a pleasant congenial companion for every day.

Platitudes like these she told herself, and swallowed them whole, trying to down that feeling of exultation in her heart, yet that heart went right on soaring like a bird, rippling out songs of joy in glad little trills. And at last she gave up. Well, nothing could take away the illusion till he came, she might as well go on and enjoy the anticipation of his coming while it lasted. Disillusionment would likely come soon enough.

And then an inner voice would remind her sharply that she was planning also to disillusion him about herself, if indeed he still cherished any illusions about her now. So really there was nothing to worry about! Why not just enjoy his coming? Enjoy that one evening with him, and then things would naturally adjust themselves. Probably she would have had enough of him and he of her before that was over.

Then she fell to wondering what kind of meeting he was taking her to. An odd place for a trysting place. An uncomfortable idea hovered on the edge of her mind that perhaps he wanted to show her that he had very little time for her confidences, and was making the time and place for them most public. He was probably wanting to make it plain that his friendship with her was to be on a strictly religious basis hereafter. And of course after she had done her part and shown him what she was, he would be even more anxious to do that.

Yet in spite of all these plain facts that she laid before her mind, and accepted bravely, her heart would lilt right on, and her eyes look glad. At least she could ask him a lot of questions about his little book in which she had been reading so faithfully. She decided to write out a list of questions and have them at her tongue's end to ask him on the way in town. Then she would be sure to have the answers before she ended everything between them.

There would be the meeting also which he was to

address. It would be rather wonderful to hear him speak in public. She felt he would do it well. Perhaps his address would even be on a subject that would answer some of her heart-longings.

She spent some time going over the parts of the Testament that she had read the most, and writing out questions that had perplexed her as she read. He might think her a fool for not knowing all these things, but somehow she felt he would answer them fully and sympathetically.

The next few days, though often full of palpitating premonition, severe self-judgment, and self-warning, were very happy ones. The family saw an immediate difference in her. There was a song on her lips from morning to night, a smile on her face, her eyes were starry, and the lilt was constantly in her voice. Her mother said: "She is so glad about her grandmother's getting well." Her father's eyes dwelt upon her with great tenderness. Her brother observed her with increasing satisfaction from day to day as he saw her continued interest in her home, and heard her various refusals over the telephone to invitations here and there. Was Connie really getting sense, he wondered?

But her grandmother watched her placidly and breathed a soft prayer. "Perhaps the little girl is learning to know her Lord," she told herself as she sat quietly in the twilight and watched the pink glow of sunset fade into the deep star-set blue of evening.

Every night when Constance read the Testament she came on more things which she did not understand, verses that she longed to know the meaning of, and her heart crooned a little melody softly. Well, he was coming. She might ask him. Before she confessed what she had done and put up an inseparable wall between them forever she would learn much.

He would probably be willing to answer questions about the Bible even if he didn't want her for a friend. He was like that. He would want to help any one, even a poor little hypocrite like herself.

Yet often as she reminded herself that she must not count on any lasting joy from his home-coming, her heart would not give up its soft singing. Well, she conceded again, she would just enjoy that one evening to the full, anyway, whatever came after.

So the days slipped by, one after another, and seemed each one a month long in the going.

Constance was with her grandmother a great deal, reading aloud, frequently reading the Bible to her, and often longing to pause and ask questions about what she read, only a great shyness was over her. The silence had been broken once between these two, but had somehow grown together again. There was new confidence, understanding, new tenderness, but it would take something out of the ordinary to make either cross again that dividing line of reticence that had existed through the years.

The evenings were the hardest. Frank was busy with Dillie, over at Dillie's house a good deal of the time, taking Dillie's mother here and there in her car, relieving her of the driving, and incidently companioning with Dillie.

Young Howarth arrived home, too, and took Frank's time. One evening Constance wheedled all three, Dillie, Frank and Will Howarth in to work over a new picture puzzle she had ordered for the occasion. They finished up the evening with singing, and Ruddy Van Arden dropped in and looked them over in puzzled gloom. He couldn't make Constance out at all. She had declined going anywhere with him. She wasn't even with Whittemore at the dance from which with a tainted breath and hazy smoldering eyes he had stolen away to find out where Constance was. And he found her singing hymns with three kids! He couldn't understand it.

He got her by herself presently after Will Howarth had left and Frank had taken Dillie home, and insisted on her going to the dance with him.

"I'll wait while you get dolled up," he announced in a surly tone, eyeing her simple muslin frock with its childish round neck and puffed sleeves.

"No, Ruddy!" she said firmly. "I'm not going over to-night. I don't want to go. I haven't wanted to go since my grandmother was so sick. I guess I've lost interest."

"Snap out of it!" growled Ruddy. "You've gotta go with me. You haven't been like yourself since you came home and you've got to get a new start. That's why I came after you. I'm not taking no for an answer. I'm going to show that cur Whittemore that I can get you when he can't."

Ruddy came over suddenly and seizing Constance's arm drew her toward him. And now she saw his unsteady balance, the strange, wild gleam in his eyes, scented the liquor on his breath, caught his look of eagerness.

She pulled away, but his grip was like a vise on her wrist, his nails biting into her flesh.

"Let go of me, Ruddy! You're hurting me!" she said in a tense low voice. She did not want to waken Grandmother who was wont to hear anything even when they thought she was asleep.

"I'll hurt you all right!" said Ruddy leering at her drunkenly. "You'll come along with me even if I have to hurt you. You've hurt me enough, haven't you? Why shouldn't I hurt you? Come along! We'll go right out here to my car!" and he drew her toward one of the long French windows that opened to the wide veranda. "You'll go with me to that dance—yes and dance with me too—or I'll know the reason why."

"Ruddy! You've been drinking!" cried Constance aghast, reaching out to grasp the piano and trying to keep her footing.

"Is that so?" mocked the young man, a flame of anger leaping into his eyes. "Well, we'll get you drunk too! Then there'll be two of us. I know a place where we can get all the drinks we want. We'll go there first and get good and drunk and then we'll go to the dance. I'm sick of all this fancy refusing. You're my girl and everybody's going to know it, even if I have to drag you there dead drunk!"

Constance had a sick feeling that she was going to faint. She never fainted. But what was she going to do? He seemed in his intoxication to have a superhuman strength, and as they struggled silently she felt her own weakness, and a frightened tightening of her throat. She cast about in her mind what to do. Must she scream?

Must Grandmother have this excitement? Oh, if only Frank were here! But he had taken Dillie home and then likely walked around with young Howarth. Her father and mother had gone out to call on some friends, and the nurse had the evening off. Only the servants were at home, but they were away off in a wing over the kitchen. They might not even hear an outcry!

But Ruddy Van Arden was getting her in his power! He flung his free arm around her waist, his hot offensive breath was on her cheek, and he literally forced her toward the window. She made herself a dead weight, but he lifted her from her feet, and she knew that in another instant he would have her out of doors in the dark. Her heart was beating wildly. Anger surged up in her but she saw she could not hold out against him much longer, and fear took hold upon her.

Then suddenly she heard a keen young voice:

"What's the little old idea, you poor fish you?" Frank bounded through the hall door and took the drunken man by the collar with a grip so hard and strangling that Ruddy Van gasped and gurgled helplessly.

"Let go of my sister!" commanded Frank, and struck the other man's wrist with a blow that sent his hand powerless to his side.

"Beat it, Connie!" ordered Frank in a stern aside. "I'll deal with him."

Constance retreated trembling to the hall and watched the conflict from the stairs, but Frank made short work of it, propelling Ruddy out of the French window. She heard an altercation out on the lawn and flew up the stairs to her window. Perhaps she ought to call for help.

But when she reached the window she could see by the light from the porch that Frank was assisting Ruddy into his car and she knew it would make him furious if she called any one else into the matter. But when she saw him spring into the driver's seat and take the wheel she cried out in spite of all her resolves.

"Oh Frank, don't!"

But the sound of the motor drowned her voice and

the car was already beginning to move down the drive. She watched it go.

The porch light flashed on Ruddy's face as they passed her window and she could see he was slumped down in the seat as if he were already asleep. But the wind in his face would revive him. There was no telling what he might do if he roused. Why did Frank take such chances? She was frantic. What ought she to do?

She rushed downstairs again and out into the drive, down to the gate. She could see the car down the street going at Frank's usual rushing pace, and—ah! it had turned into the Van Arden drive! She drew a long breath of relief. At least he was not going far away. If it only weren't for leaving Grandmother alone she would run down and see what was happening. Perhaps Frank would have trouble with Ruddy when he tried to get him out of the car. Ought she to summon her father?

Then through the summer night she thought she heard a voice calling from the house. Was that Grandmother? She turned and ran swiftly back up to her grandmother's door. Listening a moment she heard a soft stirring within.

"Did you call, Grand dear?" she asked softly, trying to take the excitement out of her voice.

"Why, yes," said Grandmother sitting up in the dark, her silver curls catching a gleam from the hall light and framing her face softly. "I thought I heard somebody in distress. What is the matter? It sounded right downstairs. I've called several times."

"I'm sorry, Grandmother. I was just outside on the walk. It is a lovely moonlight night. I came as soon as I heard you. Mother and Father stepped over to call on the Blairs. Would you like me to come and sit with you?"

"Oh, no, only I'm sure I heard some one cry out. Where is Frank? I was sure I heard his voice."

"Why yes, he was here just a minute or two ago," answered Constance trying to keep her voice steady and matter-of-fact. "He just went down the street with one of the boys. You probably heard me call him."

"But it was before that!" said Grandmother anxiously. "I heard some sort of disturbance I'm sure."

"Perhaps you had been dreaming, dear, and got your dream mixed with the noises on the street. I'm sorry we wakened you. There is nothing the matter, really, Grandmother. Suppose you lie down and let me read to you a little while."

"No," said the old lady lying down with a relieved air. "If you say everything is all right why I suppose it is, but I thought there was something terrible going on. You are sure the servants are all right?"

"Positive. Could I get you a glass of nice cold orange juice?"

"No, dear, run along. I'm all right. I'll go to sleep now. Go on out in the moonlight again."

But Constance lingered until she heard the old lady breathing softly, and knew that she had dropped to sleep once more. Then she slipped out again and softly tiptoed down to the gate, almost running into Frank as he whirled in from the street with long strides.

"Oh, Frank!" exclaimed his sister. "I've been so worried about you. What has kept you so long?"

"Why I hadta put the poor boob ta bed. He was too far gone to do it himself. Say, Connie, did he hurt you before I came? I knew he was a rotter but I didn't think he would dare touch you right in your own house. I saw he was half stewed when he came in. That's why I rushed Dillie away in such a hurry, and Bill Howarth. I didn't want them to get onto it. I didn't care to have them see what company my sister keeps. But I hurried right back in case you needed me, and it seems I didn't come any too quick. Did he hurt you?"

But suddenly Constance could stand nothing more. She tried to answer, but found speech impossible. She could only shake her head, and then without warning she threw her arms about her brother's neck and burst into tears.

Greatly embarrassed Frank put his two strong young arms around her and held her.

"You poor kid!" he murmured huskily. "I oughtta have stuck around."

"Oh, no," Constance managed to sob out. "It was all

right, only I'm so glad you came when you did! He—
he—was trying to force me to ride with him back to the
Club, and dance with him, and I couldn't seem to get
away from him!"

"The rotten little beast!" said Frank with a manly
ring to his voice. "When he gets awake to-morra I'll
have a few little words with him. Doncha worry, Connie, he'll never do that again! Good night! I wish Seagrave would come home and let you see what it is to
have a real man for a friend!"

And then suddenly Constance lifted her face smiling
through her tears, remembering that it was not long
now before Seagrave would come, but Frank didn't
know that of course.

"I was all in," she apologized shamedly. "Don't mind
me. I'm quite all right now. You're a great brother and
I'm so glad you're mine!"

He patted her head awkwardly and said in a con-
descending tone:

"Well, take a little advice from me, Kid. Get yerself
some real friends. I took your advice about Dillie and
see what a friend I got! Lay off these guys you've been
running around with and get yerself a real friend!"

To his utter surprise Constance seized his face in her
two hands and gave him a warm quick kiss, and then
fled laughing up the drive and on upstairs.

One day more and Seagrave would be here! After
that what?

CHAPTER XXI

RUDDY VAN ARDEN came over just after lunch the
next day to apologize. He had not needed Frank's
scorching remarks to make him understand how he had
transgressed. His own physical condition and his vague
haunting memories told him enough of what he had
done.

White and handsome with dark circles under his
appealing eyes, humble and beautifully groomed, he

appeared and waited for Constance to come down-stairs.

Now Constance had spent the night examining her-self and come to the conclusion that her whole life had been a dreadful mistake. She had reviewed, and re-reviewed her brief career, she had passed her former associates before her weary mind, and had found that with few exceptions they had been vapid idlers like herself. She had censured herself, her own acts, her influence, everything about herself, and was about as low down in her own estimation as one could well get.

If anything, her confession to her grandmother had only served to make her more conscious of her own failings. The approach of Seagrave and her coming interview as set in contrast with her brief contact with Ruddy last night became more and more humiliating as she saw more clearly that last night was but an outcome that might have been expected from the life they all had been leading, and that she had to a certain extent joined in with and consented to that life.

Of course she had never been a drinker. She had been brought up with a feeling against liquor, and had stood firmly on that and a few other points, but her influence had never been against it. She had been absolutely neutral about it. It was just a thing like smoking that she did not do, that was all. But she had laughed with the rest over breaking the law, had joked about those who drank too much. She had been one with the people who did it, and led the life with them as far as she chose to go. And last night when she went up to her room after the exciting events of the evening, what should she open to in the little Testament but that awful verse: "Come out from among them and be ye separate saith the Lord, and touch not the un-clean thing." Ruddy and Seagrave had been placed in startling opposition, and she, Constance Courtland, had found herself classed with Ruddy instead of Seagrave. Her conscience told her that it was so.

So it was a chastened Constance that came down to meet her erstwhile playmate, and not the haughty angry girl he had expected.

Ruddy could be the perfect gentleman when he

chose, and just now he chose. He rose with humble wistful mien and put his glib tongue through its tenderest paces. The devil himself in his rôle of angel of light could have produced no more appealing excuses.

Constance sat across the room from him, pale, quiet, reserved, and listened through to the end without a word. There were dark circles under her own eyes. She had an air of being very sad and very far away.

At last when he was entirely through and sat with humble attitude awaiting her expected forgiveness she spoke:

"Listen, Ruddy," she said slowly, "I accept your apology and all that of course, but there's something more to it than that. I feel as if I'd been to blame somewhat, too."

He stared, put up a quick protesting hand, then a sudden hope sprang into his eyes. But Constance shook her head, reading his every expression as if it were a book.

"No, Ruddy, you don't understand. I don't mean that I drove you to drink by the way I treated you. I didn't. You had no right in the world to think I belonged to you or was bound in any way to go anywhere with you, or was ill treating you when I didn't. I mean just this, that I never tried to save you from this thing that got you last night. Of course I didn't drink myself, and you knew I didn't, but I laughed at you for drinking, I laughed with you about it, I played around with you and the crowd that did these things, and we just practically threw away the time trying to amuse ourselves, and I shouldn't have been like that. Ruddy, the whole thing makes me sick!"

Ruddy stared at her.

"What's the matter, Connie, you taking this all to heart? I'm all kinds of sorry I annoyed you that way last night. I'll see that it never happens again. Give you my word of honor."

Constance studied him sadly.

"How much honor has a man for his word when he is drunk, Ruddy?"

"Aw, come now, Connie, you don't have to rub it in!"

The young man's pale face flushed impatiently, and his mobile lips set unpleasantly. He got up and walked to the window looking out.

"I thought you'd be reasonable!" he gloomed, still with his back to her. "You must own it's my first offense."

"I'm not rubbing it in, Ruddy," said Constance quickly. "You don't understand. It was only one of a hundred little things that has been helping me to see myself these last few weeks. I'm just utterly disgusted with myself and the way I've been living. I never saw it so plainly as last night."

"Gosh! Con, did it hit you that hard? Gosh, I'm sorry. Say Connie, if I thought you cared that much for me I'd even go on the water wagon. I could do it if you'd stick by me and give the other fellows the go by. Say, Connie, let's get married! I'd do any little old thing in the world if you would."

Constance gasped and rose to her feet.

"Don't, Ruddy!" she said. "Don't! You don't understand at all. This isn't a matter of getting married. I'm not choosing any one to marry right now. But I'm sure of one thing. I would never want to marry any one that was in danger of being the way you were last night. And until you can conquer a thing like that without any girl's help you wouldn't be worth marrying. Listen, Ruddy. You and I have only been playing around together amusing ourselves, and I've just come to see that some of the playing was a mighty dangerous thing. That's what I'm trying to get across to you. I'm just sorry I haven't been a more helpful friend to you. I wasn't even trying to help you. I was only trying to have a good time. I've been selfish and silly and foolish and everything else!"

Ruddy turned around and stared at her thoughtfully. "Well, if you're selfish," he said finally, I wonder what the rest of us are?"

"We've been about alike I guess," said Constance with a sigh, "and I've been getting a vision of how foolish we are. I never realized that it could lead to—well—things like last night. I wish you'd cut it out, Ruddy, and be a man."

"Will you be my girl if I do?" He asked the question doggedly.

She looked at him steadily, her face a little white, taking a long deep breath for courage. Then she answered:

"No, Ruddy. I couldn't ever be that. No matter if last night had never happened I couldn't be that, because I don't care for you that way. But I'd be your friend if that would help!"

Ruddy looked at her sullenly, a long angry look. Then he picked up his hat from the chair where he had slung it when he came in and turned on his heel, muttering:

"Friend, *nothing!* I want a girl!" Then he was gone.

Constance stood looking out of the window after him as he swung recklessly into his car and whirled away. She was vaguely conscious of having done something devastating to Ruddy, yet how could she have helped it? She searched her heart to find blame for herself and found it back in the days when she was running around with Ruddy just because he was handsome and gave her a good time. Had she led him on? Had she allowed him to suppose that he was more to her than he really was? Her newly awakened conscience would not give her absolution. All the rest of the afternoon she carried about with her a memory of Ruddy's face as he had walked away, a memory that made her shiver as she remembered how he had looked last night as he held her wrist and tried to force her out to his car. Oh, life was getting more and more terrible every way she turned, and to-morrow Seagrave was coming home and she was bound to meet him now, to go with him to a religious meeting, talk with him; have those clear eyes of his look her through and through. Probably he would see all she had done for years, or if he did not see there would be some force that would compel her to confess everything, just as she was being forced to tell him about the pearls.

The day wore on and she spent herself upon her grandmother trying to be gay, offering to read, telling bright bits of gossip, but feeling all the time that those kind sharp eyes watching her so brightly, responding with a loving smile, were searching her through and through, and often divining what was going on in her mind.

Constance brought a bit of sewing, nothing important, just a thing of lace and chiffon to adorn the neck of a dress, and sat with Grandmother all the afternoon after her nap was over, wheedling her into telling bits of her own girlhood, romances of her young friends, anything to keep her thoughts from pondering on Ruddy, and on her own useless self.

For constantly underneath every other thought was that knowledge that to-morrow Seagrave was coming and she would have to meet him and she felt more unready than ever since last night.

She had a keen memory of a day back in her very young childhood when she had been told to come in and go upstairs to her nurse to be bathed and dressed for a company cousin who was arriving presently. But instead of obeying she had run away down the back alley and played with some little children of the tenements, played in the mud all the afternoon, and arrived home just before the company tea party, torn and soiled and streaked with mud, her hair down in her eyes. She could keenly remember exactly how she looked. Her mother had taken her frowning and crying upstairs to the long mirror in her room and made her look at herself with her muddy hands and face, and torn dress, and then look down from the window at the little girl cousin in the yard by the inviting tea table with its pretty china, its little frosted cakes and pink candies and ice cream. The little company cousin was in a white dress with a wide pink sash and pink kid slippers, her dark curls tied with a big pink ribbon bow. Her mother asked her if she would like to go down there looking like a little slum girl. Her heart had been broken. She could remember just how those great sobs hurt as they broke forth from her dirty little lips, and how the big tears stung in her eyes. For Mother had said she must stay upstairs in the nursery instead of coming down to the party, because she hadn't come in when she was called and now no one had time to wash her and dress her till the party was over. She remem-

bered sitting all alone with her silent dolls crying by
herself while the tea cups jingled, and her little cousin
romped and laughed with the kitten, her white kitten,
on the lawn. She remembered her mother saying as she
led her to the nursery that little girls had to learn to
mind.

And now Constance felt as if God were leading her
away into a corner and asking her to look at herself and
see if she were fit to meet a good man and be his
friend. Constance tried to get away from these thoughts
all day.

But at last when Grandmother had been tucked
away to sleep and there was nothing more to be done,
she went downstairs to sit with the family, hoping still
to be able to further distract her thoughts. Then the
telephone rang.

"Answer that, Connie, won't you?" said her mother
looking up from her knitting and the stitches she was
counting.

Constance stepped into the hall to the telephone
booth.

It was Betty Van Arden's excited voice that greeted
her as she took down the receiver. Betty was Ruddy's
fourteen-year-old sister.

"Is that you, Constance? Oh, Connie, won't you ask
your mother to come over and talk to my mother and
see if she can't quiet her down? She's got the hysterics
and it's something awful here. You heard what's happened didn't you?"

"No!" said Constance with a sudden pang of premonition. "Has something happened?"

"I'll say there has," answered Betty's hard young
voice. "It's Ruddy of course."

Constance's heart gave a sudden terrified lurch.

"Oh, not Ruddy!" she cried piteously. "He isn't—
there hasn't been an automobile accident has there? He
isn't—?" She hesitated, not daring to speak her fear.

"No," said Betty fiercely. "He isn't dead! Though I
guess Mother wishes he was. He's just run off and got
married to that peroxide blond that serves sodas at the
drug store down next the Movie Theatre. Alma Phelps.

Do you know her? I guess that's enough to make Mother have hysterics isn't it?"

A great relief, and then a great horror went over Constance. She could scarcely summon words to answer.

"Oh—! Betty—dear!" she managed, and then added: "But how do you know it is so? Are you sure?"

"Absolutely!" said Betty dejectedly, "Ruddy just telephoned to tell us. And he's coming home tomorrow and bringing her! Can you imagine that? Alma Phelps in this house! My sister-in-law! Do you blame Mother?"

"Ohh, Betty!" gasped Constance sorrowfully. "You poor kid!" And then she roused herself. "I'll tell Mother, Betty, and I'm sure she'll be right over. And if there's anything I can do tell me."

"Can you think of anything that could be done?" answered the young tragic voice. "If he'd only married you instead, Connie!" she let out with a smothered sob, "how different it all would have been."

Constance gave a long shudder, but tried to control her voice. "Oh, you poor little girl!" she said. "I'm so sorry for you!"

When Constance had hung up she went slowly into the other room.

"Mother, it was Betty Van Arden," she said, trying to keep her voice from shaking. "She wants to know if you will come over right away and try to calm her mother. They've just had word from Ruddy that he has married some girl who serves soda water at Tait's Drug Store and she's all broken up!"

Frank looked up from a magazine he had been reading.

"Gosh!" he said, "No kidding, Connie? Is that the truth? Ruddy married? Gosh! What a mess some men do make of their lives!"

He was still for an instant and then added:

"And at that he's got a girl that was too good for him. There were three or four others he's been running around with that might have been a lot worse!"

Mrs. Courtland dropped her knitting and looked up aghast, gave a keen frightened glance at her daughter and then a reproachful one at her son.

"And you knew all that and yet let your sister go with him?" asked his mother sharply, looking straight at Frank.

"Say, listen, Mother. I did my best ta tell ya a long time ago, and you just bawled me out for talking against Con's friends! You wouldn't any of ya believe me."

"Why, Frank!"

"'s true!" said the boy grimly.

"Well, but," said his mother in fluttering indignation and bewilderment, "I don't understand. Wasn't he just here this afternoon, Constance? I'm sure I saw him as I went upstairs from lunch."

"Yes, Mother," said Constance with an anxious warning glance at Frank. "He came to apologize for something he'd done. He didn't stay long."

"Did he tell you he was going to get married?" Mrs. Courtland's gaze searched her daughter's face again as if to discover if there were any signs of blighted hopes.

"No, Mother, but he was not in a nice mood. He has been drinking a great deal lately. He was rather sore at me for not wanting to go with him."

"Say, Mother, Connie's all right. Don't put her through a questionnaire!" broke in Frank. "Connie knows what she's about."

"Don't you really think you ought to go right over to poor Mrs. Van Arden, Mother?" questioned Constance meekly. "Betty seemed at her wit's end. She said her mother had hysterics."

Mrs. Courtland thus adjured, hastily put up her knitting and hurried away.

Left alone the brother and sister looked at one another.

"I suppose," said Constance slowly as if she were thinking aloud, "that I did that to him!" There was a quiver in her words and her brother looked at her sharply.

"Don't kid yerself, sister. He'd like you ta think that. He always likes ta get it back on somebody, but he knows he's a rotten lot. Don't waste sympathy on him. Just remember what he meant ta do last night, take you over ta the Club and let everybody see ya going round with a drunken mess! I suppose he came around today

and yammered a lot and told you he'd go on the water
wagon ur something if you'd take him on again. Was
that it?"

Constance gave her brother a quick glance. What a
lot boys understood when you thought they were only
kids!

"Ferget it, Connie!" went on the boy. "He won't take
this near as seriously as his mother will. You'll see. He'll
chuck this girl as soon as he gets tired of her, won't
even bother ta send her ta Reno, just chuck her and go
off a while; and when he comes back there'll be another. I've seen 'em. He can blame it on you, but it's his
own fault and he knows it. Suppose he does blame you,
Connie? What's that got ta do with it? You couldn't go
marry him ta keep him from losing his fool head and
marrying a girl he knows his folks won't stand for. You
didn't want to be tied up ta a fella that acted the way
he did last night did ya?"

"Oh! Don't, Frank!" shivered Constance. "Of course
not. But I just feel as if I'd been an awful fool!"

"No you haven't, Connie!" burst out her brother
earnestly. "You're a swell girl. You can't be responsible
for every poor fish that gets inta a mess."

"But I've just been going around thinking of myself
and having a good time!" wailed Constance. "I've never
thought I had any responsibility about other people!"

"Well, ya haven't. When a fella's grown up it's his
own look out. You're a swell kid and a fella oughtta be
proud if he gets a look from ya. Now cut this out,
Connie, and go ta bed. You're all white around the gills
and you'll be sick ef ya don't get some rest. Ferget that
poor fish and get some sleep. He's made trouble enough
in our house and I'm glad he's married. It'll keep him
outta our house at least fer a time. He never was fit fer
ya ta wipe yer feet on. You're a swell kid, I tell ya,
Connie, and it's time you understood!"

He patted her on the back and Constance, strangely
comforted, went off to her room half laughing half
crying, to lie awake and torment herself with thoughts
till sleep came at last.

CHAPTER XXII

IT WAS late when Constance woke, but a glad thought came to greet her. Somehow the sunshine and the morning had washed away her fears and forebodings, and she only remembered with a leap of her heart that Seagrave was coming home to-day! Everything might be in a mess, she herself might be all wrong, but to-day she was going to see him, and she had a feeling now that he was going to be able to tell her how to make everything right.

She found a song on her lips and exultation in her heart.

The family rejoiced over her secretly. Grandmother was well and Constance was like herself again! Now they could begin to live again!

Mother had a dreary tale to tell of the Van Arden trouble. She had stayed until after midnight trying to quiet the frantic mother who declared she would not allow the new daughter-in-law to step her foot over the threshold. They were already planning to have the marriage annulled and send Ruddy abroad indefinitely. The mother and sister were bitter against Ruddy, and the father declared that if his son did not obey him in this matter of the annulment of the marriage that he would disown him. The whole household was in a most unhappy state.

Frank gave his sister a quick keen look and said to her in a low tone which the others did not hear:

"You should worry, Connie! Ruddy had this coming to him! It's his life not yours. Likely God knows how to work it out. You can't go around marrying every poor boob that takes a fancy to you just ta save him from unpleasantness. Trouble with him is his dad never did lick him enough! Likely all this'll be good for him in the end."

Constance flashed an amused grateful look at her brother. It was funny but somehow it was a precious thing to her to have him taking thought for her in this way. There was a lot of good common sense, too, in what he said. She really couldn't have married Ruddy of course. She never cared for him. And she couldn't save him now from the consequences of what he had done in anger. But she knew in her heart that she might have been a better friend to him, just a friend, when she first went around with him, and it made her resolve that she would never again play around without thought for those who were her companions.

But not even the pall that hung over the house next door could take the sunshine out of the day for Constance. Her heart would keep singing a melody that was entirely without foundation, and against common sense. She kept telling herself that she was going to put herself in the worst light possible to-day before the man for whose respect she cared most, and it was presumptuous for her to be so glad that he was coming.

It was a glorious day. One of those days washed clean by a shower in the night, with the earth so green and the sky so blue that it almost seemed to be too lovely for this world.

Constance gave a good deal of thought as to what she should wear that evening and decided on a simple blue organdy, cool and becoming, but very plain and childlike in its lines. She was not going to a concert or a party. It was a religious meeting she reminded herself when other more elaborate frocks presented themselves to her mind as possibilities.

So she decided on the simple blue dress, with a plain white hat and the pearls. She would wear the pearls! It was because of them that she had this confession to make. They must be present of course. And after all, only a connoisseur would recognize that they were real. Everybody wore pearl beads nowadays. To a casual observer they would look like the ordinary bead necklace that everybody wore every day.

The matter of attire settled, Constance tried to read to pass the morning away, but no book could hold her attention long. At last she tried the Testament but it turned like a knife in her soul and tortured her. If she read any more of his Testament that day it would unnerve her for the evening. She kept coming on that

"Come ye out and be separate" verse. She was glad when Frank called to her to know if she wanted to drive to the next town with himself and Dillie on an errand for Dillie's mother. Anything to take her mind off of the evening.

As they drove along amid the green fields with hills rolling off in the purply green distance on either hand somehow it seemed to her that the world had never been so lovely. Yet the ride did not do much toward occupying her thoughts. Dillie and Frank were eager about their own affairs and only cast her a bright word and a smile now and then, and there was the appalling evening hastening on.

They reached home again just in time for lunch and the afternoon stretched its interminable length before her, looking like a whole week to be lived through.

Then most unexpectedly a great box of flowers arrived, lovely feathery corn flowers, blue, white, shell pink and purple, masses of them, and a card on the top with Seagrave's name, and the words penciled, "I will call for you at seven to-night."

He had landed!

Her cheeks grew pink and her heart beat joyously as she bent her face to touch the fairy flowers closing her eyes against their feathery petals.

What unusual flowers he always sent! Hepaticas, forgetmenots, and now these lacy delicate things! What a man he was! And to think that she in her gay indifference to finer thngs had reared a wall that undoubtedly would separate her from his friendship, or at least his companionship, for life!

A bright tear dimmed its way into her eyes and fell among the flowers. Then she caught her breath and set her lips. She must not give way to such thoughts or she would never be able to go through the evening.

She hurried to search out containers for her flowers, pleasing herself arranging them. A few in a slender crystal vase, scarcely more than a stem of glass, a mass in an opalescent bowl, a graceful arrangement of more of them in a gorgeous sterling silver cup that she had won in a tennis tournament. They lent themselves graciously to any vessel that offered itself, and there was such a wealth of them!

Then she took a handful upstairs to her room. She meant to wear those to-night.

As she mounted the stairs her brother came flying down, tennis racket in hand, gave the flowers a knowing glance, half paused on the stairs and looked up after her, and then went on.

But the afternoon got itself away at last with a nap and a book and a bit of hovering over the different vases of flowers, and at last Constance could begin to get ready.

It was with an unsteady hand that she finally fastened the clasp of the pearls about her neck, dried off the stems of the lovely flowers fastening a mass of them at her breast, and went down to dinner.

"Some baby doll!" saluted Frank comically as she entered the dining room, sweeping out her chair from the table and seating her with ceremony, "And is the lady stepping out among 'em?"

There was just a shade of uneasiness in his tone as he eyed her quizzically, glanced from the knot of flowers to the flowers on the table and then back again.

Constance's cheeks flamed scarlet in spite of the fact that she wore no make-up, but she only smiled placidly and ignored his question.

"She looks very pretty!" said Grandmother who had attained to staying down to dinner for the last two or three days. "I like to see her in that little blue gown. It looks like her eyes. And I'm glad you're wearing the pearls, Constance."

Constance wondered with a pang at her heart whether she would ever be willing to wear them again after to-night, but she managed to keep her smile lighted and to get through that dinner somehow, although she was conscious of her brother's eyes continually upon her; conscious also that he studied her flowers from time to time.

Dinner dragged slowly through to the dessert, Constance managing to keep up a pretty good show of eating, and then when she had taken but one small taste of the delectable Spanish cream that was placed before her she heard the taxi drive up to the door.

She caught her breath slightly, and said hastily, "Mother, I'll have to ask you to excuse me. I didn't know it was so late. I'm going in town to a meeting."

Frank caught a glimpse of the taxi, kept his keen glance out of the window for a second till he saw who was coming up the walk and then a twinkle came into his merry eyes.

"Oh, yeah?" he said to his sister's vanishing back, and went on comfortably eating his dessert.

Constance was downstairs again with her hat on ready to go almost as soon as Seagrave entered. Indeed he was barely seated in the dim cool living room lighted only by tall candles on the wide old-fashioned white marble mantel when she stepped into the room. He came forward eagerly, and took her hand, took both hands, in his two, and stood looking down upon her for an instant, a lovely welcome in his eyes. His look took in the quaint little blue dress, the sweet face above it filled with that strange new humility, the knots of his flowers at her breast, the pearls about her throat, and his hands clasped hers with a glad warm pressure that sent the blood thrilling through her, and filled her with an ecstasy that almost frightened her. She mustn't, O, she mustn't feel this way about him. It would unnerve her.

Then he spoke, and his words went thrilling down into her soul with that same wonderful ecstasy again.

"Oh, I am glad to see you again!" There was a fervency in his tone that brought back all the dreams of him she had dared to harbor.

She went with him down the flower-bordered walk to the taxi, but every time she dared to lift her eyes, there were his eyes looking into hers, and there was that glad thrill again.

He put her into the taxi and she had one glimpse of that fiendish young brother of hers standing on the dining room porch gazing after her, waving a saucy hand for farewell and executing a clog dance for the benefit of any pedestrians who might be passing.

And Constance sat there smiling and tongue tied!

Constance, who was always so easy in her manner, always so ready with a gay word, could think of nothing whatever to say!

But it did not seem to matter.

Seagrave took his place beside her and reaching out possessed himself of her hand once more. Not as most casual free and easy young men hold hands. Rather as if it were something for which he had come a long way and waited eagerly. He looked down into her eyes and said again:

"I am glad to see you!" And again came that wonderful flood of joy in her soul, that ecstasy like to nothing she had ever experienced before. Did it mean that she had fallen in love, Constance Courtland fallen in love with a man who could never even respect her, let alone love her? Her fingers trembled in his and he released them with a lingering pressure.

"Say, aren't you the least little bit glad to see me?" he asked wistfully.

Constance trying to summon her manner of the world and say something gay and flippant couldn't think of a thing, and blundered out fervently, "Oh, I am!" and then retired into mortified shyness again. What was the matter with her? She felt as if she were going to burst into tears and run away and hide. But instead of the tears she gave him a radiant smile, her eyes growing starry with looking into his, because she could not take her gaze away. His eyes held hers.

Then all too soon they were at the station. It hadn't seemed possible to have gone those five blocks so swiftly.

He left her an instant to get the tickets, and she stood in a daze, weak with happiness. Then the train was coming and there were other people about. She noticed with keen delight the purple and gold of the sunset sky, the dash of coral against a pale green field, the flecks of gold fading into a violet depth. He stood beside her, their eyes met, and he seemed to read her thought about the sunset.

"Gorgeous, isn't it?" he assented with a fleeting glance toward the panorama of the sky. Then the train swept up and shut off their vision.

The lights in the long narrow world of the train shut off the glory of the sky, and there were people about whom Constance knew, people who recognized Seagrave and spoke. Formality descended upon them as they sat down. That brief moment alone in the taxi seemed at once a dream that had fled, too exquisite for the garish light of an evening train.

Yet still she had that sense of being waited upon, guided, protected, cared for as none of her other young escorts had ever seemed to do. That feeling of entering into an adventure of joy.

There could be no quiet personal questions here, no looking deep into eyes to search for something that words dare not go after. There were other curious eyes about, wondering who was this good looking stranger with that air of foreign travel about him. Furtive glances were cast toward them. There was Evelyn Earle three seats back across the aisle. Constance could see her eager glances reflected in the glass of her window.

They kept to conventional talk that any one might have heard. Their eyes sought out the window again as the town fled past and the open country gave another view of the dying sunset sky, wide and wonderful. But she was intensely conscious of Seagrave sitting there beside her, of the strength in every line of his face, of his courtesy, of his evident gladness to be with her, conscious of their shoulders touching as he leaned forward to raise her window a few inches higher. She wished that the way into the city were twice as long. She wanted to get her breath, find her bearings, get used to the delight of having him near. Oh, how was she ever to go through the program she had planned? But she would first have this little time to remember before she shattered her dream.

So the minutes of the ride flew, and all too soon they were in the big city station; then rushing along in another taxi for there were but five minutes before that meeting would begin and he must not be late.

The city taxi was a noisy one. They could not talk much. He did not take her hand again, but he helped her from the taxi and up the church steps as if she were something infinitely precious, not just a girl that he was

taking out somewhere. There was something about him
that made him different from all other men. She had
thought that it must have been an illusion that would
be dispelled when he came back, but it was there again,
a charm, a fascination. Oh, it would have been better
for her if he had never returned! She would have forgotten him after a while and dropped back into her
world where she belonged and where she had always
been perfectly contented until he came!

But she shivered a little inwardly and realized that
she did not want to drop back there now, would never
be contented there again as she had been.

Now they were in the great church, rapidly filling
to capacity. Hot weather, midsummer, and yet a vast
church full!

He seemed to know just where to place her most
comfortably, and people around looked at him, stirred
and whispered, and looked at her. They seemed to
know Seagrave, and a young man came down the aisle
to welcome him. An older gray-haired minister arose
from a pulpit chair and came with outstretched hand to
greet him. Suddenly Seagrave was no more an obscure
shabby stranger whom she had picked up at an Easter
communion table. He was a man of commanding
presence with many friends who were overjoyed to see
him. She noticed the stir all over the church as he took
his seat in the tall velvet cushioned chair at the left of
the old minister and bowed his head for a moment in
prayer. And at once that action of bowing his head on
his hand seemed to set him apart from her. She shrank
away into herself with an infinite pain in her heart. And
now he was the man on the hillside talking of God
among the flowers!

The singing amazed her. So many bright young
voices like jewels flashing into sound, such volume and
sweetness, such power and strength and sincerity in
song. She had never heard a great audience like that
singing as unto the Lord, singing from the heart. College choruses, even choirs of trained voices, could not
sing like that. It was different. They were singing as if
they meant every word. Offering real praise to God. She
was tremendously impressed with it.

The other men who took part seemed so in earnest too. The prayer by the old minister, sweet and tender, the scripture reading by the younger man read so impressively. Everything seemed a part of a new environment, a world she did not know, a world that she looked at wistfully as the service proceeded.

Then came Seagrave's address.

And now she was transported to the hillside as she listened to his talk. He was telling how sin began in heaven, with Lucifer that bright perfect angel, and then went on to the Garden of Eden; how we as children of Adam came to be partakers of sin, and its consequence, Death. Constance sat and saw herself an abject sinner more clearly than she had ever seen it before.

But now her sin was not just merely an act of one bright Sabbath morning, the taking of false vows upon gay lips, not just the hypocrisy she had been planning to confess to the speaker, it was something infinitely deeper and graver, more terrible than anything she had conceived of before. Something that merited a spiritual death.

She saw herself scarred and spoiled with sin, and then she was made to see how the Lord Jesus with infinite love had taken that loathsome sin upon Himself and borne its punishment that she might go free!

Before Seagrave was finished the tears were on Constance's face, and she was so absorbed she did not know it. Oh, more than anything else in life she longed to be at peace with that Saviour who had died for her. During Seagrave's closing prayer wherein he asked if there was even one soul in the audience who had not accepted that great salvation that was bought on the cross by the precious blood of Christ, that God would grant that that one might take Him now and go out of the house a saved soul, her heart cried out wistfully, "Oh, God, I do!"

The meeting was over at last, the throngs who surged up to shake hands and thank Seagrave for his message were all greeted and dismissed with that grave sweet smile, and he came down the aisle to Constance with eagerness.

"I've been thinking," he said with a smile. "We've

missed the early train by about half a minute. Do you
mind? Of course we could take a taxi all the way home,
but, how would you like instead to walk in the park a
little while? It's wonderful down there by the river. I
went down a number of times after you were gone to
college before I sailed and thought how pleasant it
would be to come there together sometime. It's moonlight to-night. It will be great! It's only a five-minute
taxi ride from here and we'd have a little over an hour
before we'd have to drive to the station for the later
train. It would be a good quiet place to talk, and cool
too. Would you enjoy it?"

Constance was trembling with the joy and the sadness of it, for she knew she must carry out her purpose
of confession now. But her eyes were bright as she
lifted them to his face, and there was a ring of gladness
in her voice.

Just a few minutes now before she must confess.
This beautiful way he was treating her was the way it
might have been between them if she had been his sort.
Oh the sweetness of it! Oh, the sadness!

She tried to tell him on the way how much she had
enjoyed the meeting! How much his message had
meant to her soul, but she could not find the right
words and stumbled along with halting speech, feeling
more and more how impossible it was because she did
not speak his language.

She was trembling visibly as he dismissed the taxi.
Now in just a minute or two she must begin her story.
There could be no more reprieve.

He drew her arm within his own and they walked
slowly along the wide paved walk amid the cool earthy
smell of ferns and other growing things, the moonlight
dripping through the feathery branches of the trees and
mingling with the garish blare of the many arc lights
along the way.

They passed several benches where people were sitting, some talking, some drowsing; a pair of lovers, the
man's arm about the girl, oblivious of the world. He led
her along till they found a seat near the river bank
deeper in the shadow than the rest, a trifle off the
beaten path. Their only neighbor was a man stretched

at full length on a bench over by the walk, his hat drawn down over his eyes. He was asleep. He would not trouble them. It seemed as if they had withdrawn into a little world of their own.

"I have thought a great deal about the time when perhaps you and I might come here," said Seagrave as they sat down. "It seems wonderful that my dream has really come true. This is a wonderful place to talk. I have been longing to tell you a lot of things. But you said you had something to tell me. Shall we begin with that first?"

Constance looked up with a frightened little shiver of a smile and knew that her time had come.

CHAPTER XXIII

"I HAVE to tell you that I am not what you think I am," she began sorrowfully. "I've been miserable ever since I found out how despicable I am, since you came and talked with Doris, and since I've been reading your little book, I have been so utterly wretched over it that I've got to be honest and tell you the whole thing."

"Yes?" he said and there was something tense and strained in his voice, as if what she had to say would mean a great deal to him.

"Don't tell me unless it will help you," he added, "I can trust you."

"No," said Constance, "you can't trust me. You think you can but that's just it. You've got to know the whole truth. I've done something that you will think is terrible! You know just a little part of it, but you've got to know the whole. I can't stand it any longer."

"Then I shall be glad to listen," said he gravely.

She put her hand to her throat.

"I wore these pearls to-night to help me to tell you," she said. "They are real and very valuable. They are matched pearls, and my great-grandfather paid a good many thousands of dollars for them. He gave them to my grandmother the day she united with the church when she was a young girl."

"Yes?" He looked down upon her with a tender light in his eyes, but she, hurrying on with her story, did not see.

"My grandmother had said for a good many years that she was going to give them to me when I united with the church. However that church part of it seemed to have dropped out of sight, and later it came to be understood that I was to have them when I graduated from college. I was most eager to have them for an especial occasion, a week-end house party to which I was invited just after Easter, and I got Mother to feel around judiciously and try to get Grandmother to be willing to give me the pearls at Easter instead of waiting for my graduation. Then, what was my disappointment to find out when I got home that Grandmother still had her heart set on the pearls being given when I joined the church. Mother found out that she had been deeply disappointed that I had not done so long ago, and when she discovered that my former Sunday School classmates were all joining at Easter, she made it a point that I join also. She seemed to feel it meant almost disgrace that I was not a member of the old church that my great-grandfather had helped to organize. She had even gone to the length of considering whether she would not give the pearls to a little country cousin of mine who could have no possible use for them, but who was quite a devoted church worker. Now, can you begin to see what I did?"

"Perhaps."

"It was Saturday night and I was going to a dance at the country club. I felt it was archaic to join the church. I didn't believe in anything. I was just a little pagan. But I went Sunday morning and appeared before the session, consented to everything they asked me, stood up beside you that Easter Sunday morning to confess before the world a Christ in whom I did not even believe! You thought I did it to please my grandmother, and even that was bad enough, and you let me see how false it was; but you did not know that I sold my honesty and mocked God for a string of matched pearls!"

Suddenly Constance felt a rough coarse hand brush

across her shoulder and touch her neck, and looking up startled she saw an ugly gun pointing straight into her face, held by a slouchy looking man with a handkerchief tied over the lower part of his face and an old hat pulled down over his eyes.

"Now you two set right still and don't you make no noise," he said in a tone that struck terror to Constance's heart. "You won't neither of you get hurt ef you do as I tell ya! Now you, lady, you just hand me over them pretty white babies round your neck, and keep still about three minutes and you won't be interrupted in yer talk anymore."

Her pearls! Constance's heart sank! Oh, why had she been such a fool! Sitting here in the open telling how valuable they were! Retribution had come swiftly. But oh, to lose them in this way! How humiliating! It would have been one thing to have to give them back to Grandmother and let her give them to Norma. That she recognized as just. But for her to have wantonly lost them outside of the family, a family heirloom! The thought added to her fright was sickening and it came in a flash as one can comprehend a whole chapter of truth in an instant under great stress. She felt paralyzed. She couldn't open her lips. She couldn't move her hand.

The man was growing impatient.

"Unfasten them pearls, sister and give 'em to me! Be quick about it ur I'll shoot yer young man and snatch 'em, see? I gotcha both covered. Ya can't do a thing! Hand 'em over! Ya don't want yer man shot, do ya?"

Constance lifted an unsteady hand toward the clasp of her pearls, but suddenly, just behind her it seemed, there came the sharp shrill scream of a policeman's whistle, almost in her ear! It was so loud and close it made both Constance and the bandit start. As if he had been but a bad dream, the intruder slithered into the shadows and disappeared. It all happened so quickly that Constance thought she must be losing her mind.

But Seagrave had caught her hand, and spoken one word: "Quick!"

On limbs that seemed powerless to bear her she fled with him across the grass, blindly, not seeing her way ahead, her breath coming in quick frightened gasps, having much ado to keep her footing as Seagrave fairly dragged her along.

It was only a moment and they were back on the safe bright pavement again where people were coming and going and a traffic cop could be seen half a block away holding up cars while a great green bus swung into its waiting place at the curb.

Straight toward the bus they ran, still hand in hand, Constance breathless and frightened, still holding her other hand tight over the pearls about her neck, and only aware that she was being guided and cared for.

No one noticed them. It was not an infrequent sight just at that spot to see people running for a bus. The world went right on about them.

Then all at once a great comforting policeman loomed ahead of them, and Seagrave drew him aside for a moment and told him what had happened.

The officer put a bright little whistle to his lips and let out that same shrill terrifying whistle that she had heard behind her ear down on the bench by the river when the bandit was ordering her to hand over her pearls, and the chills went down Constance's back.

She couldn't hear all that Seagrave and the officer were saying, but she saw the policeman look toward her pearls comprehendingly. She glanced around fearsomely half expecting to see the bandit lurking off in the shadows.

The officer was writing down something in his notebook. Seagrave took a card out of his pocket and gave it to him. Then three other policemen came hurrying from different directions to answer the whistle. A word and they were scattered hastily, one off in the direction of the bench by the river, the other two sliding away among the shrubbery like shadows on their rubbersoled boots.

Presently Seagrave came back to her where she stood waiting and put her in the bus. There was only one double seat vacant and Constance was glad to sink down into the deep puffy cushion. Seagrave reached for her hand that lay in her lap and held it firmly in a strong reassuring grasp as he sat down beside her and leaning over peered into her face.

"Are you all right?" he asked anxiously.

"Oh, yes," Constance tried to smile but it was a wan and feeble attempt, and her voice was still shaky.

"I shall never forgive myself that I let you in for that by my foolish suggestion."

"Oh, it was all my fault!" said Constance with a little catch in her voice that might easily have been an incipient sob. "I ought to have known better than to wear them. I ought not to have talked—" and she looked around furtively. "Oh, I'm such an utter fool!"

"No!" said Seagrave gently, speaking very quietly and giving her hand another tender pressure. "Please don't say that. I was entirely to blame. I ought to have realized that in this strange uncertain age in which we are living it is not safe to idle about in lonely places with a lady even so early in the evening and so near to city traffic. We have been wonderfully cared for. That was a great escape!"

"Oh, yes!" breathed Constance shivering suddenly at the memory of that sinister gun. "But, I don't quite understand yet how it all happened. What became of our policeman, the one who whistled and drove the man away from us? You don't suppose he is in any danger do you? You don't think we should have waited a while to thank him, do you?"

"There wasn't any policeman," said Seagrave turning a boyish grin toward her.

"There wasn't any?" said Constance amazed, wondering if her ears had deceived her in the general excitement. "But who whistled? It was right behind my ear!"

"I did!" said Seagrave. "It's a trick I learned long ago. I used to have all kinds of fun as a kid holding up traffic when some one was trying to speed by me. I enjoyed seeing them stop and hunt in vain for the cop who had stopped them."

"But you didn't move a muscle of your face. I could see you out of the side of my eye."

"I know," grinned Seagrave. "It's part of the trick to do it so that no one can tell where it comes from. You see it was the only weapon I had at hand. A kind of trivial thing to venture I admit in such a serious situation, but I couldn't think of anything else to do just at that stage of the game. I didn't dare try to wrest the gun out of his hand as I should likely have ventured if I had been alone, lest it would go off in your face. And I knew that the whistle was likely to startle him at least and perhaps throw him off his guard, so that I could get a better chance at him. I scarcely hoped he would fade out of the picture quite so easily, but I guess it must really have scared him."

"Oh!" said Constance suddenly taking the whole thing in. "Oh!" and suddenly she began to laugh uncontrollably, to check the tears which threatened to undo her.

And then suddenly they were at the station and had to get out of the bus.

There was still a half hour before the train was scheduled to leave, but the train was open and they found seats and comparative privacy. Only a few people were in the car, away up at the other end, and they could talk without interruption.

Constance sank into the seat wearily and put her head back closing her eyes for an instant. Seagrave eyed her anxiously.

"I shall always blame myself for having let you in for all this," he said in troubled tones.

Constance opened her eyes at that and sat up energetically.

"Oh, don't say that," she protested earnestly, "I'm glad it happened! Now it's over I'm glad for having gone through it. It was what I deserved to lose my pearls. And they would have been gone if it hadn't been for you. You saved them for me! I don't feel as if I had a right to them anymore. I'm glad, glad that I saw it all just as it must be in God's eyes. I think it took that gun to complete the revelation of myself. I found a little story in the Testament you gave me, a story about a man who found a pearl of great price and went and sold all that he had and bought it. I read it a great many times and I began to think that was like myself. I sold my finer feelings and standards when I joined the church to get those pearls."

"Ah!" said Seagrave with his eyes alight, "but don't you know what that pearl is, and what the story means? That pearl is the Church, the precious bride of Christ, the church for which He gave His life. It is a beautiful story when one understands it all. But speaking of pearls, you know how they are formed, don't you?"

"In oysters," said Constance, wondering.

"Yes, but they are made by wounds. An injury done to the animal itself is what makes it, a grain of sand perhaps, that gets inside the shell and presses against the soft body of the animal. And then the mother of pearl or nacre as it is called, which is really the lining of the shell, is deposited layer upon layer about the grain of sand till a pearl is formed. The pearl is thus, as some one has said, an answer to an injury. The offending object itself becomes, through the work of the injured one, a precious and beauteous gem. It is a picture of God's divine grace. And pearls are of different degrees of value and beauty, dependent not upon the grain of sand that gets into the oyster, but upon the number of layers of nacre that are wrapped about it. This answers to the greatness of the grace that God has bestowed upon us."

"How wonderful!" said Constance softly, her eyes alight as she watched his face.

"And it is not the things that you have done," went on Seagrave, "the depth of your own sinfulness, the measure of your own unworthiness, that makes you fit or unfit for belonging to the church of Christ, His heavenly bride. It is the beauty and glory of Him we crucified by our sin, that is put upon us as a robe to clothe us. It is not any righteousness that we could have that would make us fit for such a wondrous calling. It is Christ's righteousness, put upon us and enfolding us, that makes us as a Church a worthy bride for Him. He took the sin wherewith we wounded Him, and made of it a pearl to adorn His glory."

Constance's eyes were upon him, her mind drinking in all that he said.

"How marvelous you make it!" she exclaimed. "And

you think He could take me and make me fit to belong to His wonderful church?"

"He certainly can!" he answered in a ringing voice. "Have you accepted Him for your Saviour?"

"Yes," said Constance softly, her lashes drooping over her cheeks shyly. "To-night, while you were praying!"

"Thank God!" he said earnestly, his hand coming out and enfolding hers once more with a strong thrilling pressure. "This is what I have been praying for since that morning on the hillside."

"I hoped you were," she said trying to keep her lips from quivering. "You promised to, you know, after Doris died. And—" She hesitated shyly and went on haltingly: "And you are not ashamed to have such an unworthy one as I am for a friend?"

"Ashamed?" asked Seagrave wonderingly. "Who am I to be ashamed of you? Don't you know I am just another sinner who has been saved by His glorious grace? And you say you have accepted that offer of grace yourself? He has become your Saviour too. Then you too are justified by the blood of Christ which was shed to cleanse your sin, and you are covered by the righteousness of Christ Himself. You are now a member of His precious church, His pearl of great price. You are no longer unworthy."

"That seems too beautiful to be true," said Constance thoughtfully.

"But it is gloriously true nevertheless. We both belong to the wonderful body of Christ!"

"I cannot get used to it!" said Constance wonderingly. "It does not seem possible that such a thing can be. Oh, you don't know how I have suffered! I was afraid to tell you what I had done because I couldn't bear to lose this wonderful friendship with you. And yet I had to. God wouldn't let me keep it to myself any longer. I had to tell you, even though I was sure I would lose your friendship."

"Friendship!" exclaimed Seagrave giving her a mysterious look. "Friendship!"

Then suddenly the train came to a halt and the

brakeman drowned out any other words that might have been spoken by calling out their station.

They got to their feet in a hurry, amazed that they had reached home so quickly, and he helped her out as if she were the most precious thing on earth.

There seemed to be no taxi at the station, or perhaps some more alert traveler had seized the only one, but those two did not mind. It was not far, and the pathway seemed all paved in silver moonlight as they started.

Seagrave drew her arm within his own and gathered her hand in a close grasp.

"Now," said he. "You precious little girl, it is high time you understood me. Even if you may think it is too early in our acquaintance I've got to tell you. Friendship! Darling, don't you know I've loved you from the minute I saw you? Don't you know my heart has been crying out to God for you day and night ever since that Easter Sunday morning when I saw you in that little white dress with the pearls, standing among the lilies around God's table?"

"But," said Constance tremblingly. "Your little book says 'Come ye out and be separate!' And I was afraid, terribly afraid that when you knew what I was—"

"Dear Heart! I know! But I left all that with Him. I knew He would save you, or give me the strength to go alone. But oh, I've prayed! Darling, I've prayed! But—you say you were afraid? Did you then care a little too?"

They had been coming slowly up the walk to her father's home and now they stopped in the shade of the great lilac bushes that arched the way.

"Care?" said Constance. "Care? I've cared so much that I've drenched my pillow with tears night after night. I've cared so violently that I made a fool of myself trying to make myself forget you because I was sure you could never care for one like me. Care? Oh, yes, I've cared ever since that first morning on the hillside with the little blue flowers."

His arms were about her now, her face buried in the clear roughness of his coat. But he lifted her face and laid his lips on hers.

"My darling, my precious beloved! Tell me you love me," he said. "I want to hear you say it."

"I love you! Oh, I do love you!" she murmured softly, lifting her glad sweet face to his.

And there in the shadow of the lilacs, just at the foot of the steps of the big colonial mansion, with moonlight splashing all around wherever a lilac leaf would let one moonbeam through, they stood and plighted their troth. Then Seagrave laid his lips reverently upon hers again.

"Friendship!" he laughed softly. "Friendship! I'll say! Oh, my beloved!"

It was just at that critical instant that the front door of the house, three steps above where they stood, opened slowly, noiselessly and swung back, revealing in the dim light of the hall chandelier, the brother of the bride-to-be, clad in a violently striped bath robe of magenta and buff, his feet below the green and purple of his pajama legs thrust into pullman slippers, his hair sticking seven ways for Sunday, and his eyes blinking with sleep.

For a full minute he stood there silently blinking till they became suddenly aware of his presence and then he remarked carelessly:

"Oh, yeah?"

Constance turned with quickly crimsoning cheeks.

"Oh, Frank, you wretch! I might have expected as much! Graham, this is my pest of a brother. I hope you'll excuse his intrusion. Frank, this is—we are—!"

"I quite understand," said Frank bending low in an elaborate bow. "It is all too evident, Sister! But I'm glad to be the first of the family to welcome—that is—"

He paused with a grin.

"What I was going to remark is I couldn't have picked a better brother-in-law, Kid, not if I'd gone around the earth to choose. He's all right, and I'm with ya, Kid! Come on in! There's a whole chocolate cake in the cake box and plenty of ginger ale on the ice. Come on in and let's celebrate."